BLOOD SECRETS

BLOOD SECRETS

By Craig Jones

BALLANTINE BOOKS • NEW YORK

Library of Congress Catalog Card Number: 78-4743

ISBN 0-345-28238-8

This edition published by arrangement with
Harper & Row, Publishers

Manufactured in the United States of America

First Ballantine Books Edition: August 1979

For
Marianne, Jeanette, Frank, and Stuart

BLOOD
SECRETS

You never think this kind of thing really happens to people who've been to college. A strange consideration perhaps, but after the murder this was one of the first thoughts to strike me. And all through the trial I sensed that same thought hovering behind the faces of the jurors. In the beginning they seemed almost pleased, titillated by the fact I am an "educated, professional" woman, a teacher; each day their eyes would greet me with renewed astonishment. But as we progressed to the final stages they began to look embarrassed, and in the end, weary. In a trial as long as mine was, particularly a murder trial, there develops a bond between defendant and jury, at least on the defendant's part. After a while, you know instinctively what words, what phraseology, will make this one chuckle, that one wince. From their glances at each other you see where alliances have been formed and hostilities upheld. You recognize the leaders and the followers, and when you receive an occasional furtive look of sympathy, you end up measuring its worth by which face it comes from. Does that sound cold-blooded? It is, and so were the proceedings—cold-bloodedly civilized. Just the facts. My uncivilized crime ended up in a civilized trial: hecklers were promptly removed from the courtroom; "hate mail" was intercepted by my lawyer and burned; the first and only time the prosecuting attorney raised his voice to a shout, he sensed the inappropriateness, and he lowered it in midsentence. The courtroom experience produces many revelations, and the strangest one occurred on the last day. After all the torture I thought *I* had gone through—all the testimonies being weeded, repeated, reweeded—I stood up to hear the verdict and found myself feeling sorry for the jury. They looked more beaten than I was. Even though it was my life hanging in the balance, it had been, after all, *my* crime, and they had been dragged through every detail of it. Who can say to what degree the whole ordeal of sitting in judgment taxed, perhaps even changed, their lives? One murder, yet who knows how far the reverberations can reach? However, I'm not going to tell you much about the trial. I'm going to tell you about the murder itself and the circumstances leading up to it. Not surprisingly, those circumstances were defined and determined by love, my own and my victim's. Since love is neither static nor isolated from everyday events, it journeys through a number of stages, from one place to another. And for some, love's last stop is a public courtroom. The newspaper implied as much when it printed my wedding picture next to a later photograph of my husband, my daughter and myself, our smiling faces looming above copy that detailed the grim events surrounding the murder. This juxtaposition was calculated to dramatize not only the death of a person but also the death of a marriage, the disintegration of a once happy family—and, of course, calculated to strike suspicion and fear in the hearts of the complacent.

I hope I am as objective and detached as I sound. During the trial, I had plenty of time to become that way, and I'll try to remain so as I tell you the story. If at any point I feel I'm losing that detachment, I'll do my best to let you know it so you can be on your guard. After all, you have your own powers of judgment to rely upon; *mine* only got me to where I am now. . . .

DETACHMENT. It was the very thing that first attracted me to Frank. I was working on my master's degree at the state university and was quite content with being the fair-haired favorite in the English Department. As an undergraduate, I had made the dean's list every term and had been admitted to the Honors College, a distinction which carried all sorts of practical advantages, including a private room in an overcrowded dormitory. I stayed on at State for my master's even though I was courted by fellowship offerings from five more prestigious universities. I was secure, comfortable and smugly superior. At the time I met Frank, I wasn't consciously aware that I was tiring of my niche. Had I been as satisfied as I thought I was, I probably would have dismissed him at our first encounter.

I had only one girlfriend, Gloria Davidson, who lived in an apartment off campus. There were many reasons for my liking Gloria. Being number four scholastically in the English Department, she never begrudged my being number one, and she never competed. She was forthright and witty, more glamorous but less vain than I, and uncommonly loyal. Despite the fact that we were the same age, I called her "the kid," an endearment she would smile at and one that succinctly defined our relationship. I had no sister, only two younger brothers; she had one older sister, whom she disliked, and so the chosen roles in our friendship were perfectly suited to each of us. Whenever we double-dated, she had a childlike and charming way of showing off our friendship by directing most of her attention to me while her date was drooling over her. She enjoyed my mock cynicism and was dazzled by the impression I gave of being totally self-sufficient. Whenever possible, she signed up for the same classes I did. Sitting next to me, she would take copious notes while I slouched in my seat, lost in a crossword puzzle or a newspaper bridge column. Now and then, when there was a lull in the lecture, she would glance at me, amused, and yet admiring my "rebelliousness." I helped her shop for clothes and passed judgment on the men she went out with. Secretly, I reveled in the knowledge that I was the rock and she the tide. However, the self-serving incompleteness of this metaphor escaped me at the time: for it is the movement of the tide which shapes the rock. Later, Gloria was to become a major influence in my life—and a witness to the murder.

Frank lived in Gloria's building, and we met at a party given by another tenant. After my first glimpse of him standing in the middle of the room, I turned to Gloria and said, "Where did they dig up Abe Lincoln?" I assumed immediately, and correctly, that he was a history major, since that department had a reputation for corraling the oddest-looking people on campus. He had the uniform black-frame glasses and the pipe filled with Cherry Blend, the requisite tattered turtleneck (although it was the middle of May) and the worn trousers shiny in the seat. His stiltlike legs seemed to compose more than half his height of well over six feet. Actually, he didn't look at all like Abe Lincoln; his face wasn't that dramatic. I remember thinking his features were actually recessive, because there was nothing distinctive or imposing about them. His eyes were simply oval, his nose short and straight, his mouth neither too thin nor too ample. Viewed full face, he was average; in profile, forgettable. For 1958, his hair was rebelliously long, the color of mud, the texture of straw. He was nothing the movies were looking for and not what *I* would have looked for—had I been looking.

The party was quite successful. Most of the people were serious students who on the weekends became serious drinkers. Long before midnight, most of us were drunk and playing a vicious game called Speculation, wherein each of us matched up two unpopular faculty members, created an unlikely dialogue between them, then speculated on what they could possibly find to do with each other in bed. I loved this game (I played only those games I was good at) because my speculations

4

usually made me the center of attention. At these parties, I was the rock, with all kinds of crosscurrents caressing me. This party was no exception—until I went into the kitchen to freshen my drink. Just before I reached the doorway, I heard Frank say inside: "It's the purest form of love there is."

I rounded the corner in time to see the other man responding with a smirk. "What is?" I asked.

Frank blushed at my intrusion. "It's too involved," he replied.

"Don't you history people ever *relax?*"

He smiled indulgently, and his silence indicated the conversation would continue only after I left. I took my time mixing my drink. They waited. Not a word. At parties, there were damned few conversations I was not welcome in. *I* was the one who did the picking and choosing. Just where did this recessive Abe Lincoln get off being a snob?

The more I drank, the larger the slight became, and I grew sullenly discontent with the attention the others were paying me. The next time I went to the kitchen, I stood on the other side of the doorway and eavesdropped.

"A good historian is never completely objective," Frank was saying to his companion. "Without subjectivity, you might as well let those computers write the textbooks."

This was my cue. I stepped in and said, "We *could* use those computers to replace some of the dialogue that goes on at parties. Really, boys, didn't you get your fill of profundities back in your sophomore year?"

"Maybe not," said Frank, "but long before then I learned eavesdropping is rude."

I had always appreciated a good rejoinder, but Frank's voice did not carry the typical *touché.* His smile remained polite and unchastising. I withdrew again, but when I returned to the group in the living room I took up a new position on the floor, which gave me a partial view of the kitchen door. The game of Speculation continued, but I bowed out so as not to have my attention divided.

Finally, Frank and the other man came out of the kitchen and stood next to our seated circle. I was drunk, so drunk I could feel the tiny contortions my face was going through trying to find the smirk I wanted. The effort was pointless. Frank said goodnight without singling me out by word or gesture. And off he went.

He was, I told myself, too tall, too skinny, too humorless, too *forgettable* (and gap-toothed, besides), to get away with that condescending attitude. I hadn't had a challenge in a long time, and as petty as this one was, I decided to finish the evening with it: I turned to Gloria and asked which apartment he lived in. She looked at me in amazement.

"Him? You don't know the first thing about him," she said, implying *she* did.

With my opening line decided upon, I left the party and knocked on his door. It took three knocks before he answered. He was wearing a bathrobe that was meant to reach the shins but only made it as far as his knees.

"What *is* the purest form of love there is?" I asked.

His smile was tight and tolerant, enough to push my courage back into reserve. "Right now," he said, "the purest form would be the consideration we give our neighbors when they want to sleep. Good night."

Well, I thought, not bad. Not bad at all. It could be he was not half so dreary as I imagined. And different, much different from the other men I'd met at these parties.

As always when I had drunk this much, I stayed at Gloria's. She rolled her eyes when I came in. "My God"—she laughed—"you must really be smashed."

"Why?"

"Going up to the weirdo's."

"The weirdo?"

"That's what they call him."

"They who?"

"People in the building." She cocked her head, her smile now puzzled. "Why *did* you go up there?"

"To"—thinking quickly—"apologize."

"Apologize! For what?"

"I was rude to him in the kitchen. How is he weird?"

"The girls come and go at all hours. He ought to put up a revolving door."

"Him? Come on! He's not the type."

"No, he's not the type—for anything *conventional*. And you ought to get a load of the girls."

"Cheap?"

"No. But pathetic. Homely and kind of lost-looking. And very young. Some of them must still be in high school."

"Maybe he's a counselor or something."

"Yeah, and I'm Greta Garbo going to college. Listen, Tom Kennard's apartment is right next to his and he hears everything through the wall. He says there's always a lot of crying."

"Crying?"

"I'm telling you, he is *weird*. Even the guys in this building think so."

I laughed. "Oh, well, then, that should settle it!"

I didn't see him again for over a month. I had six dates with a basketball player who at any other time would have been just the nourishment my ego delighted in. He was considerate, affectionate, very sexually interested, but gentleman enough to take no for an answer and still keep calling, and he wanted to read some of the authors I said were my favorites so we could discuss them. He even wanted to take me home with him over Memorial Day weekend to meet his parents. For a while, he balanced the scales of my indecisiveness perfectly. On the one hand, he was kind and sensitive; on the other, dull and persistent. The only way my conscience would let me unload him was by lying. I told him I had rekindled an old flame and there was no future in our continuing to see each other. He took it with the kind of graciousness that made me want to slug myself.

Spring term ended, and I signed up for two classes over the summer. I moved out of the dormitory and in with Gloria. She was short on money and took a part-time job in a travel agency, so that three days a week I had the apartment to myself. During the first week I saw nothing of Frank, and I thought maybe he had gone away for the summer even though his name remained on the mailbox. With too much time on my hands, I became friendly with Tom Kennard, a likable bore, and his girlfriend, Janet, a harmless twit whose most memorable features were a sorority pin and a lisp. The three of us spent several afternoons drinking beer in Tom's apartment, and I sometimes turned the topic of conversation to "the weirdo" living next door to him.

Frank, they said, was something of a prodigy, having finished his master's at twenty-one and now, at twenty-five, nearly through with his doctoral dissertation. His area of concentration was Asian-African Studies ("Very faddish," affirmed Janet, puckering the *f*), which probably accounted for the sparseness of his living conditions. Tom had been in Frank's apartment only once, and according to him, once was enough. Old cushions and pillows substituted for furniture, the walls were absolutely barren, and except for one study lamp and the fluorescent tubes in the kitchen and bathroom, the entire place was lighted by candles. The living room, said Tom, looked more like a hut than a home.

"What about those girls who come to see him?" I asked.

"God only knows what they do in there," said Janet. "I wouldn't be surprised if he practices voodoo."

8

When I finally saw him again, it wasn't in our apartment building but in the student union grill. Sitting alone in a booth, he had a book in front of him, from which he read only bits at a time. He would lift his eyes from the page and squint pensively, giving the impression he was not about to accept anything until he had taken it apart for himself. While I stood in the cafeteria line waiting for my cheeseburger, I stared at him, but I was analyzing myself. Why in hell did he interest me? There had been other guys, much more appealing in every respect, whom I had found unattainable, and I had never compromised myself by pursuing them. Here I was a student of Literature and therefore, I figured, a student of human motives and emotions; still, I could not put a finger on the motives behind my own behavior. I wasn't out husband-hunting, I didn't suffer from nymphomania, I had no penchant for tall men, I wasn't a masochist who enjoyed rejection, I had little interest in history or politics or anything else he was likely to talk about, I was unimpressed by his bohemian appearance, and I *certainly* wasn't one of those lost little girls who need a man to tell them who they are.

"Hi. Remember me?"

He looked up and blinked. He was still absorbed in his book and his own thoughts. I felt like the violator of some intimate connection.

"Yes," he said, "I remember. The eavesdropper."

I sensed I wouldn't be invited, so I sat down immediately.

"Well, eavesdropping is one way of finding out things. Another thing I've found out is that you make your girlfriends cry."

His mouth tightened. "Let's put it another way: I *let* them cry."

"Oh? And what do they have to cry about?"

"Things you probably wouldn't understand." Said

oh, so politely, but it was a definite swipe. An emotional snob, I thought.

"Do you run ads in the paper? 'Strong shoulder seeks tears'? Or 'Have compassion, will travel'?"

He inhaled deeply and looked away.

"Well," I continued, "how *do* you meet them?"

"You don't strike me as the type who goes in for small talk. Why are you doing it with me?"

"I wouldn't classify this as small talk. Unless you consider your personal life small."

"You're very good at passing the ball. If you'll excuse me, I—"

"No. Please. I don't like eating alone."

"You came in here alone."

"But now I'm not. Please stay."

"I'm too uncomfortable," he said.

"I make you uncomfortable?"

"Yes."

"Why?"

"Because . . ." His face reddened, his tone hardened. "I don't know what you're up to. But whatever it is, it's not attractive, and I'm not amused."

"You mean I'm not your type?"

He winced at this, picked up his book and left.

I sulked the entire evening. Gloria and I played Scrabble. I drew nothing but vowels, cursed my luck, snapped at Gloria, smoked one cigarette after another, criticized Rita Hayworth's acting on the midnight movie, and went to bed with a headache.

When I woke up on Saturday, I resolved to pull myself out of this slump. But the very fact that I did not understand the slump irritated me all the more. I began working on a paper due on Tuesday, but Ugo Betti and his "emblematic themes" could not compete with Frank's words going round and round in my head: "Things you probably wouldn't understand" and "I'm not amused." How dare he! If I considered myself to be anything, it was bright and amusing. I was the

10

"star" of the dormitory I had lived in, always the center of attention when I wanted it. I was also famous for whipping up a paper in five or six hours, and I had often been propositioned by the other girls to write theirs for them. I wanted to tell *him* about the time a girl from Shaker Heights laid a hundred dollars on my desk (tempted, I still declined it) and begged me to write something on Sinclair Lewis so she could spend the weekend shacked up with the mechanic who had replaced the spark plugs in her Corvette.

But *this* paper I was working on did not come together. By Sunday night it was still disjointed and lacking focus. I pushed it aside and asked Gloria if she wanted to go out for a beer. Although she had to get up for work the next morning, she sprang from her chair and got to the door before I did. All weekend she had been watching me the way I imagine doctors watch a terminal case; obviously, she equated my suggestion with improved health.

Just as we reached the parking lot, Frank and a girl were getting out of his car, each with a bag of groceries. Instantly, I consoled myself with the fact that the girl was pale and mousy. But as Frank looked at me and quickly turned away, I was struck by something else: because the girl was so puny, she could easily have been seventeen or eighteen, but she could also have been as young as fourteen. What really got to me were the groceries; somehow, they seemed just as suggestive as a toothbrush and pajamas.

"What a sorry-looking little thing she is," I muttered as we drove away.

"That's exactly what I told you about," said Gloria. "And she'll probably be sorrier for getting mixed up with him."

I didn't answer. I waited until we got to the Campus Keg and had a beer in front of us, then told her what had happened in the union grill. She looked at me in surprise.

11

"You mean *you* went over to *him?*"

"You don't have to say it like that," I protested.

"Oh, brother!" she said, rolling her eyes. "Are you suddenly developing a taste for strange excitement?"

It was bad enough being angry at *him,* but Gloria's criticism of me tempted me into playing devil's advocate.

"Don't get dramatic," I said. "What is he—Jack the Ripper?"

"Meet him in the fog sometime and find out." She lifted her glass of beer and was about to sip, when suddenly her face turned sly. "Waaaait a minute. Is that why . . ." She leaned forward. "Is that little incident with *him* the reason you've been obnoxious all weekend?"

"Of course not," I answered irritably. "I just don't see why you're so critical of him."

"*Me* critical! Look who's talking—Irene Rutledge, verbal lampoonist *par excellence*. Compared to you, I'm Little Nell."

"All right, Nell, let's drop it."

As we drove back home, I was fully aware of the subtle side glances she was giving me. When we pulled into the parking lot, Frank's car was gone. Gloria looked at the empty spot and said, "Well, that must have been a quick meal."

"Maybe the girl took off with his car," I said sullenly.

"I hope you're not going to knock on his door to find out."

"Let's just forget it."

"Exactly my sentiments."

For the next two weeks I busied myself with reading, working on a tan at the campus swimming pool, and deliberating over which classes to take in the fall, when I would enter the Ph.D. program. Gloria had a party and conspicuously left Frank uninvited; if she expected a reaction from me, she didn't get it. I was regaining the old grip on myself, the rock reassuming its comfortable firmness.

Then came the incident with Larry.

One morning in July, I saw a group of fraternity boys, identifiable by the pins on their sport shirts, running around blindfolded in the grassy area between the auditorium and the river which cut through the center of the campus. The mysterious game turned out to be Blindfolded Football, wherein the *un*blindfolded quarterback of each team called the signals and yelled out directions to the other team players. I thought it thoroughly ridiculous but just comic enough to watch a few minutes before moving on to my class. Standing on the dirt footpath about three feet from the river, I was soon noticed by one of the quarterbacks. He smiled and before the next play he shouted to his team, "All right, you guys, there's a gorgeous redhead standing over here who's waiting to see what you can do!"

Coming toward me on the footpath, but a good distance away, was a blind boy. In one hand was a briefcase, in the other the white stick he used as a "sweep" in front of him. Even farther in the distance, but approaching in the same direction, was Frank. Although I pretended to watch the players, I kept Frank in my sights, and I noticed quite plainly that the second he saw me, he turned abruptly and began to cut across the grass toward the auditorium. He kept his eyes on the ground and quickened his step until it was almost a sprint.

God! I fumed. What does he think I am—poison?

"To the left! To the left! The *left,* Donovan, you dumb jerk!"

I turned in time to see a wave of players heading toward the river—and the blind boy. The boy stopped immediately, his head making the same back-and-forth sweeping motion his stick had made.

"Look out!" I yelled. "Look out for—" It was too late.

Some of the players did halt, but three crashed into the boy and sent him tumbling right into the river. For a few seconds, my legs wouldn't move, and when they did, I found myself converging on the scene simultaneously with Frank. The boy was flailing the water, and the others, blindfolds removed, were shouting, "This way! Swim *this* way!" Fortunately, there was a good-sized stick right at my feet. I picked it up and called, "Use this—get him to grab hold of this!" (The reason we were all unwilling to jump in unless the boy went under was that the river was practically stagnant and notoriously filthy, not so much a river as an elongated cesspool. Upstream from where we stood there were patches of green slime beneath an overhang of trees.) The boy stretched out his hand, but a few inches remained between him and the stick. One of the quarterbacks surrendered it to Frank, whose long and lanky arm filled in the needed inches. The boy was pulled out, and Frank sat him down on the ground. The smell of the river on his clothes was atrocious; the players backed away from it.

"My briefcase! Where's my briefcase!"

I turned and saw the last corner of it sinking into the water.

Frank said, "I'm afraid it's gone."

"It can't be! Everything's in it! My notes, my . . ." He was almost crying.

My panic gone, I was quickly filled with anger. Eying the quarterback, I said, "I hope you're satisfied, you stupid ass!"

"Me? *I* didn't run into him."

"You were calling the directions! You know there's a footpath here, you know people use it, you saw *me* here, you certainly saw *him!*"

"I didn't. I—"

"And the rest of you, running around like five-year-olds—blindfolded, for God's sake!" Their blindfolds were off; they could walk away as freely as they

14

pleased. But the boy couldn't. The grim irony of the situation made me furious. "He could have drowned!"

"Look, we're sorry."

"Sorry isn't going to rescue his briefcase."

Satisfied that Frank was looking after the boy, the players retreated, mumbling to each other. I heard one of them say, "Man, what a bitch *she* is."

I bent down in front of the boy. "You know, you'll have to have a tetanus shot."

"My notes, everything . . ." He bit his lip.

"His stick went into the river," I said to Frank. "I'd take him to the health center, but I have to get to class. I have a test. Could you take him?"

"Sure," he said, actually smiling at me.

I was in the middle of supper and telling Gloria about the incident when the doorbell rang. It was Frank.

"Come in. Did he get his shot?"

"Yes, he's okay. I spoke to three of his professors this afternoon and told them what happened. They'll arrange to have someone dictate the notes he lost. By the way, I invited him over for dinner tomorrow night. I wondered if you wanted to come too."

The invitation came too unexpectedly for me to be anything but direct. "Sure. Why don't you sit down and have some coffee? We were just finishing."

"Thanks, but I have company." He looked past me and said, "You're invited too, Gloria."

The double invitation annoyed me. And "I have company" conjured up a picture of that mousy girl with the groceries.

"And what are *you* looking at?" I challenged Gloria after he left.

"The willing fly about to enter the web."

"You mean you're not going?"

Her only answer was a smirk.

FRANK made spaghetti and clam sauce and presented Larry with a new briefcase. After dinner we sat on cushions and drank wine. My face was as placid as Buddha's, but my insides were roiling, first with anticipation, then with resentment. Frank turned the whole conversation over to Larry, asking about things like the Braille facilities in the library and the note-taking device blind students use. Larry needed little encouragement. He rattled on about his childhood, and the two of them tossed around the subject of who were more fortunate—those who had never seen or those who had lost their sight. I contributed nothing, even though Frank tried to rope me in by asking my opinion here and there. I kept pouring wine from the half-gallon jug and staring at Frank's bare legs. They were so skinny that the thighs were barely wider than the knees. Why, I asked myself, would someone with those legs wear shorts? But then, why should I be staring at them? Why did I want to reach out and run my hands down them? Up to this time, I had slept with only two guys. Both of them had been handsome, nearly perfect specimens, but even so, I never became aroused simply by looking at them. Maybe because this new attraction was so alien to me, I was able to get hold of myself and switch from wine to coffee. The coffee kept my eyes off his legs, but watching his face and listening to his voice didn't help my resistance. He listened to Larry with the same facial expression he had had while reading that book in the union grill: he wasn't being merely polite, he was *interested*. Sullenly, I told myself he'd listen to a grasshopper if it could talk.

Finally, Larry said he had to be getting back to the dorm. Boldly, I told Frank I wanted to go along for the ride. He nodded and smiled, but even in the candlelight I could see him coloring.

Before he got out of the car, Larry asked if he could feel our faces. He did Frank's first. When it came my turn, I expected his hands to be as clammy as his eyes looked. They weren't. As a matter of fact, there was something comforting in the touch, as though I were being examined by an old family doctor. When he finished, he said we made a nice-looking couple. Frank was clearly embarrassed, and I was ashamed at having said practically nothing to Larry all evening.

Riding back home, I tried to think of anything except where we were heading. Inviting myself along to the dorm was one thing; I could not suggest that he invite me back up to his apartment. I looked over at his white, white legs as we passed under a streetlamp.

"Do you ever go out in the sun?" I asked.

"You mean lie in it?"

"Yes."

"I don't have the patience for it."

"Really? You strike me as the very essence of patience."

No response.

"Besides the sun," I said, "what else are you impatient with?"

He smiled. "Other people's impatience, I guess."

"Ohhh, impatient with impatience. Very Philosophy 101. Shall we go on to falling in love with love and I hate to hate? Anything else you're impatient with?"

"I'll have to think about it."

"What about . . . aggressive girls?"

"They make me nervous."

"Why is that?"

"They usually have too many expectations. They want soft bells and sirens and violins and calliopes all at the same time."

"I see. Tone deaf emotionally. Your, uh, little girl-

17

friend with the groceries—she's very retiring, I suppose."

"Yes." It was a "yes" that meant "Back Off: Dead End."

"The aggressive girls—how do you handle them?"

"Would you like to get some ice cream?"

The thought of taking it back to his apartment squelched my objection to the evasion. "Anything but strawberry."

For the first time, he took his eyes off the road and looked at me. *That's* how I handle aggressive girls." He smiled.

"Very cute. You *are* smug."

"Oh, no." He chuckled. "When it comes to smugness, you've got the market cornered."

We pulled up to a small grocery store, and he went in.

I was not aware of any hidden chord in me aching to be plucked. Yet as I sat there staring through double glass—the windshield and the store window —I was determined to make him want me. He stood at the counter talking to the clerk, a middle-aged man whose face and manner were so thoroughly bland that his conversation just had to match. The man propped his arms on top of the cash register as if his listener were going to stay for a while. Frank smiled, then laughed. I saw him laugh, but I had never *heard* him laugh—not in the open, forthright way he seemed to be doing it now. A storekeeper, not clever Irene Rutledge, caused him to laugh. It didn't make sense.

We took the ice cream back to his apartment. Coming up the steps, we met Gloria on her way to the incinerator. The look she gave me would have wilted a nun, but nothing short of an earthquake could have altered my course.

He spooned my ice cream into a dish and ate his from the container. Gospel music was playing on his transistor radio, and the flame of the candle seemed to flicker with the voices. The barrenness of the room, which I had found unpleasant earlier, now seemed comforting.

"How did you happen to go into Asian-African Studies?"

He shrugged. "I guess because so much of their history has yet to be made. Right now they're the world's underdogs, and underdogs are always interesting to watch, if just to see which way they'll go— Look, I don't want to bore you."

"You're safe until I yawn."

He laughed. Out loud. Very good, I thought. You're making *some* progress. What he didn't know was that he could have read me the Betty Crocker cookbook, for all I cared. At least he was talking.

There was a storytelling lilt to his voice as he enumerated historical examples of underdogs turned top dogs. He talked about turnabouts in national identities, the role of chance in determining world powers. What really impressed me was that he did not sound academic or pedantic. History, it seemed, was a very *personal* matter to him.

"History," he said, "has always proven one cliché: After you get what you want, you don't want it. It'll be interesting to see what Asia and Africa *give* up as they try to *catch* up—what they give up willingly and what they give up unknowingly. Look at Japan. Someday they'll put all their chopsticks in museums and pick up the plastic fork." He pressed his palms together and bowed. "Ah so. End of honorable and pompous lecture."

"What inspired this interest in the underdog?"

He hesitated, scraping the bottom of the ice cream container. "I guess most of my life *I* was pretty much the underdog."

"In what way?"

"I was raised in a small town, where your name sums you up. There were two rock-bottom families, us and the Hooples. Old Man Hoople was a drunk and eventually went to prison. None of the Hoople kids except one made it beyond the tenth grade. But we were considered respectably poor because my father always worked. Most people pitied us, but they had contempt for the Hooples. Even my mother. If any of us complained about something we didn't have, she'd say, 'Just be glad you ain't a Hoople.' She spent half the day reading the Bible, but she pulled rank on the Hooples every chance she got. She was too ignorant to see that what she was doing to them, everyone else was doing to us: clustering us under one name as if we'd all been stamped out of some inferior mold. She didn't know there was one Hoople she could never pull rank on." He stared wistfully into the flame of the candle between us. "Wanda Hoople," he said softly, as though caressing the name. "I haven't thought about her in years. Not until yesterday. It hit me when I was holding that stick out for Larry to grab. Suddenly I wished I'd done the same for Wanda."

I began to picture Wanda Hoople as the girl with the groceries. "She drowned?" I asked.

"In a way," he said, still looking at the candle. "Every year the high school put on a Holly Hop, a dressy Christmas dance where the girls asked the boys. I had never had a date in high school and I sure wasn't planning on being asked. But Wanda asked me. Three days in a row she stood on this street corner in the morning when I came to school and then again in the afternoon when I went home. She lived in the opposite direction, so there was no reason for her being there. The third day we saw her, my friend and I started joking about it. I said maybe she was trying to get picked up. Her sisters were all whores, so it was easy to figure she would follow the same path. Since it had been drilled into me that the Hooples were below us, I didn't want to admit even one of them could be different from the rest. But Wanda *was* different. Her skirts were always safety-pinned in the back and her ankle socks were so limp they kept sliding down into her shoes, but her face and hair—shiny as glass. The other girls in school were experimenting with make-up, but she never wore it. Her *sisters* wore it in layers, but she didn't. Her face and hair were sort of a badge, something that would show everyone she was *clean*. Her sisters were loud too, always egging on the boys to prove they could talk dirtier. But Wanda was a mouse. That third afternoon we passed her, she called out my name. Her eyes looked terrified when she asked me to step over to the curb. There was this pause and when she finally asked me to go to the dance she didn't look at me, she looked at the fire hydrant. For a minute I thought it was a joke, or maybe I was hoping it was. I didn't answer her; I just stared at the rip in her coat and felt my face getting hot. Then she began to back away, very slowly. I stood there, she stopped for a second, then backed up some more. I heard my friend snickering and I felt the heat in my face, but I didn't say a word. She gave me one last look, like I was going to kill her or something, and she ran off down the street. I could have called out to her, but I didn't."

"Did you ever speak to her after that?"

He shook his head. "My friend spread the word and it became a big joke for a while. I wanted to hate her for embarrassing me, but . . . I couldn't get past that look on her face. Or those socks that went down in her shoes. Whenever we saw each other in school, we both looked the other way. I didn't want to admit to myself I was ashamed. When she asked me that day, it must have taken every ounce of courage she had, and all she got for it was humiliation. She quit school in the middle of the twelfth grade and got married to a much older man who was a farmer. That was just about the time I was looking forward to getting out of that town and going to college."

He lit his pipe and blew smoke rings, staring at each

one as it drifted upward to build a hazy scaffolding of gray. When he spoke again, he continued in that soft, storytelling tone. But his face appeared cautious, as if he were veering away from an emotion that would interrupt him.

"The PTA gave me a one-year scholarship, something they'd never have given a Hoople. I got my picture in the paper and then I got a letter from Wanda. It said: 'Dear Frank, I'm sorry about that day. Good luck in college and in the future. Sincerely, Wanda Lowell—parentheses Hoople.' You know what got me? The parentheses. Reminding me as if she were *forgettable*. No one should ever have to feel that way." Then in the next breath, but out of nowhere, he said: "I hate it when people just *breed*."

The mixture of sadness and repugnance startled me, but I had no time to respond. He looked at me full face and said, "Why have you been showing an interest in me?"

"Because I've never gone out with a history major." It was a stupid cover-up, far beneath my talents, and that tolerant smile of his made me feel more ridiculous. "I don't know," I mumbled.

"Well," he said, "it's not because I look like Clark Gable and it's not because you've seen me driving around in a Cadillac. I'm not one of the campus lovers." He smirked. "It must be my reputation as the life of the party."

"Don't toy with me."

"Don't *you* toy with *me*."

"What are you talking about?"

"I don't enjoy being a diverting amusement. Although in your case . . ."

"You haven't given me a chance to. I'm surprised you even bothered to find out my name!"

"I found out a lot this morning. Your name is Irene Abigail Rutledge. Student number: 111314. Hometown: Cedar Run. Major: English. Birth date: June 1,

1936. Two younger brothers. B.A., summa cum laude. The English Department's model student and secretly —or semisecretly—leched after by two esteemed members of same department."

"What!"

"You're very confident, probably too bright for your own good, susceptible to alcohol, aggressiveness and sarcasm, charming when made to feel secure, intolerant of carelessness (yesterday's incident), and lovely to look at in *any* mood." He paused, lowering his voice. "And perversely fond of shaking up scarecrows."

There seemed to be tiny fish swimming through my blood: my hands felt twitchy although they were perfectly limp in my lap. "How did you find out all that?"

"I never reveal my sources."

"You're not a scarecrow," I said, "but I'd like to hear how I shook you up."

"I'm sure you would. But you have a capful of feathers already. I'll tell you about it later—when I'm over it."

"Maybe I don't want you to be over it."

He got up and brought over the wine. We drank and stared at each other. He gave in and lowered his eyes.

"I guess," he said, "this is where I'm supposed to take you in my arms."

"Why don't you?"

He shook his head. "I'd rather wait. If you don't mind."

"Until when?"

"Next time."

"Tomorrow night?"

"No; I'll have quizzes to grade tomorrow night."

"Are you backing off now?"

"Can you meet me for lunch day after tomorrow?"

We set the time and place, and I got up to leave. Before he opened the door, I stood on my toes and put my hands behind his neck.

"How about a down payment?" I said.

His body trembled and his lips quivered against mine. It was the tenderest and most awkward kiss I had ever gotten, and I hung on until he pulled away.

FOR the next few weeks, Wanda Hoople took up daily residence in my thoughts simply because Frank's description of her also applied to him. Around me, he was hesitant and timid. *I* had to reach for *his* hand when we walked together or take him in *my* arms when I wanted a kiss. He always waited for me to let him know when I was "free" to see him. And the first time we slept together it was at my insistence.

"I'm not very experienced," he said, looking away. It was a Saturday afternoon in August, pouring rain. He had just taken off his wet socks, and I was drying my hair with a towel.

"I don't want experience. I want you."

We sat down on the cushions; I leaned over and kissed the arch of his foot.

"We don't have to do anything," I said. "We can just lie naked together."

I stood up and undressed. The look on Frank's face was almost reverential; for a second, I felt like Botticelli's Venus on the half shell. When I sat down next to him, he gently pushed my knees up under my chin, held all of me in his arms, and kissed my hair and eyes. Then he released me and stood up. He tried to hide his apprehension as he pulled off the shirt and trousers. When he stuck his thumbs into the waistband of his boxer shorts, he paused and said, "I'm not circumcised." He said it as though this were equivalent to being a hermaphrodite.

"That's all right," I said. "Neither am I."

It worked. He laughed out loud and pulled off the shorts.

"Why does it bother you?" I asked.

"I've heard a lot of women don't like it. They find it repulsive."

"I don't see why." I reached down and slowly pulled the foreskin back. "Look, it's like watching something being born."

"In more ways than one." He was becoming erect.

The first time we made love, there on the floor, it was awkward but not embarrassingly so. We were both intent upon pleasing each other, but he was too large and I was too tight.

"Can we stop for a while?" I said. "It hurts."

"Sure. It hurts me too."

This surprised and pleased me. I had thought anything that hard must be invincible. Knowing that he hurt too made the pain almost pleasurable. We lay back on the cushions and had several glasses of wine.

By the time we went to sleep that night, we had made love six times. It would have been five, but just as we were drifting off, he suggested we make it an even half dozen. The whole afternoon and evening I experienced a new and wonderful feeling of abandonment: he was like a starving man, and my body was the banquet.

I returned to my apartment Sunday night riding on a balloon even Gloria couldn't puncture.

"Well, well, look who's back from the stud farm."

"Is there anything to eat?"

"Why? Didn't you have time for that?"

"No, as a matter of fact."

She looked me up and down, as if overnight I had become defective. I made a sandwich and sat down opposite her while she lacquered her nails. Her intense concentration was an obvious ploy to irritate me.

"And what's wrong with you?" I said.

"There's nothing wrong with *me*. I don't understand

it. I've known you four years and I'm just finding out I don't know you at all."

"Why? Because I spent two days with a man?"

"With *that* man."

"What exactly is wrong with him?"

"That's just it—*you* don't see it. That's what's so crazy!"

"Suppose you spell it out for me."

"Spell it! All right, he's w-e-i-r-d. You're way out of his c-l-a-s-s. He can't function socially, he has no friends except those pathetic creatures he drags in, he's always got his nose in a book, he looks like he's never seen sunlight or decent food, or soap and water for that matter."

"Now wait a minute—"

"His hands are filthy, or didn't you notice?"

"That is grease on his hands because he works on his car instead of paying some half-wit mechanic to do it."

"Well, hooray for the handyman. What gets me is you don't mind being one of *that* harem."

"There is no harem. You're being awfully presumptuous."

"I suppose those girls are phantoms. And the one we saw in the parking lot—I suppose that's his sister."

"He's discussed all that with me. He just happens to feel sorry for them. That girl we saw is a freshman in the class he teaches. She's from a small town and she's having trouble adjusting. She has two horrendous roommates who—"

"Spare me the details. All I'm going to say is I thought you had better sense. I thought it would take only a few dates for the novelty to wear off. And now" —she shivered—"you've slept with him."

"You bet I did," I said to get even for her shiver. "Slept and slept and slept."

"Irene, there's something wrong with him. I can *sense* it."

"That analysis is medieval."

"You listen to me. 'The kid' has something to say."

" 'The kid' has had plenty to say."

"Be quiet, for a change. I thought you, of all people, would keep your eyes open when you met someone. A good relationship has to be equal, one where both parties bring something valuable to share. The scales have to balance or else someone gets cheated. And it's always the one who had the *most* to offer."

"Thank you, Ann Landers."

"I've watched it happen. It happened to my mother."

"Yes, you've told me." Her father was an inveterate lecher, her mother now an alcoholic. "But I don't plan to go down the same path. Now can we drop the subject? No one has said I'm going to marry the guy."

"Famous last words."

GLORIA's appraisal of Frank did not soften. Whenever he came into the apartment she managed to be civil, *too* civil; then she would retreat to the bedroom and stay there until he left. Even on the nights I had him in for dinner, she refused to join us and often went out to eat; sometimes she would call from a public phone to make sure he was gone before she got back. Aside from Gloria's behavior, I was angered by Frank's complacent acceptance of it.

"She loves you very much," he said. "I never had a friend like that. You're very lucky. I think it's better if I don't come down here anymore."

"I'm not going to let her rule my life."

"Irene, it's her apartment, it's her name on the lease. We can see each other at my place."

"We can at least come here when she's out."

27

"Honey, what's the point? She'd find out. Doing it behind her back would insult her."

"Frank, why are you giving in to her like this?"

"Because she's upset and hurt and I'm not."

So far as he was concerned, it was that simple. Before he got carried away with this consideration for her, I was itching to tell him some of the things she had said behind his back. But I didn't. No matter how magnanimous he might be, there was still room for hurt. Besides, I didn't have to wait long for him to admit she was way out of bounds. He admitted it the day my parents paid a surprise visit.

I had spent Saturday night at Frank's. We were just finishing a late breakfast when the bell rang. Fortunately, I had brought my own robe and had it on when Frank opened the door to my mother and father. My first emotion was murderous: their sheepish smiles told me immediately that Gloria had engineered this intrusion.

"We went to your apartment first," was my mother's weak excuse, "but we didn't know how long it would take you to come down."

"Frank has a telephone," I said. "And so do I. Why didn't you let me know you were coming?"

They had visited me only three times during my college career, and always reluctantly. They preferred my coming home to visit them.

"Well, your father and I thought we'd start doing a few things on the spur of the moment."

"Did you bring Neil and Barry?"

"No. Neil had a date to go bowling with his girlfriend. Barry went camping this weekend."

What she said was plausible but not very probable. Neil loved the campus and would go off on his own to explore whenever he came. I couldn't imagine him passing up this opportunity, especially if he had a girlfriend to show it to. And Barry, who ranked me even higher in his affections than he did his catcher's mitt and hockey stick, was not likely to let a camping trip interfere with visiting me. Unless he hadn't been told.

"Would you like some breakfast?" said Frank.

"Oh, no," said my mother. "We stopped on the way."

"Coffee, then?"

"That would be nice."

My father's eyes were crawling all over the place, until they found my brassiere draped over the desk chair.

"Quite a place you've got here," he said to Frank. "It's really . . . different."

"Different from what?" I said.

Frank flashed me a look which meant "Be gracious," and my mother jumped in to steer the conversation.

"Those big cushions there look comfortable," she said. "And they're so practical too."

Frank brought the coffee, and we all sat down to a grating silence. I broke it with the suggestion that we invite Gloria up too.

"Oh, no," my mother said, flustered. "She was just going out when we came in."

"How convenient for her."

"You'll stay for dinner, won't you?" asked Frank.

"We don't want to impose."

"You're not imposing. I was just going out to the store for vegetables. Any particular kind you like?"

"No, really—"

"They both like green beans," I said.

As soon as Frank was dressed and gone, I put on another pot of coffee and took the chicken from the refrigerator to prepare it for the oven. I wanted them to see that I was familiar with everything in the apartment.

"Are you ready to tell me the truth?" I said casually.

"How long have you been living here?" My father's

tone was too nonchalant, the tone people sometimes use when they find they have been shifted from offense to defense.

"I don't live here. And you didn't answer my question."

"We just hadn't heard from you. . . ." My mother was too unpracticed in lies to complete this one.

"Frank will be back soon," I said, "and I'm not going to discuss this in front of him. Let's not waste time beating around the bush."

"We thought you might be in some kind of trouble," said my father.

"Where did you get that idea?" Neither of them answered. "I know it had to be Gloria. She called you, didn't she?"

"Yes."

"Kenneth!" My mother winced. "You promised you wouldn't—"

"Because she was concerned. It sounds as though you're in a situation you're not aware of," he said.

"Is that so? What did Gloria use for evidence?"

"Now just hold on. We'd like some explanation from *you*. What do you know about this guy? How come there's no furniture in this place? And just what in hell is your brassiere doing over there?"

"Obviously I spent the night here."

"Obviously. And quite a few other nights, it seems."

"That's right."

"I'm glad you're so proud of it!" he snapped. "Maybe you wouldn't mind your brothers knowing about this, either."

"Kenneth!"

"That's up to you," I said. "I didn't ask you to come spying. I'm twenty-two years old. If you care to remember, you got married at twenty and Mom was eighteen."

"That's right. Married. Not shacking up!"

I knew what I was about to say would hurt my

mother more than him, but I couldn't resist. "Married January second. I was born June first. And I wasn't premature."

"Irene! We were engaged!" said my mother.

"You don't have to justify anything to her, Millie. She's just trying to turn the tables." He lit a cigarette and took a deep drag. I had seen this gesture often enough to know he was shifting to his imperious pose. "You know, young lady, you think just because this college hands you some honors you've got the world by the tail. You've got all the answers—past, present and future. Your parents don't know anything and you've got nothing left to learn. You're so clever that everything will go your way, doors will fly open at the mention of your name. Let me tell you something, Miss Honor Student: the world is not holding its breath for you. You may be big stuff on campus, but a university is not reality. Nowhere near it. But you won't find that out until someone knocks you on your smug little butt."

"And you'd like a ringside seat for that event, wouldn't you?"

"Yes, I would." Pause. "And I'll probably end up hating whoever does it."

His frown, as always, was irresistible. I went over and tousled his hair. "You won't have to hate anyone. I've got a pretty good punch of my own."

"That's your trouble," he said, slipping his arm around my waist. "You've always been more independent than the boys. Maybe because you're the oldest. Sometimes you make me feel I have three sons."

"I'm glad Frank doesn't see me that way."

"And how do *you* see *him?*"

"I love him."

"You're sure?"

"As sure as I can be."

"And he feels the same?"

I nodded and felt my face shining. "You can't possibly know him from just one visit. If only you could see him—even the way he reads a newspaper."

He smirked. "He reads it upside down?"

"He *feels* what he reads. The expressions on his face—it's more than just gathering information. He gets involved with what's going on in the world, and that's good for me, it really is." I went on like a mute who has just found a voice. I told them about Frank's shyness, his insecurities, how I had had to go after him. I told them about the incident with Larry, about Frank's childhood of poverty, even about Wanda Hoople.

"So that explains why he hasn't had a haircut since he was ten."

"Oh, Dad, that doesn't matter. It bothered me at first too. But there are other things."

"There must be. He's a rather . . . unlikely-looking man. And a little undernourished. You might lose him to the first strong wind that comes along."

"I don't know what I'd do if that happened. I wouldn't ever want another man to touch me."

This embarrassed them both. They didn't completely look away, but their eyes shifted just slightly to avoid mine. My father rescued himself by joking. "Your mother was crazy about me that way. She was so anxious and nervous the first time I kissed her that the second we touched lips, she farted."

"Kenneth Rutledge, you are a liar!" She reddened, and her mouth puckered to stifle a smile.

"Pop! Just like bubble gum."

"Oh, what a liar you are!"

The telephone rang. It was Frank.

"I'm outside the store," he said. "Should I get some ice cream for the pie?"

"Sure. And hurry back."

He smacked a kiss into the phone.

My father lit another cigarette, imperious once again. "Irene, you've always enjoyed playing devil's advocate. That wouldn't have anything to do with your taking up with Frank, would it?"

"I don't know what you mean."

"I think you do." He looked me squarely in the eye. "He's not exactly what anyone would expect you to choose. It would be cruel to let him fall for you if he's only a novelty to you."

"Novelty—you sound like Gloria. You make me out as some kind of prize going to waste. Did it ever occur to you I might consider Frank the prize?"

"It's just that Gloria made it sound—well, we pictured Frank as the local Lothario making a conquest of our daughter. And now here I am, looking out for *his* welfare. Just promise us one thing: Keep your head and go slowly. Because, like it or not, you're *our* prize. You're our only daughter and that's the way it is."

"That makes us even, since you're my only parents."

He shook his head and sighed. "I can't remember when you didn't have an answer for everything."

The afternoon proved to be a victory over Gloria and her scheme. At first, Frank and my father had little to say to one another. Then they landed on the subject of cars, and my father explained the trouble he was having with his transmission. Together, they went down to the parking lot to look at it. When they returned, we spent the rest of the day playing bridge. Frank and my mother established an easy rapport because they discussed *me*. My mother got a little tipsy on the wine, and by evening the two of them jokingly exchanged suggestions for improving my humility, and ended up assigning me the title Irene the Arrogant.

I lived up to that title the very next night, when I returned to Gloria's apartment to confront her. Initially, she wouldn't even deign to justify what she had done, but by the time I finished packing the first suitcase, she was well into a defensive oration on friendship. In the bathroom, where I scooped my toiletries into a box and snatched up my bath mat and toilet-seat cover, she finally apologized by saying she didn't know what had come over her. Back in the bedroom, she grabbed my wrist as I unplugged my clock-radio.

"Don't, Irene. Please. I was wrong, I'm sorry. I'll apologize to Frank, too, if you want me to. You don't have to do this."

"Let go," I said calmly. She released my wrist.

"I've made a mistake. Nothing like it will happen again, believe me. This is all so ridiculous."

"It *has* been ridiculous." Matter-of-factly, I wrapped the cord around the clock-radio.

"Friends make mistakes; you don't walk out on them because of that. Let's at least talk about it!"

In perfect deadpan, I said, "Consider yourself lucky I *won't* talk about it."

Frank and I settled into a comfortable routine. Since I had more free time than he did (as a graduate assistant, he taught two classes and was adding the finishing touches to his thesis), I took almost full command of running the apartment. To my surprise, I actually enjoyed those menial tasks I had always hated. Growing up at home, I had sneered at cookbooks and dirty dishes and had complained about having to iron blouses and clean my room. All the while I had known Frank, I was amazed at the enthusiasm he had for working on his car. It didn't mesh with his

34

intellectual pursuits, but he explained that working with his hands on a motor gave his mind a much needed change of activity. Quickly, it dawned on me that I had no hobbies at all except reading, going to movies and honing my tongue on some poor, amazed soul at a party. I turned up my nose at Frank's suggestion that I buy some plants. To my mind, plants were something old ladies fussed over after their children left home. Then one day he walked in with a philodendron and told me it was one of the easiest plants to care for. I set it in the window and doused it with water each day until it began to droop, then shrivel. I easily dismissed it as an insignificant failure. But it was the source of my first real argument with Frank.

"You're giving it too much water," he said.

"If I don't water it every day, I'll forget about it completely and never water it."

"That's ridiculous. You have to take a plant on its terms, not yours."

"I'm not going to be a slave to a plant."

"No one's asking you to be a slave. Just considerate."

"For God's sake, it's not a pet."

"It's alive. And you're letting it die."

"What do you want me to do—call in an undertaker?"

"If you can't take care of it properly, just leave it alone."

"With pleasure. It's dead anyway," I said, pulling off a leaf.

"Just don't touch it."

"All right! You don't have to make it sound like I'm the Dutch elm disease." I pulled off another withered leaf. He got up and carried it from the living room into the bedroom and placed it on the window sill near his side of the bed.

I was furious.

"Maybe you'd like me to give it a 2 A.M. feeding with an eyedropper."

"I said leave it alone."

"Oh, who the hell wants to touch the damned thing!" He sat back down at his desk and opened a book. "I'll bet your little girl with the grocery bags has green thumbs."

Silence.

"I'll bet whole greenhouses burst into bloom when she passes through. She's probably an absolute Flora. I can see tulips sprouting in her footsteps, breaking right through concrete. What an enviable talent—to be able to bend your wrist just right as you tip the watering can."

"Don't belittle something you can't do. And someone you don't know." He didn't bother to look up.

"I don't think I can bear going through life now being responsible for the death of a philodendron."

He smiled incredulously. "You're unbelievable. Unbelievable."

"And you're being redundant. Redundant."

"If Irene Rutledge can't do something, then it's not worth doing. It's much more comfortable to look down your nose at it."

"Don't lecture me. I'm not one of your students."

"And don't bother to listen, either, because there's not the slightest chance someone else knows something you don't. Or if they do, it can't be very important. Besides, if it's not in a book, it's not worth knowing."

"Oh, go play with your jumper cables."

"Right now, they'd be better company."

I turned and walked out. I flounced down the steps and threw open the door to the parking lot, only to run smack into Gloria.

"Jesus!" she gasped, staggering backward.

This was all I needed, to have her see me angry at Frank. "I'm sorry. Are you all right?" She had dropped a folder full of travel fliers from the agency she worked at. I stooped and picked them up. "I left a book in the library; now I have to go all the way over and pick it up."

"It's after ten," she said. "The library's closed."

She was right. During the summer term the library closed early. It was a stupid lie. Still, I couldn't go back upstairs. I thrust the folder into her hand and said I'd call her sometime.

I walked ten blocks to the student union, but in the grill the custodian was already putting the chairs on top of the tables. There was still time for a quick cup of coffee, but I didn't feel much like sitting in a place that was closing up around me.

The campus was quiet, dismally so, and that was fine with me. One strolling couple, hand in hand, passed by. I muttered some obscenity under my breath, but apparently loud enough to turn their heads.

I ended up at the botanical gardens, sitting on a bench and smoking one cigarette after another. The lamppost globes lit up only the first few rows of flowers. The rest of the garden was a shadowy arrangement of spikes and clumps. What I couldn't see didn't matter. I didn't know a peony from a petunia. I had never bothered to learn flowers, since I had no plans for becoming a gardener or a Southern writer.

If it's not in a book, it's not worth knowing.

That remark kept crawling around in my mind. I couldn't dismiss it in my usual fashion because I couldn't dismiss the certainty in his voice, the authority on his face. I couldn't even keep a grip on my self-righteous anger, my only source of protection.

He was right. Since high school, I had been so wrapped up in myself that I dismissed anyone or anything that didn't in some way profit or amuse me. That night Larry had come to dinner, I could have taken an interest, but I hadn't because a blind boy didn't serve *my* interest. Looking further back, it occurred to me that when Neil was in Little League, I hadn't gone to a single game. Of course he had asked me, but I figured if my parents put in an appearance, that was sufficient. Not one game. He had been on the team three years, and I didn't know what position he played. I couldn't even remember the name of the team. And there was Barry, little Barry, who had written me letters my first two years of college, letters which went unanswered because I was much too busy.

Suddenly, I began to cry. Over Neil and Barry, over being a fool about the plant and a bitch to Frank. And to Gloria. And I kept crying because Frank saw through me before I did, because our relationship was going to require an honesty I wasn't sure I was capable of.

I thought I had finished crying when I got up and started back to the apartment. But shame was not a familiar feeling to me, and I had no way of fighting the swelling in my throat and the recurring tears. I kept wiping my eyes as I took side streets to avoid the main avenue. I was still wiping them when I reached our building and opened the door at the parking lot entrance. Not since I was twelve had I let anyone see me cry. All right, so he would see me cry; wasn't that something lovers did in front of each other? I would apologize, slip into his arms, and the whole silly mess would be over. I started up the stairs.

I was halfway up when I saw her coming down. The grocery girl. Her eyes were still red and moist from crying. A cold, dull tremor passed through me as the look of recognition was exchanged. She ran down the rest of the way and out the door.

I didn't ring. I opened the door with my key.

He was lying there on one of the cushions, and he jumped up before I got the door closed. His eyes were wild and fearful, but he said nothing. We stood staring at each other.

"Where . . . did you go?" he said at last. Voice

shaky. Face flushed. My eyes slid around the room for evidence.

"I just walked. To the campus." I could hear the chill in my voice.

"Do you—do you feel better now?"

"I'm not sure," I said, letting my eyes drill into his. I went into the kitchen and poured a double shot of bourbon. When I turned around he was standing in the doorway, looking imploringly at me. I sensed he wanted to come closer but wouldn't. Or couldn't.

"Are you still angry?"

"I'm not sure about that, either."

He attempted a smile, but it faded in the silence.

"Do you want to talk about it?" He almost whispered.

"Do you?"

"I'll do whatever you want."

I couldn't even manage a smirk. I was too hurt and angry. "Why the sudden compliance, Frank?"

"I just don't think we should let an argument come between us."

"Why are you so nervous?"

Another attempted smile. "Honey, I don't like arguing. It depresses me."

"And what do you do for consolation when you're . . . 'depressed'?" He cocked his head questioningly. "Do you call someone up for a little reassurance?"

"What do you mean?"

"Since you're not going to tell me, I'll tell you. I just passed your little friend on the stairs. It was pretty obvious she'd been crying. From hearing *your* side of things, no doubt."

"Irene!"

"One argument, and she's back in the picture."

"It's not that way! She just dropped by—"

"Out of the sky."

"Honey, please! She came by about two minutes after you left. She was upset and so was I. I guess I was a little abrupt with her. She had a problem with one of her roommates again—I've told you about that. I was too distracted because of *us;* I really couldn't concern myself with someone else. I didn't tell her we'd had an argument, but I did tell her about you. I kind of wanted her to meet you but not under tonight's circumstances, so I guess I rushed her out of here."

"Quite a rush to make her cry."

"She wasn't crying when she left."

"And *quite* a coincidence."

"But it was a coincidence." He made a fist and held it between his head and the doorjamb. "It was a coincidence."

I started to slip past him, but he spread his arm to block me.

"Don't, Irene."

"Let me past."

"Don't keep running out on me." I nudged against his arm. "Can't you be angry and *stay?*"

"Let me past."

"No." He put his arms around me and pulled me to his chest.

"Don't, Frank." I tried to wriggle free, but his arms tightened.

"Honey, please, how can you think—"

"Let me go."

"I have to tell you something. I'm a . . . freak." That's all he said for a moment. His chest quivered, then his whole body trembled, but his arms grew even tighter around me. I couldn't believe it: he was crying. "I—I love you much too much, I know that. I love you more than it's healthy to love someone. I try to hold it back so I won't smother you and—Jesus! I know it's my fault if I'm so afraid of losing you, but I never thought I'd meet anyone like you who would . . . want me too. I'm guilty of that and probably a lot of other things, but don't accuse me of even *thinking* of someone else. That's not fair, Irene, it really isn't."

He went on stroking my back and my hair. Finally, my arms went around him.

"Maybe I'm the freak," I said. "I don't *want* to be selfish, Frank. Help me not to be."

He picked me up and held me so I was looking down into his face. He smiled, but his cheeks were still wet. "You give me more than you know."

"Including a little grief now and then."

"Yes, indeed, but I'll take it." His smile widened. "You really *were* jealous for a few minutes there?"

"Frank, I don't want to——"

"Come on, were you?"

"Well, what did it look like?"

He was beaming. "No one was ever jealous over me in my life. It's a nice feeling."

"Don't plan on any repetitions, mister."

"And no more running out?"

"No more running out."

The next day, I dropped the philodendron in the trash and bought another one. Its longevity has been remarkable. For years it flourished on the window sill in the bedroom of our house. In fact, it was the last thing I looked at in that room the night I picked up the gun and slipped it into my purse.

FEARING that time and opportunity would allow me to retreat into my emotional armor, I made it a point to visit Gloria while my mood would make it easier for me to apologize. Her disapproval of Frank did not have to become an insurmountable problem; the simple solution was to keep them apart and to see her alone.

"Irene, you don't have to apologize." She was embarrassed.

"I'm not excusing what you did. But there's no excuse for what I did, either. You've been good to me; you're the best friend I've ever had. What I did was mean and—well, shabby."

This made her squirm. "Did Frank suggest this apology?"

"I may love him, but I still have a mind of my own."

"I hope so. It's too good a mind to give up. To anyone."

Fall term began, and I carried a full load of classes. For the first time, Gloria did not choose any of the ones I took. We established a routine of having dinner together one night a week, followed by a movie or a concert on campus. Too often, I caught her looking at me with that sidelong glance of hers, but I refused to confront it. I was determined to keep the friendship running smoothly, even if that meant sacrificing it to superficiality. After my argument with Frank over the plant, I was on my guard against being glib and overcritical. On a few occasions, Gloria and I went out for a drink, but I no longer scanned the bar in search of material for snide remarks. She viewed me then the way I imagine historians view great civilizations in decline. But it was pointless for me to explain my new contentment. I would just have to wait until she herself found someone who would make the same difference in her life as Frank did in mine.

She met him at midterm, but it seemed she made more of a difference to his life than he did to hers. His name was Patrick Malone. A veterinarian who had moved up here from Indianapolis, he had the kind of appeal women rarely find outside their fantasies. Though he was close to Frank's height, he had twenty more pounds distributed among his chest, arms and legs. From a distance, his face was as symmetrical as a mechanical drawing, but with sharp green eyes which pierced that distance. Up close, a slight hump on the bridge of his nose added character, and his cheeks were dotted with tiny indentations, the rugged remains of teen-age acne. His smile was quick and boyish, his laugh full-bellied and richly masculine. His conversation, his gestures, everything about him, was affirmative yet gentle. My conversations with him flowed easily, sliding comfortably now and then into friendly gibes at one another. He loved the title my mother and Frank had given me—Irene the Arrogant —and he used it every chance he got. He liked to kid me about having had skin surgery: no one, he said, could have hair as naturally red as mine without having freckles as well. In return, I nicknamed him Craterface and told him he probably hadn't had acne at all, but purposely poked those little holes in his cheeks because he was too pretty. Gloria loved our repartee and looked happiest when she could sit back, sip on a drink and just listen to us.

Unfortunately, the happy threesome became a tense foursome whenever Frank entered the picture. I saw the guardedness in Pat's manner the first time he met Frank, and I could well imagine the source of it. But I felt mildly victorious as Pat and Frank began to relax around each other. Pat loved to talk and Frank was a probing listener, always asking questions and pursuing explanations. Gloria's icy civility toward Frank had mellowed to become an artificial and awkward friendliness, and we all felt the strain. Whenever she had a few drinks in her and her defenses were down, she would slip into staring at him, watching his every movement and judging it. Frank's reaction was to avoid conversation with her; when he did address her, he never looked her in the eye.

The foursome was short-lived. Frank bowed out gradually, at first with excuses of having to work. Later, excuses weren't necessary. Measured against Frank's "exile," Pat's presence made me resentful, and I soon went back to seeing Gloria alone.

43

FRANK and I spent an increasing amount of time alone together. We were both working very hard; sometimes during the week our only amusement was reading to each other the papers we had written. Up to the time I met Frank, I had always mailed my papers home for my father to read. He taught English at Cedar Run High School, and he was more than a little proud of his influence in getting me interested in the same field. I knew my working on a Ph.D. would complete the dream he once had for himself. Naturally, he wanted to keep tabs on that dream. When I forgot to send the papers home after reading them to Frank, I soon received a one-line note from my father which read: "Ph.D. candidates don't write papers anymore?" Chuckling, I showed the note to Frank, but he was not amused.

"You shouldn't forget your father like that," he said seriously.

"I hadn't meant to."

He reached into his desk drawer and pulled out a large envelope. "Here, get your papers together in this and mail it tonight."

I sat down on a cushion and arranged the papers in the envelope, then wrote a short note of apology.

"Do you ever send your papers home?" I asked.

"No."

"Why not?"

"No one to send them to."

"What about your parents?"

"They're dead." It was a simple statement, and he flipped a page of his book as he said it.

"Frank, you never told me!"

"Didn't I?"

"No, you didn't! I can't believe you never mentioned it."

"I would have gotten around to it."

"When?"

"I don't know. It's not a subject I particularly enjoy."

"But you'll tell me about it *sometime,* won't you?"

"Sometime."

I always did my studying at the kitchen table so we would be out of each other's way. But that night I couldn't concentrate. I could hear him flipping pages in the other room, and I tried to imagine what I would be like if both my parents were dead. Then I realized something else. Frank had told me he was the youngest of nine kids, yet so far as I knew, he had never got a phone call or a letter from any of them during the three months we had been living together. I sat staring at the flecks in the Formica tabletop and wondered how I could have been so blind—and selfish. Although he had chosen to say nothing about his family, why hadn't it occurred to me to ask about them?

I went to bed and lay waiting for him. I kept telling myself it was ridiculous to be jealous over something I didn't know. Yes, I was jealous of withheld information. I wanted to know everything that had ever happened to him. After all, the death of one's parents was not a casual scrap of information.

I didn't move when he got into bed. With a short groan he stretched out on his back. We had lived together long enough to have established communication in the dark; I knew that still as I was, he knew I was wide awake and waiting.

"My father was killed in a bar when I was eighteen. My mother died of pneumonia four years ago." He said it quickly, dispassionately, then sighed heavily to signal me he wanted to sleep.

"Killed? How?"

"He was shot."

"Why?"

"It was a holdup. When the bartender wouldn't surrender the money, they shot up the place. My father was hit by accident, along with two other men."

I was about to say "How did you feel?" but realized how ridiculous it would sound. Instead, I asked how often he saw his brothers and sisters.

"I don't see them at all. Not since my mother died."

"Why not?"

"Our house was so small, we spent half our time trying to get away from each other."

"But now that you all live apart, surely you can see each other once in a while."

"I don't care to see any of them," he said flatly.

"But weren't any of you close to each other?"

"Too close; privacy was at a premium. When you're scraping elbows at the dinner table and using the bathroom three at a time, you don't want to spend your free time exchanging intimacies. You want to spend it alone."

"Not all large families are like that, are they?"

"I guess not. But I'm not going to have a large family to find out."

I remembered him saying: *I hate it when people just breed.* In a way, he was making the same statement again.

I said, "Are you sure my living with you isn't disturbing your privacy?"

"You're living here because I want you here. You're my family now."

"Am I?" I moved over and put my head on his shoulder. We lay still, saying nothing for several minutes. His chest rose, and he held his breath.

"Irene, would you marry me?"

I didn't intend to keep him in suspense, but I wanted the words to linger.

"I mean," he said, "would you think about marrying me?"

"No, I won't *think* about it." I pressed my mouth against his ear. "Just promise me we'll make it soon."

GLORIA took the news standing up and with a look on her face that said: "I knew this would happen." But all she said was "Congratulations": from past experience, she had learned not to verbalize her thoughts about Frank and me.

We went to Cedar Run for Christmas and told my parents. My mother seemed genuinely pleased, while my father made a pretense of being pleased. From my recent experiences with Gloria, I was sensitive to being watched, and I felt my father watching me the more he pretended not to. I suspected he knew he had not been told everything, and I was not looking forward to the task. The night before Frank and I were to leave, I stayed up late and alone with my father to confess the rest.

"I'm taking a leave from the Ph.D. program," I began.

"You mean you're *leaving* the program."

"I'm going to take education courses next term and practice-teach in the spring so I can get a job in the fall. In a couple of years, I'll go back and get the degree."

He was sitting in his recliner. He laid his head back and sighed. "I might have expected this."

I bristled. Gloria had done her best to suggest my life was taking a downhill slide; I did not need the suggestion reinforced by my father. "It's my life. Don't you think I have the right to make a few decisions about what I want to do with it?"

"You have every right. I suppose *I* have no right to be disappointed. But I am. Was this Frank's idea?"

"No, it wasn't. In fact, he was against it at first."

"But he's going along with it?"

"It's what I want to do. Dad, do you remember what you said that day you and Mom came down to Frank's—about college being removed from reality? I've thought about that a lot, the way I've been living in a shell. I've lived away from home, but I've never really been on my own. The English Department has been my guardian and I've been its good little girl."

"So now you're Frank's little girl. I wouldn't call that being on your own, either."

"Yes, it is. Since I've known Frank, I've been on my own in a very painful way. I've had to admit things about myself that aren't very pleasant."

"Like what?"

"Just the *way* I've been, the way I never paid any attention to Neil and Barry."

"That's natural. You're the girl, you're older, you've had different interests."

"I've never had a job, not even a summer one, and before I met Frank I never had to consider anyone else or even meet them halfway. I've never allowed myself to be challenged. Do you remember in tenth grade how I hated gym and we got Dr. Patterson to write that phony letter so I could get excused? I've been doing that kind of thing all my life. When I got to college, if I didn't like a class the first two weeks, I dropped it. If I didn't bowl or play tennis well the first few times out, I quit doing it. I could always run back to the books and get my A's."

"You're blowing this way out of proportion. Studying is hard work. Dedicating yourself to a goal demands discipline, and you've always had perfect discipline, the kind most people never have. I won't let you minimize that. As for bowling or tennis, no one can excel in everything."

"I know that. But it's easy to hide yourself away in a niche and pat yourself on the back and never try anything else for the simple reason you might fall flat on your face."

"Honey, not having a niche is what makes people miserable. Be thankful you've got one."

I kept quiet for a few minutes until I found another argument. "When you fell in love with Mom, what did it feel like?"

"What do you mean?" He was wary of being sidetracked.

"How did you feel?"

"I was happy, of course. I guess I was flattered too, when I realized how she felt about me. There were a couple of others who wanted very much to be in my shoes. But I don't see what—"

"Then it's natural to feel happy when you love someone?"

"Certainly. What's your point, Irene?"

"Just this. When I first knew Frank I was miserable. Can you imagine why?"

"Because he bowls and plays tennis better than you do."

"Don't be cute. It was because for once in my life I was doing something I couldn't do well—loving someone."

"What makes you think you can't love well?"

"*Couldn't*. I think I'm learning."

"Well, then, what are you learning?"

"That I'm not as terrific as I thought I was and . . . that I can be better than I am. That loving someone requires making allowances."

He frowned. "What kind of allowances?"

"I didn't know until a few weeks ago that both his parents are dead. When I found out, I was insulted he hadn't told me, and I was so busy stewing in the insult that I didn't stop to consider *why* he hadn't talked about them. It was just too painful for him. I couldn't understand it because I've never had that kind of pain. Frank's been anything but sheltered and I'm tired of being sheltered. I'm sick of being so damned comfortable. I guess I'm sick of myself. I want to take those education courses and then teach for a while. I want to get out there and *do* something."

"Those who can't do, teach."

"Stop it. You of all people know better than that. I've had plenty of professors who aren't half the teacher you are."

"How would you know? You were never in a class of mine."

"I had friends who were."

He spread his fingers out on the arms of his chair. "I should know better than to try to change your mind. But let me exercise the ancient parental prerogative and give you some advice. I know I told you academic life was not reality—whatever that battered term means. And maybe it is a niche, but it's one that gives you plenty of spare time, and time is freedom. If you teach in a high school, you'd better be prepared for some intellectual shrinkage and a drastic trimming of your ideals. And don't think that your enthusiasm for your subject is going to spill out and saturate all your students. There *are* rewards, but they're quite different from what you're used to. I liked it the first few years, but then when you kids began to grow up, somehow it got stale. Maybe it'll be different for you. At least you won't be starting out as a parent."

"Maybe not."

"For God's sake, you can at least wait for *that!* Don't build your fence on all four sides."

"Do you think I'll make a good mother?"

"If your kids are like Frank, yes. God help you if you have just one who turns out as headstrong as you are."

I said good night by pressing his shoulder and kissing his hair. I knew he was disappointed, but that the disappointment would pass. As I climbed the stairs to my old room, I was confident that he, like myself, would be more than pleased with everything I did.

IT was true Frank opposed my leaving the Ph.D. program and joining the masses in the small auditorium of the Education Building. Dr. Denning, the chairman of the English Department, greeted my decision with absolute repugnance. I had to pedal very softly with him for two reasons. During the past four years he had assumed a regard for me that was as paternal as it was academic. And in addition to hitting him with this decision of mine, I had to ask him to use his influence in getting the Education Department to allow me to take their three sequence courses all in one term. At first, he countered by offering me an instructor's position for the spring term and practically promised me a job after I got my degree. When he saw I would not be swayed, he granted my request, but not before telling me that given the odds, my leaving the program would most likely be "terminal." As I put on my coat to leave, he stood up and, actually misty-eyed, offered his hand; he assured me his door was always open if I ever needed him.

Naturally, I was hungry for encouragement, yet I was not going to stumble over the disappointment of my father, Dr. Denning, or even Frank. Emotionally, I felt like a pioneer heading west; if the going got rough I could always turn back.

Denning carried through, and I got the three education courses concurrently. I also got a dose of boredom more excruciating than I had expected. There was nothing "entertaining" in the reading or in the papers I had to write. By the third week I was keeping a countdown calendar aimed at the end of the term. Three weeks before finals, I got the notice that my student-teaching assignment for the spring was in Elkton, thirty miles from campus. I hadn't looked forward to living away from Frank for even one term, but fortunately Elkton was close enough for me to commute.

That spring term went smoothly enough to convince me I had made the right decision. My supervising teacher was impressed enough with my scholastic record to give me her senior class—her "plum," as she called it—instead of one of her sophomore classes. The class and I took to each other beautifully, and my "shrunken expectations" were revitalized when I discovered how enthusiastic and verbal many of the kids were. I worked them as hard as I worked myself, and the results were gratifying. I came home every evening bubbling with stories and anecdotes about my day. Even Frank began to concede that my decision had been a good one, that this change was what I needed.

"Since you're adapting so well to change," he said, "when are we going to make the big one?"

"Which is?"

"Change of name. From Rutledge to Mattison."

"What comes with it?"

"Oh, nothing much. Just a man who can't live without you."

"In that case, I accept. I never could resist a worthy cause."

"Bitch." He grinned.

Before the wedding, we moved out of the apartment and into a house trailer. It was owned by a student in the History Department, who offered to let us live in it rent-free while he went off to study in Mexico. I was thrilled about the move, regarding it as another installment in the continuing adventure of changing my life. Since Frank had next to no furniture, there was very little to pack for making such a move.

The first day after being set free for the summer, I decided I would take over the packing and organizing. Frank was preoccupied with the upcoming meeting where he would have to defend his thesis and with the preparation of materials and reading lists for the summer classes he would be teaching.

He was off at the library when I began the chore of packing boxes and crates and labeling them. My adrenaline was running high, so high that by mid-afternoon everything was squared away and ready to go, everything but the bed and the contents of Frank's desk. I took a break with a cup of coffee and a few cigarettes and debated with myself whether or not I should go ahead and clean out the desk. Frank was extremely well organized, so there wouldn't be any problem transferring his material. It was simple: each drawer would be assigned to a separate box. Still, I hesitated. The desk was Frank's only private turf in the apartment, and I had never invaded it. I sat looking at it for quite a while, until I convinced myself it was silly to put him through the task while I had time on my hands.

Everything in the four side drawers was neatly filed in folders and big envelopes and clearly labeled. The top middle drawer contained personal items. Although I promised myself not to look through anything as I packed, I broke the promise almost immediately when I saw the paper with my name and "statistics" on it —the exact information about me that he had recited our first night together. He had obviously had a connection with someone in the registrar's office. I smiled at the fact that he had gone to the trouble of checking up on me. Had I really appeared *that* forbidding?

The next thing I came across was a yellowed newspaper clipping that included a picture of Frank and five other scholarship winners in his high school. I stood there staring at it because it was so poignant: compared to the others, Frank was conspicuously ill-dressed. Instead of a sport coat he wore a snowflake-patterned sweater far too small for him; the sleeves ended a good four inches from the wrists, that remaining space taken up by a clashing checkered shirt. My God, I thought, he really was *that* poor. Looking at him in that outfit, I immediately flashed back to my high school senior prom. No dress in Cedar Run or in any of the neighboring towns was good enough for me. I had made my mother drive over a hundred miles to go shopping for something better. Even when I settled on something better, it was the style I wanted but not exactly the color and I complained about it right up to the minute my date rang our doorbell.

I took a large envelope and put the clipping in it so it wouldn't yellow or wrinkle any more than it had. Someday, I thought, if our children ever complained about what they didn't have, I could pull the clipping out and show them how far their father had come on next to nothing.

I removed the last layer of memorabilia—some concert and play programs from university productions —and found one remaining item in the corner of the drawer. It was a photograph of Frank and a girl, taken when he was probably fifteen or sixteen, both of them dressed raggedly and sitting under a tree. The girl's face was turned and smiling up at Frank. She was a pretty thing, but her sagging shoulders coupled with her low brow line gave the impression she was somewhat "slow." In striking contrast to the girl's smile was the smoldering expression on Frank's face: his jaw was clenched so hard it looked as if it had been wired shut, and his eyes were two slits behind his eyeglasses. I had never seen him look at anyone in that way; I knew if *I* had been the one holding the camera to take that picture, Frank's face would have withered me on the spot.

I had finished filling the box for this drawerful, and I laid the picture down on top of everything else.

A couple of times later in the afternoon, I stopped to glance at it again, although that face was already imprinted on my mind. It was not just an angry face. It was livid.

I was in the shower when Frank came home. By the time I dried off, combed my hair and got dressed, he was loading up the car with the boxes.

"What's the rush?" I said. "Don't you want to go have dinner first?"

"I want to do this now before I eat and get drowsy."

He had worked so quickly that by the time we were ready to go, I only had to carry one shopping bag down to the car. When we arrived at the trailer, he did the unloading while I cleaned the toilet and washbowl. As we were tossing around suggestions about where to go for dinner, I happened to glance at the box that had the top desk drawer things in it.

"Hey, what happened to that picture that was sitting on top of this stuff?"

"What picture?"

"The one of you and a girl. It was right here on top of everything."

"Maybe it slipped down in. Come on, let's get going."

"Just a minute." I lifted everything from the box, but the picture was gone. "Oh, damn it! Didn't you see it, Frank? It was right on top."

"No, I didn't."

"It was you and this girl; you were sitting under a tree. I found it in your top desk drawer while I was packing."

"We'll find it later. And if we don't, it's not important."

"It certainly *is* important if you kept it all these years."

"No, it's not, really."

"Who is she?"

"Just a girl I knew once."

"A girlfriend?"

"Not in that way."

"She looked—well, a little retarded. Was she?"

"Mildly, yes."

"And you looked like you were going to bite some-one's head off. Who *took* the picture?"

"I don't remember. Some relative or neighbor. Now will you come on—I'm starving."

The next day I went through all the boxes I had packed, looking for that picture. But I never found it. And Frank was blandly unconcerned over its disap-pearance.

At the time, it didn't occur to me to think anything of it. . . .

WE were married in July in the Cedar Run Presbyterian Church. Frank had his hair cut for the wedding although I told him not to do it on my account. But he insisted, knowing it would please my parents. It did. My father must have mentioned a hundred times what "an improvement" it was. Frank merely smiled and said nothing.

The day of the wedding and the day before it were eventful, to say the least. Since Frank had no really close friends, he had asked Bernie Golden, another graduate instructor in history, to be his best man. Dur-ing the rehearsal, Bernie walked around telling every-one, "I don't know how Frank got her. He ought to write a book about it. Send his secret in to *Playboy*." My annoyance with him was fast approaching verbal-ization, but every now and then Frank would squeeze my hand and whisper, "Patience. You can afford it."

I had had a real debate with myself over asking Gloria to be my maid of honor. It was Frank who talked me into making the offer. Her acceptance was pointedly unenthusiastic, but I chose to write it off as a cover-up. When she arrived in Cedar Run, she had given up her subtle sullenness and replaced it with a look of stoic resignation. And so between Gloria and Bernie and my father (whose disappointment in me I felt was still potent), there was enough friction in the air to keep me on edge.

But there was more.

Frank and I had come close to having several arguments over his refusal to invite any of his family to the wedding. His only guests would be two professors and their wives and nine students.

"I don't see why you can't invite a few of your brothers and sisters."

"I know you don't see why," he said. "But take my word for it, it's better this way."

"Imagine how strange it's going to look in the church with your side almost empty."

"I know how it's going to look, honey, and I'm sorry. But I'll be more comfortable this way."

"Do you really hate them that much?"

The blood rushed to his face. "I just don't have anything in common with them."

"What does that matter for one afternoon?"

"It matters a great deal. To me."

"I can't understand this hostility of yours."

"Irene, considering the family you come from, I know it's hard for you to understand. It would kill something in you to give your family up. But it'll kill something in me if I *don't* give mine up. Starting now."

"But why? Why does it have to be so absolute?"

"All right," he said stiffly, "I'll tell you. My sister Doris ran off with a married man fourteen years ago. When I left to go to college, his wife and kids were still waiting to hear from him. My brother Tom was a traveling salesman until he lost his license because of so many drunk-driving charges. Now he's a night custodian so he can drink on the job and get away from his wife. Jack's decided to follow in my father's footsteps. He drives a delivery truck and his wife has a baby almost every year. Terry's serving a prison term in Pennsylvania for manslaughter. He had a fight with his girlfriend one night and ran down a man at a crosswalk. Marian and her husband left town right after they were married and haven't been heard from since. Bill and Mike are as close as brothers can be— they both share Mike's wife." He was breathing like an exhausted runner. "They're not going to touch me. They're not going to touch *us*. Irene, what you come from and what I come from are worlds apart. The only way for it to work is to make one world between us. We keep your family and we drop mine."

More than his words, it was the look of repugnance and fear on his face that convinced me not to press any further. It was his family and up to him to deal with them as he saw fit. Wanda Hoople had escaped from her family and had forgone a high school diploma to do it. Frank certainly had the same right to escape at the age of twenty-six.

The evening before the wedding, we had our rehearsal, followed by a dinner for the wedding party. My spirits were dampened by my father's and Gloria's reserve; they went through the rehearsal matter-of-factly, totally bland-faced. Whatever bolstering I got came from my mother's smiling enthusiasm and Frank's caressing eyes.

My father and I were halfway down the aisle in the final run-through when I saw Frank's face go white and rigid. We continued on, but Frank kept looking past us to the rear of the church. The minister cleared his throat, then spoke Frank's name. Frank recovered himself, but when he stepped up to me I could see his eyes were wild, his hands trembling. The second we were finished I turned around and saw a man and woman sitting in the last pew. Frank didn't move. He kept his back to them and muttered, "God damn her, God damn her!"

"Frank! Who is it?"

"Vivian," he gritted.

"Who's Vivian?"

"My sister. She found out. I knew she would, I knew she would!"

"So she found out, so what? Come on, you'd better introduce me." He wouldn't budge. "Frank, what's the matter with you?"

His voice cracked. "She's the worst! And now she's here, she just walks right in!"

"And whose fault is that? I imagine she feels pretty insulted. Are you afraid she'll make a scene?"

"Yes, yes!"

"We can't just leave her sitting back there. Now come on."

By this time, everybody was staring at the couple. I took Frank's hand and started down the aisle toward them. The man's face was expressionless, but the woman was smiling, first at Frank, then at me. Although she seemed a good deal older than Frank, there was no mistaking that she was his sister. Her features were similar to his, but stronger, her eyes larger, her mouth slightly fuller. Like Frank, she was quite tall, but well built instead of gangly, and her squared shoulders contributed to her impeccably confident posture. A solitary streak of gray hair among the dark brown lent a dramatic touch to her striking appearance.

The man stood up, still expressionless, and offered his hand to Frank. Frank only glowered at him.

"Hello, I'm Vivian Snell, Frank's sister. This is my husband, Leo."

Leo turned his hand to me and I shook it. Then Vivian offered hers. There was a momentary silence. Finally, I spoke. "I really don't know what to say."

"And neither do I." Vivian smiled. "Maybe Frank has something to say."

If Frank's eyes had been bullets, Vivian would have been dead on the spot. "I have nothing to say to you. There's no reason for you to be here."

Her smile disappeared but she remained unruffled. "Frank," she said softly, "if you choose to walk out on your family, that's your business. But I think we all have the right to know who you're going to marry."

"You have no right. How did you find me?"

"There are other people in Ridgeway who go to the university. The word got back to us." She turned to me. "You're very pretty. Very pretty. Have you known Frank long?"

"A little more than a year."

"Oh, then it wasn't a whirlwind courtship?"

"No, it wasn't."

"I'm glad. The two of you had plenty of time to get to know each other. Are those your parents down there?"

"Yes. Come meet them. And since you're here, why don't you have dinner with us? The whole wedding party's going out."

"We'd like that very much. If Frank can put up with it."

"Don't be silly," I said, even though I saw the sick look on Frank's face.

The introductions were made. When we left the church, Frank saw to it that no one rode in the car with us on the way to the restaurant.

"Why! Why did you have to do that?" His voice was quivering with rage and his eyes were tearing. I was frightened.

"Can't you bury the hatchet for one evening?" I said timidly.

"Bury the hatchet? You think it's that simple? This isn't like one of those arguments *you* have with your father, where you make up the next day and everything's forgotten. You don't seem to understand that I hate her. I've always hated her; I'll never stop hating her; I don't want her around me! Is that clear?"

"How can you hate her so much? You never even mentioned her to me."

He swallowed hard and tightened his lips. We drove for a few more blocks before he spoke again. "Irene, I hate her as much as I love you. Maybe you can't understand that, but please try to accept it. All my life I've watched her butt into other people's lives and twist them to her advantage. She started with my —my mother, and then the rest of us. Doris and Marian ran away because of her and so did I."

"But what did she do?"

"It's not what she did; it's what she *is*. She controls everything around her. Just watch Leo for two minutes."

"Does she have any children?"

"No."

"Maybe that's the reason she wants to hang on to the rest of you. Frank, it's just for tonight. She wants a share of her baby brother's happiness, that's all. How old is she, anyway?"

"Forty-two."

"That's sixteen years' difference. It's only natural she wants to mother you a bit—"

"After tonight, that's it. She stays away permanently."

"Whatever you say. Now how about a kiss?" I nestled up to him.

"Please, Irene, I'm trying to drive."

We were the last ones to arrive at the restaurant. The waiters had pushed three tables together to make one long one; at the head of it were two empty chairs waiting for us. I sat directly at the head, with Frank on my right, Vivian on my left. Vivian was on her second martini. Leo was nursing a club soda.

"It was nice of you to ask us," said Vivian. "We hadn't expected it."

Frank glared at her, then ordered a double Scotch. Although there were conversations all along the table, I had a feeling everyone was keeping an ear turned to Frank, Vivian and me.

"You have a nice family," said Vivian. "There's just you and the two boys?"

"Yes, Neil and Barry."

"What do your father and mother do?"

"My father teaches English at the high school. My mother's a dressmaker. She had our front porch glassed in and uses it as her shop."

"You look as if you all get along very well."

"We do. I'm quite proud of them."

"Yes, I can tell." She twirled the olive in her martini glass. "And I'm proud of Frank. We all are."

"I am too," I said.

"Frank's proud of himself too," she said teasingly. "He'd like to think we don't have much in common. But we do have one thing. Ambition. Leo and I started out with one lumberyard. Now we have three."

"And you have no children?"

"We couldn't have them. But I have my nieces and nephews. I'm satisfied with that. We're a very close family."

She picked up the surprise in my voice. "All except Frank, of course. He's always been the loner. He's more . . . private than the rest of us. It's hard to tell what's going on in that head of his. Even as a kid he was secretive."

Yes, I wanted to say, he *is* secretive. That wild anger had left Frank's face, replaced now by a look of contempt.

"Anyway," continued Vivian, "now that he's proven himself and done it all on his own, maybe he won't have to be so independent. Maybe he'll let his family do a few things for him."

Frank laid his napkin on the table, excused himself and went to the men's room. Immediately, Vivian opened her purse, pulled something from it and put it in my hand under the table.

"Don't let anybody see it," she said, "and don't say a word about it to Frank."

I drew my hand into my lap and looked down. It was a check.

"Vivian!" I whispered. "This is for a thousand dollars!"

"It's made out to you so Frank doesn't have to know anything about it. You spend it the way you see fit."

"Oh, Vivian, I can't. He didn't even invite you to the wedding and now you're giving us this——"

"In our family we look out for our own. Frank's a strange young man. I know; I watched him grow up. Maybe that's part of his charm. If he chooses to cut us off, there's nothing we can do about that. But I want you to know we're always there in case you need us."

"Why does he feel the way he does? I don't understand it."

"Don't try," she said. "I gave up a long time ago. We're a large family and every one of us is different. We were very poor and we all had our share of hurt, in and out of the house. I think Frank indulges himself. I think part of him enjoys hanging on to the hurt. He never forgets, and he doesn't forgive easily. But maybe now that he's found you . . ." She leaned back in her chair, looked me over and smiled. "You really *are* a beauty. You're sure to have lovely children. You do plan to have them, don't you?"

"Of course. A little later, though. But about this check. I can't——"

"Yes, you can. And not a word to Frank."

"Then come to the wedding tomorrow. Please."

"No. The way Frank feels right now, it would be

too much for him. I'm satisfied just to have met you."

I glanced at Leo, and he smiled woodenly. He appeared to have been only half listening, and he had not said a word to anyone else. It flashed through my mind what an incongruous pair they were: she was so animated and outgoing and he was such a stiff. But then, who was I to judge? Gloria, I knew, considered Frank and me incongruous.

"Here comes Frank now," said Vivian. "Remember, this is just between us."

Frank sat down and looked suspiciously at Vivian and me. So did Gloria and my father. The five of us barely spoke during the rest of the meal.

Vivian and Leo said good-bye in the parking lot and drove off. Pat Malone suggested that Frank and I come out for a drink with him and Gloria, but Frank refused before I could say a word. We got into the car and drove a few miles out of town on the highway. He turned off onto a gravel road and pulled over to the shoulder.

"Don't tell me we're going to neck," I said, trying to offset the gravity of his manner.

"There's something we have to settle right now. You know how I feel about my family. Do you or do you not intend to respect those feelings? I have to know now."

"That sounds almost like an ultimatum."

"I guess it does," he said firmly.

"Do you think it's fair to be handing out ultimatums the night before our wedding?"

"A lot of things are unfair, Irene. That's the way life is."

"Thank you, Philosopher Mattison!"

"Please don't take that tone."

"What tone am I supposed to take when you get sanctimonious with me? I know what brought this on. It's because I was civil to Vivian."

"You were more than civil."

"All right, I was. But I must say your behavior left a lot to be desired. Whatever resentment you have for her could be put aside for just one evening. To tell you the truth, I was shocked by you. And disappointed. You know, that first night I came to your apartment, you treated Larry like a prince and I was impressed. Then tonight you treat your own sister as if she were . . . some kind of vermin. Even when it's apparent she cares so much for you." A muted snort came through his nose. "Go ahead and shrug it off, but you might just as well shrug off the fact the earth is round. She's obliging and cautious with you and all she gets in return is the most childish rudeness. She had nothing but praise and consideration for you and she gave us—" I stopped dead, remembering too late the promise I made to her.

"Gave us what?"

"Her blessing."

"Gave us what?"

"All right, she gave us a check."

"A check? Let me see it."

"Frank—"

"Let me see it."

I took it from my purse and handed it to him. He stared at it, then calmly tore it up.

"That's just wonderful," I said. "You won't even allow her that pleasure."

"She's not going to buy her way into our lives."

"That wasn't what she was doing."

"That's exactly what she was doing. This is the kind of thing I'd expect from her."

"I don't understand it. If it's a matter of pride—"

"It's more than that. All I'm asking of you is that you respect my feelings."

"Even when you won't explain them?"

"You didn't grow up in my family, Irene, and I didn't grow up in yours. Would you like it if we moved far away from your parents and your brothers?"

"No, I wouldn't."

"All right, so we won't. I'll respect your wishes. All I ask is the same in return."

It *sounded* reasonable, yet I couldn't *feel* it was reasonable. But there was nothing I could say.

"I want nothing to do with any of them," he said. "I don't want to live near them, I don't want to hear from them—no birthdays, no Christmas cards, nothing."

"All right, all right. Let's not fight over it."

"Let's not, ever again. I don't want them to have the power to make us fight."

The next day, all my father's reservations seemed to slip away with the smile and the kiss he gave me before we started down the aisle. After the ceremony, the reception was loud and festive. My mother had two glasses of champagne and had to sit down. Lazily, she rested her head on my father's shoulder. He whispered something in her ear, she smiled, then turned and kissed him tenderly on the cheek. Frank saw it too, and he said to me: "That'll be us in twenty years."

When we were ready to make our escape through one of the rear doors, I saw Gloria sitting alone in a far corner of the room. The sight of her made me hesitate a moment. She was sagging forward, her head bowed; and in my brief glimpse I could see her hands lying in her lap, limp and curled like a pair of dead birds.

THE first three years of my marriage I was recklessly happy. I wore my happiness like a badge, oversized and well polished, ostentatious in every way. And I was most ostentatious whenever I was around Gloria. For a long time, I was haunted by that single glimpse of her at the wedding reception, and I wanted to refute any unspoken predictions she might be making about my marriage. She went on being propitiously polite to Frank and guarded around me when he was present. I knew her disappointment in me struck more deeply than she let on, and that alone cast the first solid shadow on the turn my life had taken. I resented that shadow; to eliminate it, I chose to pity Gloria for her blindness.

She got her Ph.D. and married Pat Malone. Without any apparent resentment, he packed up his veterinary practice and moved it to Los Angeles because Gloria received a job offer there.

I had got a job teaching at Peck High School (the most desirable school in town because it was new and many of the students were the children of professors), and Frank was hired by the university as an assistant professor. We bought a nine-room, fifty-year-old house and the vacant lot next to it. The first few nights we were in it, we wandered through the large, empty rooms sipping on wine and making plans for the paint, wallpaper, rugs and furniture. A few times, when the second or third glass of wine had mellowed him, Frank would turn misty-eyed, slip his arm around me and assure me that *his* family was never going to be crowded. I clearly recall the urgency in his voice, as if he were saying we would never starve or perish in a flood or contract a fatal disease. *We were never going to be crowded.*

Two months later, I became pregnant. It was verified by the doctor on a Wednesday, but I waited until Friday night to tell Frank. I wanted the weekend right there with no work interruptions, so we could celebrate and play with the future. We stayed in bed talking until Saturday afternoon. That night he took me to the best restaurant in town. In candlelight and over champagne, we suggested names back and forth. By the end of the evening, we were leaning across the table, holding hands, whispering.

"Why are we whispering?" I whispered.

He smiled lazily. "Because no one else in the world has to hear us. I want you always to be just a whisper away."

That weekend I fell in love all over again, but this time painlessly, luxuriously. Sunday night, Frank gave me a bath in that old chipped tub we would eventually replace. He washed me, oiled me, dried me off, and wouldn't let me lift a hand to any of it.

"Until the baby comes," he said, *"you're* the baby."

When we got into bed, he stroked my belly in a soft, circular motion, then laid his head there and kissed it.

"It's going to be loved," he said. "It's going to be so loved."

I finished the statement in my head: "The way you *weren't*."

"Yes," I said, "it's going to be loved."

He kissed me there again, soft and lingering. "It's the purest form of love there is," he murmured.

I knew I had heard him say that before, but I was too drowsy to recall where and when. I went to sleep with my fingers in his hair.

SHE was born on June first, my birthday, and we named her Regina Frances. I had had my heart set on Mary (I was always fond of alliterative names), but Frank argued it was too common and too religious. There was really no other name I wanted, so I gave in when he insisted on Regina. At least, I thought, it sounded dignified: Regina Mattison would be quite suitable for a writer or an actress or a Pulitzer Prize winner. Naturally, I never pictured it in newspaper stories about a murder trial.

She weighed just under seven pounds and had no

hair whatsoever. The first few times she was brought
to me for nursing, my joy over this tiny creation was
undercut by apprehension. The veins in her head
were so large, so near the surface, that I feared she
was missing a necessary layer of skin. The doctor assured me she was perfectly normal. But it was really
a nurse, Miss Pennington, who put my fear to rest.
Whenever she brought Regina to me she would quip,
"Here's Mrs. Mattison's little road map." And Frank
studied Regina like a road map. He would hold her
and look searchingly into that little face, then say he
was sure she was going to look like me.

"Don't be silly," I said. "It's too soon to tell. She
hasn't even got hair yet. I just hope baldness doesn't
run in your family."

"It doesn't," he returned seriously.

I knew by now he did not welcome *any* reference
to his family. But the day we left the hospital with
Regina, he was faced with more than a reference:
Vivian was waiting for us in the lobby.

Smiling, she stood up and came toward us. She had
cut her hair since we saw her last, and she looked
more like Frank than ever. She was still far from
beautiful, but quite striking and obviously unself-
conscious about her height, because she wore heels
and did not slouch in the least. I was carrying Regina
and Frank was carrying the two plants some of my
students had brought me. As soon as he saw Vivian,
he tucked one of the plants under his arm, then
gripped my shoulder to steer me to the door. Vivian
halted and made no attempt to follow us: that alone
made me angry with Frank.

"You can't do this to her," I said, pulling away
from him.

"*She* can't do this to *us!*" he hissed. "Come on!"

I glanced over my shoulder at her. She stood there
tall and proud, yet looked at me helplessly.

"You can at least let her look at the baby."

"No."

"You're acting like a child."

"You don't know her. She's not worming her way in. You made a promise to me, Irene. Now keep it."

We continued on to the parking lot. I got into the car but Frank didn't. "I'll be right back," he said, and started for the lobby doors. Vivian came through them and met Frank on the steps. Frank spoke, then she spoke, then she reached out to touch his hand and he pulled back from her. He said something else as he backed away from her. She remained on the steps. We drove home without saying a word to each other.

A few days later, a typewritten envelope with no return address came for me. Inside was a note from Vivian explaining the accompanying check: a thousand reoffered as a wedding gift and a thousand to begin a savings account for the baby. I debated with myself over telling Frank and finally decided not to. I stuck the check in my jewelry box and for a week considered opening a secret savings account. I watched Frank carefully that week, the way he lingered at the crib staring at a miracle, the smile on his face as he sat with his arm around me while I nursed the baby.

I tore up the check and the envelope with it.

During the months that followed, I was quite naturally preoccupied with Regina. And with Frank. His energy astounded me. He hired a plumber from the university and the two of them went to work rebuilding and modernizing the kitchen and the upstairs bathroom. By the end of the summer, he was buying the materials for building a recreation room and laundry room in the basement. Yet when classes began, he assigned himself extra office hours and tutored the poorer students in our living room for midterm and final exams. Still, there was always time for the house and for the baby. He worked incessantly, sleeping only four or five hours a night, but the harsh routine he set for himself seemed to nourish rather than debilitate him. Within a year, the basement was completed, every floor in the house refinished. My initial reservations about having taken on an old house instead of a new one dwindled each time I drove up to it. The neighborhood was settled and comfortable, with fully grown oaks and maples that stood like sentinels on both sides of the street. The houses were all large and quite modest in their trimmings: standard white was the reigning preference for wood and brick alike. Ours was a dark green, but within two years we would paint it white, following suit. And within five years, our adjoining empty lot—the sunniest patch on the block—would contain a vegetable garden. Having that extra property gave us a certain prestige among the neighbors, but the feature I loved most about the house was its location at the end of the block, where the street dead-ended. I liked the feeling of being tucked away even from the minimal traffic on the rest of the street, minimal because most of our neighbors were much older, with their children already grown. However, our empty lot did attract children from neighboring streets, and I was happy that Regina would have playmates close by. Frank, in fact, encouraged kids to play in the lot by hanging old tractor tires from the oak limbs to serve as swings. "When she has friends," he would say, "I want them to feel comfortable here. I want *them* to come to *her*." I thought at the time she would always be surrounded by friends if they came to her the way her father did. When Frank was finished preparing his lectures and reading his students' papers, when he put aside the hammer and the sandpaper and the paint, his total recreation was Regina. I was instructed to take a nap or read or go to a movie while he played with her on the living room floor. He bought a couple of dimestore wigs, a rubber nose, wax lips, and kept her entertained for hours with impersonations. He built a little stage with a cloth curtain and put on shows for her with hand puppets. I was not the entertainer Frank was. For Regina, the drawing and coloring and games I taught her were inferior substitutes for her father's performances. As soon as she heard Frank come up the front porch steps, she would scramble to her feet and toddle to the door with hand puppets dangling from her fists.

As much as I loved my daughter, my heart was not really in most of the activities we did together. While playing with her I found myself daydreaming about teaching and going back to it. The short time I taught before she was born was the happiest period of my life. When I left Peck High to have Regina, the principal, Hugh Lance, told me firmly I had damned well better plan on coming back, that he didn't want to see my talent wasted. He was not given to compliments, so I was genuinely flattered by what he said. As comfortable as I was at home, nothing in the world rivaled the sensation of being in front of a class giving my performance, which would encourage the kids to give theirs. Naturally, there were disappointments, scores of them, but somehow they were always outweighed by the accomplishments. And while I was at home with Regina, it was those accomplishments I kept thinking about. Although I said nothing, I would catch Frank every now and then giving me a knowing, sympathetic look. Finally, a few months before Regina turned four, he suggested I call Lance and ask if I could come back the following September. I wanted to leap for the phone, but I said no, another year wouldn't make any difference one way or the other. I was apprehensive about turning Regina over to a stranger before she started school. The last thing I wanted her to feel was abandonment.

I called Lance and the arrangements were made. I would start back to work when Regina started kindergarten. Frank's plan was to get Regina into the morning session and to schedule his own classes for the morning as well. That way, she would come home to him, not to a baby-sitter.

That last year alone with Regina, I managed to keep my disposition in top form: knowing I was going back to work made my patience invincible. When Regina whined and crabbed, I was stolidly serene. I didn't even mind playing chauffeur and chaperon when she and her friends wanted to go to the zoo or to the south-side swimming pool every day it didn't rain. Before that, during the winter months, I took them sledding three days a week.

Then in August came the end to my serenity. Regina began to complain of feeling cold, of aching in her ankles, arches and knees. The doctor said it was probably a summer cold or a strain of flu. I was content with that for three or four days, until she turned pale and developed dark circles under her eyes that looked as if they had been there forever.

It turned out to be rheumatic fever. Along with the prescription for the medication, the doctor handed us the news that there would be no school for Regina until January, and possibly not even then. She was to have constant rest and no excitement. That, of course, meant she had to be watched. So for me it would be good-bye to teaching for another year.

"You're going back," said Frank.

"But we'll have to hire a baby-sitter."

"No, we won't. I'll stay with her."

"But how?"

"I'll get evening classes. I'll take care of it."

And he did. He managed to get his chairman to go along with it, although he had to schedule his office hours for Tuesday and Thursday mornings. Mrs. Lorimer, a widow who lived down the street, came in for three hours on those mornings. She was a compulsive worker and very fond of Regina, two factors which made me feel lucky to have her. However, I would catch her giving me looks of disapproval as I gulped down my morning coffee and reviewed my lesson plans for the day. None too subtly, she liked to remind me that she had raised five daughters, all of whom had turned out exactly the way she wanted them to because she had stayed at home to keep her eye on them. I could have pointed out that my staying home would have put her out twenty dollars a week, but I said nothing. Yet her disapproval of me was mild compared to her disapproval of Frank. She avoided him entirely, except with her eyes: they crawled over him like hands that can't quite figure out the texture of the object they're touching. I imagined what was going through her mind: How could a man let his wife work when there was a sick child in the house? Why would a man who *is* a man shape his life around his wife's job when his own job was more important? Naturally, the answers to these questions were two of the answers to why I loved Frank. But I felt no need to explain that to Mrs. Lorimer.

That school year, 1967–1968, and the following summer proved to be a pivotal period in our lives. Trying to assess all the events and their separate impacts puts me in the position of an editor trying to decide on the right headline. First of all, I returned to Peck High in a state of ebullience that was soon diminished by an amorphous tension among the students. The summer riots in Detroit had been given tremendous publicity, and every now and then I heard "Those niggers" being mumbled in the corridors. The black population at Peck was less than ten percent, but there was already talk of redistricting to bring that figure to twenty-five percent. The majority of black students slunk around the building as if they expected the walls to open up and discharge troops against them. But there was a small group of black boys to match the group of whites who were longing for confrontation. The confrontation came in February, two days after a white woman was raped and murdered by a black man in a downtown transient hotel. It broke out in a gym class, and because the seven students involved were black and white, it was the first incident in the school's history to earn the term "racial." Hugh Lance expelled all seven and the next day called a special assembly at which he warned every student that fighting of any kind would result in automatic expulsion—girls included. The school was quiet the rest of the semester, but the fights were continued off school property, where Lance could do nothing about them.

At home I didn't think about school problems. I was too involved with Frank and Regina. Regina was crushed when she couldn't start kindergarten with her friends and crushed again when the doctor refused to let her go in January. This second blow turned her disappointment into resentment, and we had an even harder time keeping her off her feet. Television, books, games bored her. For the first two months or so, her friends were faithful in their visits—one at a time, as the doctor ordered—but as the novelty became a chore for them, they came by only when they had nothing better to do. Perhaps to punish them, Regina was petulant in their presence. She fought with each one of them so often that by the middle of the year, they stopped coming altogether.

After work and on the weekends, I took charge of her. In the rocking chair, I marked papers and wrote lesson plans to the din of the television and was interrupted constantly by her requests for juice and crackers and toys and dolls. One night while Frank was teaching, she turned to me and said:

"I have to go to the bathroom." The tone of her voice hit something in me. It was the same tone a number of my students were beginning to use, a tone that had more than an edge of command in it.

"Then go," I said.

"Carry me."

"What?"

"Carry me."

"Regina, you don't need to be carried. You can get up to do *that*."

"Daddy carries me. He always carries me."

"I'm sure he doesn't always do it."

"Yes, he does."

"Well, you can walk to the bathroom and back. That little bit won't hurt you. In fact, it'll be good for you—just that little bit."

"Daddy wants me to get well."

"I want you to get well too, but you can walk to the bathroom and back. I'll come with you."

"No, I'll go alone."

I watched her from the corner of my eye. She did a dramatic wavering out of the room, and there was a long, almost ominous silence. When I heard the crash, it suddenly seemed as if I had been waiting for it.

The bottles of bath oil and cologne we kept on top of the toilet tank were scattered on the floor. Regina stood there watching one of them roll in a circle and come to a stop.

"I bumped into it," she said, without looking at me.

"It had to be bumped pretty hard."

"I fell."

The doctor's primary warning had been: "She must not become excited." "All right," I said. "From now on I'll come with you so you won't bump into things." She looked uncertain for a moment, then stooped down to pick up the bottles. "I'll pick them up," I said. "You just go to the toilet."

"I don't feel like going now."

Frank came home that night the way he always did, exhausted and pretending not to be. I couldn't hold back from approaching him with this bathroom business, so I decided to do it lightly. He said he had been carrying her to the bathroom, but he would explain to her why I couldn't.

"I don't think you should be doing it, either," I said. "The doctor says she can get up to do that."

"She can do it when I'm not here. If she likes to be carried once in a while, there's nothing wrong with that."

"She knocked over those bottles on purpose."

"Irene, she's a sick and very lonely little girl. Don't be so hard on her."

I was stung by the accusation. I looked at the philodendron on our window sill and remembered that night back in college when I had been hard and unreasonable. "You're right," I said. "Come to bed." I knew he was tired but I had to have him make love to me. I had to show him the tenderness that would prove the accusation wrong.

It may have been a few days or a few weeks later when we had our first serious argument over Regina. We were figuring the monthly bills at the kitchen table while Regina was supposed to be taking her nap. When I walked into the living room, she was off the sofa and standing at the window that faced our empty lot. Her fists were clenched against the glass, her face stony with rage. Outside, four of her friends were swinging on the tractor tires. Before I could speak, she turned to me and said: "Get them out of our yard."

"You know you're not supposed to be up."

"Tell them to get out of our yard."

"They're just playing. Now get back on the sofa."

"I don't want them there!"

"You won't know they're out there if you stay on the sofa."

"I know they're there."

Frank came in and asked what was wrong.

"She wants the kids out of the yard," I said, trying to slough it off.

"Daddy, make them get out. I don't want them there!"

"We'll just close the drape," I said, "and you won't even see them."

"Daddy, make them go," she said, ignoring me. "It's *our* yard."

"Okay, pumpkin, but you've got to get back on that sofa."

"Frank—"

He flashed me a look of angry warning, then turned and walked out the front door. I took hold of Regina's shoulder and told her to get onto the sofa. She pulled away and said she wanted to *see* Daddy tell them. I watched with her as Frank ambled up to the kids with a smile. For a minute they looked at him blankly, but one boy caught on more quickly than the others; he looked immediately toward the window where we were standing. His eyes slid from me to Regina, and his expression became fiercely identical to hers. As he walked away with the others, he glanced back over his shoulder. I understood his sneer.

"How could you do that?" I asked after I motioned Frank up to the bedroom and closed the door.

"None of them come to see her anymore. It's natural for her to be angry."

"They're only kids, Frank. They don't understand."

"What about her? She doesn't understand, either."

"But she has to understand that her getting sick was . . . accidental. She can't punish everyone else for it."

"She has to understand, but they don't?"

"It's happened to *her*, not to them. I realize it's hard for her, very hard, but—"

"I would think your first loyalty would be to your daughter."

"It has nothing to do with loyalty."

"Were you ever confined to a bed?"

"That has nothing to do with what I'm saying."

"It has everything to do with what you're saying. I'd think you'd be a little more tolerant. She's sick, she deserves to be indulged a little. If it makes her upset to see those kids out there, then I don't see anything wrong with making them stay away."

"She has to learn she can't have everything her own way."

"You mean the way you have?"

That remark sliced deep. "If that's what you think, then you don't know me very well." I left him there and went down to start supper.

I breaded the pork chops, peeled the potatoes, and didn't start to cry until I got to the salad. Then I felt his arms slide around me and his lips graze my ear.

"I'm sorry," he said.

"Don't. Just leave me alone."

He held me tighter. "No, I won't leave you alone. You're going to let me say I'm sorry, because I mean it." I turned and he held me against his chest. "I do love you," he said. Then, kissing me: "I'll set the table. We'll use candles tonight."

He took down the dishes and was fishing for the silverware when Regina's voice shot in from the living room.

"Daddy, a piece of my puzzle is gone. Come find it for me."

"Coming, pumpkin." He squeezed my shoulder and said, "Be back in a minute."

I finished the salad and set the table and called them both when everything was ready.

He forgot about the candles.

THE end of the school year was punctuated with the assassination of Bobby Kennedy and a massive anti-Vietnam rally at the university. Frank took part in the rally and got the expected reprimand from the university president's office. Accompanying the reprimand was a clear-cut threat that any further activity of this sort would jeopardize his position on the faculty. He was undaunted, but I was frightened and told him so. I agreed that the protest was honorable, but I didn't want him to lose his job because of it. There was a great deal of freedom in the university newspaper, but unsponsored rallies and spontaneous gatherings were prohibited on university property. Until there was a softer policy, I wanted Frank to adhere to the present one.

The day of Kennedy's funeral, Frank used our living room for a kind of wake. Bernie Golden and another professor were present, along with a dozen students. I was on tenterhooks the whole evening because I thought somehow this meeting was going to violate a university rule. And if that didn't happen, I figured a neighbor might call the police. And frankly, I was intimidated. Everyone in the group had taken up the badge of long hair—and there I was with my pageboy and bangs. One girl with hip-length friz and jungle-loop earrings looked me over suspiciously when I came down from putting Regina to bed. She eyed me several times while I sat silently at the edge of the group, and once she stared outright until I stared back. A few minutes later, she reached into her shoulder bag and pulled out three joints and held them up triumphantly.

"Can we, Frank?"

"Just let me turn up the air conditioner," he said.

"Frank," I said, "will you help me in the kitchen a minute?" It was the most clichéd trick in the world, but it was all I could manage on the spot. The girl with the joints looked at me and smirked.

"We'll wait till you get back," she said to Frank.

As soon as we closed the door, I said to him, "I don't want that stuff in the house."

"Irene, it's harmless. It's like taking a drink."

"Except that you can go to jail for it."

"We're in our own home. Do you think the police are out setting up dragnets for a little grass?"

"The neighbors have eyes. When they see a few carloads of people with long hair pull up to our house, they're going to start wondering—"

"I've had long hair ever since you met me."

"I *like* long hair, and as for them, I don't care if their hair is green and pink. That's not the point. The point is we don't live on a desert island. We have neighbors with big eyes and bigger mouths."

"You're being paranoid."

"Stop accusing me! What about that presumptuous bitch in there bringing that stuff into our house?"

His eyes narrowed. "That presumptuous bitch, as you call her, spent half an hour in my office today, crying. And do you know why? Not because her parents forgot to send her her allowance or because some sorority rejected her. She was crying because she loved a man she never met, a man she thought was vital to her country. And even though our opinions differ, I have to respect that kind of conscience."

"Good for her. I hope her conscience keeps her company when she's sitting in a jail cell."

"Irene, this country's in big trouble. If there's going to be any change, a lot of people are going to have to take chances with their lives."

"We're off the issue. We're talking about a chance that's so foolish—"

"You like liquor, they like grass. Your preference

is sanctioned, theirs isn't. That's what's bothering you."

"It's *my* house. That's what's bothering me."

He nodded. *"Your* house."

"I don't mean it that way."

"I think you do."

"All right," I said. "Do what you want."

His face lit up like a child's. "You come have some too."

"No; I'm going upstairs to read."

He cupped my face in his hands. "I want you to try it. With me. I want you sitting right next to me."

"Really, I don't want to."

"Please. In another hour, we'll toss them all out and go to bed."

I loved the idea of tossing them out, and I was reassured by the fact that *he* had suggested it.

"Fraaaank?" the girl called from the living room.

"In a minute," he answered.

"Let's get in there," I said. "The natives are restless."

"The natives can wait." He kissed my eyes, my cheeks, my forehead, then filled my mouth with his tongue. "I know I ask to be indulged sometimes, but I indulge you too, don't I?"

Back in the living room, Frank adjusted the lighting, a ritual which I had heard usually preceded grass-smoking. He lit the kerosene hurricane lamp on the mantelpiece and brought in the two candles from the dining room. It was apparent he had smoked before; aside from wondering how often, I wondered where and with whom. I sat on one side of Frank and the friz girl, Sylvia, sat on the other. When the joint had been smoked down to a stub, he held it for her. I didn't like the way her lips pressed his fingers as she sucked in the smoke.

For twenty minutes or so, I didn't feel a thing. But when I stood up to get the jug of wine, a flush of cold blood ran from my head to my legs, and I had to stand still before moving.

"She's *stoned*," said Sylvia, as if I had won some kind of victory.

"Hey, Irene, how d'ya feel?" Bernie asked, laughing. The others tittered; their voices sounded hollow and metallic. Since I was the only one standing, I was the center of attention and I didn't want to be. I didn't want to walk and I wasn't sure I could sit down gracefully, so I just stood where I was, in line with the blast of the air conditioner. I felt Frank's hand grip my wrist, his other hand grip my waist, and in one blurred movement I was sitting next to him again. We were all sitting in a circle and for the longest time nobody said anything. Half of them had their eyes closed, their chins lifted in the attitude of receiving a vision. I caught Bernie Golden staring at me with a bold expression I had never seen before. I stared back, dumbly, wondering if I was imagining it. When his mouth formed a crooked half smile, I quickly turned away. What I turned to was no better. Sylvia was leaning against Frank, whispering in his ear, leaning back to giggle, leaning forward to whisper again. She had on one of those muslin Indian tops and no brassiere. When she whispered to Frank, her breasts nuzzled his arm. I made another attempt to get up, but Frank caught my shoulder.

"What do you want, honey? I'll get it."

"The wine," I lied. I wanted to go upstairs.

"And some music, Frank," said Sylvia. "We need some music."

"What kind?" he asked.

Don't ask her what kind! That bitch doesn't run this house!

"Got any Jefferson Airplane?"

"No."

"Rolling Stones?"

"Uh uh. We've got Mamas and Papas."

"That's good. They're mellow."

Frank got up. Sylvia lit a cigarette, then turned to me and said, "How do you feel?"

"I feel fine."

"Good, good."

Good, good. Who do you think you are? The goddam hostess?

"Look at Tim!" she laughed. "He's spaced out!"

Everyone looked at Tim and tittered. The boy's eyes were closed, his mouth open. When he sensed everyone looking at him, he shook his hair off his shoulders onto his back and said, "Wow, am I stoned!"

The Mamas and the Papas came on with "Monday, Monday." I thought: Good, the music will shut them up.

Frank refilled wineglasses and sat down again. Sylvia shifted her weight onto one hip, the one closest to Frank, and leaned on an arm, which touched his leg. I pretended to stare at the rug, but I had an adequate view of Sylvia. Suddenly, I thought of that girl, years ago, who had got out of Frank's car with the bag of groceries. Sylvia resembled her in that she was equally plain, almost homely. But Sylvia was not meek and retiring. Far from it. As I looked at her and at Bernie Golden, who still had that crooked smile, I wished I had Gloria next to me, someone who would see the same things I was seeing.

"All right, gang, ready for the zinger?" she said, holding up a joint the size of a small cigar.

Everyone said, "Oh, wow," "Far out" and "Too much."

When it got to me, I passed it up. I was thinking of what Frank had said about tossing them out.

"Hey!" Sylvia clapped her hands and began singing "Chicago, Chi-cago." The others joined in.

"Man, we're really gonna open their eyes," said Tim, who was not about to open his.

"Whose eyes?" I said.

"The hawks and the pigs," said the boy next to Tim. "Those capitalist killers and political money grubbers."

I turned to Frank. "The Democratic convention, honey," he said. "It's going to be one hell of a demonstration."

"What about it?"

"Well, we're all going in a kind of caravan—"

"*You're* going?"

Lightly, he put his hand on the back of my neck and nodded.

"When was all this decided?"

"Let's not go into it now," he whispered.

Part of me wanted to get up and out of the room immediately, but another part didn't want any of them, especially Sylvia, to see my anger. I closed my eyes, pretended to be absorbed in the music, and waited until the record ended before making my exit upstairs. My whole body felt weighted as I climbed the steps. I looked in on Regina, then went to our room, where I tried to stay awake so I could talk to Frank. It was no use. The combination of grass and wine and standing up made me want to sleep forever. And I wanted to shake the picture I had of Sylvia holding a bag of groceries.

I woke up to the sound of giggling, muffled and sporadic. It took me a few seconds to realize that it was coming from downstairs and a minute more to recognize two voices, Regina's and a woman's. Frank was lying next to me, his arm slung over his eyes and his mouth wide open, snoring. I got up and into my robe. My head was throbbing, my eyes felt puffed and raw. I wanted to get downstairs quickly, but my body wouldn't keep up with my mind.

In the living room, I found Sylvia on her elbows and knees, bent forward and shaking her head so furiously that her hair ballooned into a huge globe of fuzz. Regina, giggling, sat with her arms extended and almost lost in Sylvia's hair.

"What's going on?"

Sylvia stopped and fell back on her elbows, panting. The four buttons on her Indian top were unfastened, and I could see the side of each breast. "We're playing," she said breathlessly. "I didn't think we were being that loud."

"How . . . did you get here?" For some reason, I couldn't broach the obvious.

"I passed out on the floor and woke up on the couch. Frank must have put me there." Very matter-of-fact, not a trace of apology in her voice.

"What time is it?"

"I don't know." And obviously didn't care.

"Mommy, Sylvia said you could grow your hair long if you wanted to. Will you?"

"I don't want my hair long."

"Well, I'm gonna grow *mine*."

"It'll get in your eyes."

"I like it in my eyes. I can look through it."

"You've got pretty eyes," said Sylvia. "Just like your father."

I walked past them into the kitchen. I set up the coffeepot. While it perked, I made myself a cup of instant. Their giggling started up again. I sat at the table, seething and preparing what I was going to say to Frank. I wanted a clear head, I wanted to be alone with Frank for the whole day, and more than anything I wanted the night before to be completely erased. I wanted Sylvia out of my house and I wanted to forget that bold, suggestive look on Bernie Golden's face.

The giggling stopped. Everything was too quiet. When I got to the living room, they weren't there. I knew they couldn't be outside, because Regina was still in her nightie. I didn't want to suspect what I was suspecting, but the shrill laugh—Sylvia's laugh—that shot down the stairs was a clear invitation to battle.

I found the two of them on the bed, tickling Frank. He was squirming around, wrapped up in the sheet, and he had the pillow over his head. No one noticed me, so I stood and watched. Until Sylvia's hand went *under* the sheet.

"Since everyone's awake," I said, "I think we'd better have breakfast." The announcement was for the three of them, but my eyes were on Sylvia. She looked back dumbly. *All right, bitch, let's see you start hopping.* "Sylvia, would you take Regina downstairs? Frank and I have to get dressed." She took Regina by the hand and left. Frank sat up against the pillows and smiled until he read the look on my face.

"Honey, what's wrong?"

"You haven't got the slightest idea?" He shook his head. "Well, *that's* what's wrong."

"Tell me. What is it?"

"It's so obvious! What is she doing here?"

"She passed out last night and slept on the couch."

"Yes, she told me that much."

"You don't think . . . You know better than that."

"Do I?"

"Stop it. She passed out and slept on the couch. Why make something out of that?"

"Why? Because this isn't a flophouse! Because she thinks she can do as she damn pleases here. She pulls out the grass as if she's running the place, she decides what music everyone is going to hear, she doesn't leave your side the whole night, she feels perfectly free to pass out on our floor, and then she has the gall to come into our room while you're still in bed and to run her hand under the sheet. Now ask me what's wrong!"

"Come sit next to me for a minute."

"No, thanks, I'll stand. I want her out of here. She has plenty of brass and you polish it for her. Don't think she didn't enjoy the fact that you said nothing to me about going to that convention."

"I was going to tell you about it today."

"*Tell* me? Obviously, then, we're not going to *discuss* it. It's all been decided."

"I have to go, Irene. The bigger the number, the louder the voice. This is a chance for the people to show they won't have policy pushed onto them."

"Let's start determining a little policy around here. First of all, this is not a place for self-appointed rebels to flop. If she wants to try moving in on you, let her do it at your office, not here."

"She's not moving in on me. She's got a slight case of hero-worship, that's all. She's a little mixed up right now and she doesn't quite know how to handle her emotions."

"It's not her emotions she wants to handle."

"Will you stop being so hard on people? I told you last night what she's going through—"

"I don't want to hear any more about her 'political conscience.' She's aggressive, presumptuous and ill-mannered. And I'll tell you right now I don't like the idea of your going off to that convention with her."

"And I don't like the idea of your not trusting me. Besides, eleven of us are going. Come on now, let's not fight anymore." He rolled to the edge of the bed and put his feet on the floor. "If you don't like her, I'll make sure she doesn't come here anymore. I don't want to fight with you."

"I don't want you to give in just because you don't want to fight. I want you to *understand* what I'm saying about her."

"I understand; I just *feel* differently about it. If she makes you that uncomfortable, we won't have her here."

Over breakfast, Sylvia reversed her tactics. She directed all her attention to me, asked questions about teaching, about Regina's long illness and how I coped with it, then complimented me on *my* taste in fixing up the house. Frank listened to it all without a trace of "I told you so," something I both admired and resented. Relief came when he and Regina left to take Sylvia home. I needed the house to myself and I worked quickly to set it straight. I emptied ashtrays, vacuumed the rug, washed the wineglasses, and removed the candle stubs from their holders. It was the clean-up after the invasion, a grand sweep to wipe out every trace of the enemy's occupation. I sprayed Lysol until the air was thick with it.

When Frank and Regina returned, I was washing up the breakfast dishes and humming as I envisioned the three of us spending this lazy day working in the yard. Frank gave Regina a Popsicle, then went up to change into his yard clothes. She sat down at the table behind me.

"Regina, don't slurp like that."

She continued to slurp, but more quietly. "What's repressed?" she asked.

"Repressed?"

"Uh huh."

"Where did you hear that?"

"Sylvia. She told Daddy you were repressed. What's it mean?"

"It means 'quiet.' " And I told myself to keep quiet but asked her anyway: "And what did Daddy say?"

"He didn't say anything."

"What else did Sylvia say?"

"She said I could come to her apartment for a whole day and play with her cats."

Over my dead body.

I made plans to take Regina with me and stay at my parents' while Frank was in Chicago. Neil was just back from Vietnam; I thought being around him would reassure me that Frank's trip was meaningful and necessary. But the day before Frank left, Gloria called from Los Angeles to say she was flying in to see her mother. (Her father had died two years earlier.) I grabbed at the opportunity of inviting her to spend a few days at our house. Pat was not coming with her, but she was bringing their three-year-old son, Brian. At first she hesitated at my offer, but when I said Frank would be gone, she readily accepted.

She timed her arrival just right; her rented car pulled into our driveway three hours after Frank pulled out of it. Instead of running out to greet her, I stood near the window, out of sight, and watched her lift Brian from the front seat and take the luggage out of the trunk. She was radiant. Her blond hair was blonder—I assumed from the sun—parted in the middle and drawn back in soft waves to form an old-fashioned bun. Instead of slacks or something else casual, she wore a cream-colored tailored suit. It was a style that seemed to be disappearing, and I was somehow proud of Gloria for hanging on to it. It made her look soft yet determined, behind the times but beyond them too. My stomach churned all the way up to my throat: I felt like a kid whose favorite grandmother was coming to visit.

I finally got myself moving to help her with the luggage. When we got it inside, I hugged her so hard that she laughed. It was good to hear her laugh, the way she used to before I met Frank.

"This is Mommy's friend," she said to Brian, who was gripping her skirt. "See, I told you her hair is red." She turned to me. "I don't think he's ever seen a real redhead. Just about everyone in California is a blond." She brushed his fleecy locks.

"Regina's taking a nap right now. Are you hungry? Do you want a shower?"

"Just some coffee." She looked around the living room and into the dining room. "This is beautiful, Irene. Really beautiful."

"It's a little too dark. We're surrounded by trees."

"I'll take this any day over that California glare."

"Stomach hurts," said Brian.

Gloria put her hand on her stomach and said, "No, it doesn't."

"Stomach *hurts.*"

"Feels fine to me," she said.

"*My* stomach hurts."

"Ohhh, why didn't you say so? I think you should take off your shoes and lie down on that couch over there."

"You lie with me."

"No; Irene and I are going to sit at the dining room table. You'll be able to hear me."

He took off his shoes and crawled onto the couch. "I'll hear you?" he said.

"Now don't you dare go to sleep. You have to hear me."

"I won't go to sleep," he murmured, his eyes already closed. "I can close my eyes but I can hear you."

"That's right. You can close your eyes, but don't go to sleep." As we moved into the dining room, she shook her head and smiled. "Oh, the little games they teach us."

I nodded but said nothing. Already I was running a comparison: the past year with Regina had not been a light-hearted experience. She had taught us a game, all right, but it was one Frank and I reacted to differently and argued over. At the end of March, when she had recovered from the rheumatic fever, the doctor warned us to watch her carefully if she ever complained of a sore throat because it could lead to strep, which in turn could bring on a relapse of the rheumatic condition. Frank relayed this information to Regina and told her to let us know if she felt even the slightest tickle. Too many times, when she wanted to stay up late or found out she was going to spend an evening with a baby-sitter, she would begin hinting about her throat. The doctor would come, only to discover that her throat showed no trace of redness at all. Finally, one night when Frank was working, I decided this game had to come to a halt. I told Regina if her throat really did hurt, we could not take chances: she would have to have a penicillin shot to protect her. She decided her throat really didn't hurt. Frank was livid when I told him what I had done. "You've made her afraid to tell us," he said. I said I hadn't, that I had explained to her the difference between real danger and no danger. After that, her complaints did subside a bit, but when she had them, she always went to Frank.

"How's Regina?" asked Gloria.

"Fully recovered, the doctor says. Naturally, she's anxious to start school. It's been a tough year for her. Her friends sort of abandoned her and I don't think she's quite forgiven them. There's a new family on the next block and she's taken up with their little girl, so she does have someone. I must say Frank made everything a lot easier for both Regina and me." I told her how he had arranged his teaching schedule so I could go back to work. She looked a little embarrassed, then said:

"I'm happy things have turned out well for you and Frank. I think I've grown up a little since—well, since I've had Brian. And since my father died."

"How's your mother?"

She shook her head. "Hopeless. She's drunk all the time now. I was going to stay three days with her, but all I could take was one night. She won't hire a housekeeper or a gardener; the place is in a complete shambles, yet she won't sell it and move into an apartment. She won't listen to anything I say; she just wants to be left alone to drink. I'll tell you, there's no one explanation for a bad marriage, I realize that now. She was miserable when he was alive, but she's more miserable now that he's dead. I've decided she's just lazy. I know that sounds callous, but . . . happiness takes a lot of work. Misery takes no work."

"Amen."

"I've had to change my mind about a lot of things, mainly her and him. And you and Frank. Obviously you've made a go of it."

"Yes. But the differences become more sharply defined as we get older. You know he went to that demonstration. He's very political and I'm not at all."

"I'm not, either. I can't make up my mind about politics. Sometimes it all seems so complicated and other times I feel it's so damned simple-minded, just a lot of sloganeering." She smiled. "I feel the same way about Brian. Sometimes I look at him and think he's only three and therefore just a simple little soul. Then he turns around and does something that makes me say, 'No, he's already a complex little individual.' Do you ever feel that way about Regina?"

"Oh, yes. She's got her tricks and her stratagems. Not all of them pleasant, I'm afraid."

"Frightening little creatures, aren't they, when you realize they have thoughts of their own."

"Who's that?"

We both looked at Regina, standing in the archway. She was pointing to the couch, which we couldn't see. "Who's that?" she repeated.

"That's Brian," I said. "And this is Gloria."

"Hello, Regina."

"Hello. When's Daddy coming home?"

"I told you, not for a few days. Gloria and Brian are staying with us. Daddy will be back after they leave."

"Daddy's coming back when they go?"

"Yes."

"If they go now, will he come home now?"

Gloria laughed. "She's way ahead of you, Irene."

"Are they sleeping here?"

"Yes, they're sleeping here. Do you want some cookies and milk?"

"Is Sylvia going to stay with us too?"

"Sylvia's out of town."

"With Daddy?"

"Yes, they went to a convention. Now let's stop with the questions. What big plans do you have for the afternoon?"

"I want to go to Susan's."

"Fine, but be home by four-thirty. That way you can play with Brian for a little while before dinner."

She looked disdainfully in the direction of the couch. "I don't want to play with him. He's a *baby*."

"He's small," I said, "but he's not a baby. He's three."

"I'm six. Three and three is six."

I could see Gloria was amused by this exchange, but I was growing impatient. "You can still have fun together."

"Babies aren't fun. You have to take care of them."

"That's enough, Miss Priss. You just be home by four-thirty or I'll take care of *you*. Make sure you're nearby when I call."

"Suppose I'm in Susan's house?"

"They have clocks."

"Suppose we go to the store?"

"Suppose you stay home."

That was enough to send her skipping out of the house.

"She's so tall and she looks just like Frank," said Gloria. "But she takes after you. Sharp and sassy."

"Kindergarten will smooth her corners."

She asked who Sylvia was and I poured out the story. Talking about it made me angry all over again, but this time I enjoyed the anger. Gloria's knowing smiles and nods reassured me I was talking to someone whose opinions were aligned with my own.

"So you didn't like the grass?" she asked.

"Not particularly. But then, I was drinking wine with it."

"No good. And you were with strangers too."

"Yes, I suppose that makes a difference. But I don't even drink much anymore."

"How about smoking with *me* tonight?"

"You smoke grass?"

"Once in a while. I've been dying to smoke with someone who has more to say than 'Oh, wow.' We'll smoke an official peace pipe."

I liked the idea immediately, partly because, as Gloria suggested, this was our reunion, and partly because she was the picture of propriety except for the sly grin she was giving me. She tapped her purse with her perfectly manicured painted-peach nails and said with a mock-Southern drawl: "Whah, Offi-suh, ah have no idea how six li'l ol' joints got inta this heah purse."

"Six! They could lock you up for that." Then, a little apprehensive, I asked, "How often do you smoke that stuff?"

"Once or twice a week. Just a couple of puffs to get me to sleep when I'm wound up. Purely medicinal, my dear. I never smoke with anyone; that's why I'd like to do it with you. In fact, maybe I should have a little nap now so I don't pass out on the stuff later."

"Sure, go ahead. If Brian wakes up, we'll get acquainted."

She stood up and looked around the room again. "You really have done a beautiful job with the house. It *feels* like a home."

After she went upstairs, I sat and took in the room. She was right, it did feel like a home, and I was especially proud of the dining room, with the light oak moldings around the windows and the archway, the roughly cut hutch and wine rack, the green Tiffany lamp hanging over the round, dark oak table. Spacious and uncluttered, it was a room that made you think of children getting out of wet boots and mittens and gathering around for cookies and cocoa. I was glad Gloria approved; I was glad she found Regina so amusing. And I was glad we were having this reunion. Having been involved with Regina and the house and then my job again, I had not cultivated any close friendships like the one I had once had with Gloria. Obvious as it should have been, it didn't occur to me what I had been missing until I heard her laugh again and saw her listening, really listening, to me.

I was reading a magazine in the living room when Brian woke up. He gave a big yawn, sat straight up and pressed the corners of his eyes with his fingers, then put his hands flat on his legs and said hello to me very matter-of-factly. To me, this little routine was hilariously adult, like that of an executive emerging from a stolen nap in the office. I told him his mother was sleeping upstairs; he nodded and looked out the window as if that were what he had expected me to say. After cookies and milk, he stretched out on the floor with one of Regina's coloring books. He chose a picture of Alice meeting the Queen of Hearts. Before he would touch a crayon to each item, he consulted me about the color he should use. He worked slowly, clamping his tongue between his lips and squinting his eyes when the crayon got close to the borders; when he was safely away from the borders and had more freedom of movement, his face relaxed and his hand sped up. I compared his work with Regina's on the page next to it. Her strokes jagged out of the lines and were put down with varying degrees of pressure. And like most of her pictures, this one was unfinished. I felt a twinge of jealousy as I watched Brian's steady concentration. But of course, I thought, he had not suffered a confinement to make him frustrated and impatient.

As if my silent comparison had summoned her, Regina was standing in the archway, staring at Brian.

"Aren't you the quiet one," I said. "It's only ten to four. Didn't you play with Susan?"

"Her grandma came," she mumbled, not taking her eyes off Brian. Brian looked up for only a second, and went back to his work.

"Why don't you get your other book and color with Brian?"

"Who said he could color in my book?"

"I said. He's only coloring one picture."

"I was saving that picture."

I doubted it. "I'm sorry, I didn't know. You can color one in your other book."

"I hate that other book."

"You don't hate it. You color in it all the time."

"I hate it. I was saving *that* picture and now he spoiled it!"

Brian put his crayon down and backed away to the couch.

"It's all right, Brian, you can keep coloring." He stood where he was and stared at Regina. "If you've got any notion about throwing a tantrum, young lady, you can forget it right now. I didn't know you were saving that picture and that's that. There are plenty of other pictures for you to color."

"He spoiled it! You let a baby color in my book!"

"*You're* acting like the baby. I don't want to hear another word about it."

"Daddy wouldn't give it to him."

"Daddy would have. Now that's enough. Brian, go ahead and finish your picture."

He started for the book but Regina shot forward and grabbed it.

"Regina, put that down!" She backed up a few steps and hung on to it. "I said to put it down." I could tell by the defiance in her eyes I was going to have to take it from her. I started out of the chair.

In one quick movement, she tore the page from the book, then hurled the book to the floor. As I came to her, she crumpled the picture into a ball. I grabbed her arm and headed for the stairs. "You are going to your room and you're staying there until I tell you you can come out."

She began to cry. "I want Daddy. I want Daddy to come home!"

"Get going," I said, aiming her up the first step.

"I want Daddy," she sobbed, and slid down against the wall.

"Regina, I can't carry you, but if I have to I'll drag you up. Now get moving."

She spread herself face down on the steps and wailed, "I want Daddy. I want him *now!*"

"Get up." I tugged on her arm, but she was determined to stay where she was.

"Irene, what's wrong?" It was Gloria at the top of the stairs.

"Just the Queen of Sheba throwing a tantrum." I took hold of Regina by both wrists and started walking backward up the steps.

"Irene, don't! You'll hurt your back."

"She is going to her room—one way or the other."

"I want Daddy!"

Gloria came down. "I shouldn't butt in, but let me help you. You can't pull her like that; you'll both get hurt." She went for Regina's feet but had to pull away when Regina began to kick.

"Don't touch me! You don't live here! Go away and let my daddy come home! Don't touch me, don't touch me!"

I was furious and ashamed. I had to stand still for a minute because I was afraid I might yank Regina's arms right out of their sockets. I saw a look of sympathy, almost pity, on Gloria's face, and I hated Regina for putting it there.

When I got her into her room, I closed the door

and took a few deep breaths to steady myself. She flung herself onto the bed and buried her face in the pillow.

"You can go right on crying," I said, "but you listen to me and you listen well. Gloria is my friend and she and Brian are guests in this house. When you have guests, you share things with them. So you'd better start learning how. You've had a few little taps on your butt before, but you've never had a real spanking. You're going to find out what one feels like if you dare to act the way you did just now. Do you understand?" I knew better than to wait for an answer, so I left immediately.

When I got back to the living room, Brian was uncrumpling the picture to show to Gloria. I felt helpless, with nothing to say. If only Brian had cried or thrown a tantrum himself. But there he was accepting his mother's assurance that a few wrinkles wouldn't hurt his good coloring job. When he looked skeptical, she asked him who the prettiest woman in the world was. He said it was she. "Well," she said, "someday I'll be wrinkled just like that paper, but I'll still be pretty, won't I?" She pressed her forehead against his and said, "Won't I?"

He smiled and kissed her mouth with a loud smack. I could tell the kiss was a ritual between them and for the moment I couldn't help feeling cheated.

Regina refused to come out of her room to eat, so dinner turned out to be quite pleasant. Maybe because I was so disappointed in Regina—and myself —and because I admired the tenderness between Gloria and Brian, I set out to win the boy's attention. When I served the pudding, I gave him a side dish of whipped cream shaped like a snowman, with raisin eyes, lemon-peel mouth and a maraschino cherry cap. Once again, he showed that uncanny adult expression as he adjusted the cherry cap to his liking.

"I can see it coming," sighed Gloria as we watched him. "He's going to be a nit-picker like his father."

We had our coffee in the living room. Brian sat on my lap, running his fingers through my hair and murmuring, "Fire." Gloria watched us with the same contentment she once had when she used to listen to Pat and me kidding each other.

"Don't you think we should take something up to Regina?" she said.

"I told her if she wants to eat she can come downstairs."

"Why don't you let me take it up, as a kind of peace offering. After all, we've invaded her territory."

"All right, if you want to."

She prepared a tray with the ham and the potato salad and made a whipped cream snowman as I had done for Brian. She went upstairs, knocked and called Regina's name. There was a long silence before she came back down.

"She wouldn't answer me. I left the tray on the nightstand."

"Then let her stew." She sat down with a look of amusement. "I know. You think I'm being too hard."

She shrugged. "Not at all. I know your expectations, Irene."

"And you think they're too high?"

She cocked her head to the side. "Do you really doubt yourself that much?"

"Sometimes. Especially when it comes from all sides. Frank and I see eye to eye on all the important things except Regina. I think he's too indulgent, he thinks I'm too hard. The same thing at school. The trend now is less homework and practically no writing. Complete sentences are out of fashion, spelling is unimportant, knowing the parts of speech is considered passé. And when it comes to literature, everyone seems to be on this kick of reading what's supposed to be *relevant*—the implication being that anything written before 1950 is irrelevant. I'm not very popular with the other people in the English Department. If it weren't for the principal's support, I'd feel like a total dinosaur."

"It's no better in college. You should see the papers I had to read. But let's not talk shop."

We put Brian to bed in the same room where Gloria would sleep. We only had to promise to leave the door open and the hall light on.

"Do you want one of Regina's dolls or bears to sleep with?" I asked him.

"No," said Gloria. "He hates things in bed with him. Likes the whole place to himself. Don'tcha, kiddo?"

He smiled and stuck his arms out to the sides. "Can't fall out," he said.

"After the crib, we put him in a twin. He fell out of it six times, so now he's got a double."

I checked on Regina. She was reading comic books in bed, and the food was untouched. She would not look at me, and we said nothing to each other. I simply closed the door and went downstairs.

"How about some more coffee to go with the grass?" said Gloria. "It'll keep everything in check."

I perked a pot and we sat down at the dining room table. Gloria pulled out the joint. When we got it smoked down too far to hold, she produced a roach clip and showed me how to suck in the last of the smoke. I soon felt the mellowness come over me, and the room seemed to cool off considerably.

"How about some music? I can put on FM."

"No," she said. "No music, if you don't mind. You know what I love to do? I love to take a few puffs, settle into bed and read. But always the same stuff—S. J. Perelman or Dorothy Parker or Flannery O'Connor. I read them over and over again. I tried Waugh once but it didn't work." She giggled. "Waugh was a flop in bed."

"Doesn't Pat ever want to . . . you know?"

"Have sex? We take care of that earlier. And without grass. Then he goes to sleep and I puff and read." She smiled wistfully.

"You miss him?"

"Ummm. Every now and then I need to be away from him. But I do miss him. I learned my lesson."

"What lesson?"

"He left me once. When he found out I was having an affair."

"*You* had an affair?"

"For about two months. I was pregnant with Brian. That just about killed Pat. 'You let another man put his prick in you while you've got *my* baby in there?' 'Don't worry,' I said, 'it isn't touching the baby.' I was an out-and-out bitch."

"Who was he? How did it start?"

"He was a cashier in the supermarket, a drifter, forty-five years old. I knew I had to leave the college to have Brian and I guess I was afraid of the middle-class setup I'd be falling into. Anyway, this guy kept giving me the eye and I was dazzled by the fact he had no roots and didn't give a damn. That was before I realized half the state of California is filled with drifters and they're a dime a dozen. So one day he's ringing up my order and he says to me, 'Did you ever lie naked on pine needles?' He was so matter-of-fact, it fascinated me. We never made it to the pine needles, but I went to his house every morning for two months."

"Every morning?"

"Weekday mornings while Pat was working." She lit a cigarette. "Hal was quite violent. I had to keep warning him against leaving marks."

"What did he use—a rubber hose?"

She laughed. "Not violent *that* way."

"How did Pat find out?"

"The usual way. The only day I ever went out with

Hal for lunch, Pat saw us and followed us back to Hal's. He didn't tell me. The next morning he drove by Hal's and saw my car in the driveway. Then he confronted me and I confessed. Then he walked out for two weeks. He wouldn't let me in his office and he hung up every time I called. I almost went crazy. I thought I was going to lose him, I thought some woman would get him and that would be the end of it. When he came back, he said if it ever happened again, he'd leave me for good and take the baby too. And I knew he meant it. You know what's crazy? I don't think I really loved him until he said that. I was very lucky. Sometimes I get the chills when I think how it could have all gone another way."

"Yes, it could have."

We sat quietly for what seemed a long time. I watched her circle the ashtray with her cigarette butt.

"It's all chance, isn't it?" she said. "Who we meet and who we don't. I know it sounds sophomoric, but when you realize it *emotionally,* it's frightening. If I'd never met you or Pat . . . Are you happy, Irene?"

"I . . ." Maybe it was the grass, maybe an echo of the past, but suddenly I suspected a trap. "Yes." Her eyes rolled up to meet mine. "I guess so. Reasonably."

She smiled. "A reasonable answer."

"Sometimes I'm afraid."

"Of what?"

"Of change. This damned war, King and the Kennedys assassinated—it's gotten Frank all worked up and involved and it scares me. And then Regina, the whole last year. And school, of course. We had so many fights last year, all that racial stuff. And some problems with drugs. And here *I* sit smoking grass with you. It's just so strange. Even a year ago I couldn't have pictured myself doing it."

"Well, you're doing it and it's all right, so relax. In fact, I think I'll send a little news item to our alumni paper: 'Irene Mattison, nee Rutledge, Queen of

Sparta, renounces crown and scepter for daily dose of dope and relaxation.' "

"No one would believe it."

"That, my dear, is why it makes good copy."

She suggested we switch from coffee to Coca-Cola and have another joint. When I hesitated, she assured me we had eaten recently enough to keep us from getting too stoned. Just as she struck the match, the doorbell rang.

"Oh, my God, the cops!"

She laughed. "Very unlikely. Probably a moon-lighting Avon lady. I'll get rid of her."

I watched her walk through the living room and open the door. The porch light wasn't on, so I couldn't make out the figure on the porch. "Oh, yes," I heard Gloria say, "I remember you. Come on in. Irene, you've got company."

Vivian stepped into the living room.

"Hello, Irene." She smiled meekly and looked quickly around the room. "Is Frank here?"

"As a matter of fact, he's not." *Get on your feet, you idiot!* I stood up. "He's in Chicago. On business."

"Oh? He's not teaching at the university anymore?"

"It's university business."

We stood there awkward and silent. Finally, Gloria said, "I think I'll do the dishes. If you'll excuse me . . ." She picked up the coffee cups from the dining room table—and the joint along with them.

"I know I'm not supposed to be here," said Vivian. "I just took a chance that maybe Frank has softened a little."

"I don't think he has. I'm sorry." *What are you doing standing here in the dining room while she's standing in there? Get moving!* "I really don't know what to say." I moved forward a few steps. "Would you like to sit down for a few minutes?"

"I'd better not, since Frank's not here." But she

didn't move. "You never cashed that second check I sent you."

"I couldn't. I—"

"I understand, believe me." She bit her lip and looked at the floor. "Irene, I'm going to ask you a big favor. I've *got* to ask it. Can I see the baby?"

"The baby?"

"Sorry. She must be six now, going into first grade."

"Kindergarten. She was sick last year."

Her face darkened. "How sick?"

"Rheumatic fever. She was in the house for eight months."

"Is she all right?"

"Oh, yes. Spunky and sassy."

She smiled. "Could I see her. Just *see* her. I won't say a word to her. You don't have to tell her who I am. Please, you don't know what it would mean to me."

I couldn't stand hearing her beg. "If Frank ever found out . . ."

"Irene, I know it's asking a lot, but I promise you he'll never know. *No* one will know. Even Leo doesn't know I came here."

"Yes, you must promise me that."

"I do promise you."

We found Regina sprawled out on the bed, still dressed and sound asleep in a pile of comics. The food on the nightstand hadn't been touched; the raisins and lemon peel and cherry lay in a puddle of cream.

"She was being punished," I whispered in hasty explanation. "She didn't want to tare her shoys—" *Idiot!* "—I mean share her toys." God, I thought, I hope she can't smell that stuff.

She smiled and bent down closer to Regina. "Lovely, lovely. She's going to be tall like Frank."

"Yes, she looks just like Frank."

"I hope she's not going to slouch. Tall girls have a

tendency to do that. I had to teach myself not to. What's her name?"

"Regina."

She looked as if she didn't believe me. "Regina?"

"Yes."

"Then Frank must have named her."

"Yes." I watched her bend even closer, until her face nearly touched Regina's. "She's a light sleeper," I lied. I was beginning to feel a vague resentment. Vivian took the hint and followed me out of the room.

"What did you mean—'Frank must have named her'?"

She looked embarrassed. "It just seemed a little coincidental. It was our sister's name."

"What sister?"

"Didn't he tell you? Our sister who died. Her name was Regina."

"When did she die?"

"She was fifteen. It was Frank who found her. In the woods."

"In the woods?"

"She was retarded. She drank a bottle of lye."

"Lye! But was it—was it by mistake?"

"No one knows. She was secretive, like Frank. They were very close and apart from the rest of us."

"Frank never mentioned her. In fact, he never mentioned you, either, until you came to the wedding rehearsal."

"Who knows what goes on in that mind of his."

"Vivian, why doesn't he like you?"

She sighed and looked away. "I don't want to give you the wrong impression, Irene. I love Frank very much. But he's always been quite committed to having his own way. We were a big family and I had to look after him a lot of the time. And discipline him. Frank does not like discipline, and he holds grudges better than anyone I know. That's why, for your sake as well as mine, I wouldn't tell him I was here."

"But I want to ask him why he never said anything about his sister."

"Don't, please. Maybe it's just too painful for him to talk about, maybe he just wants to forget about it. In time, he might tell you about it."

"In time? We've been married nine years!"

"We all have our secret torments no one knows about. There are some things people *can't* share. I shouldn't have told you."

"No, I'm glad you did."

"One more thing before I go. I know you won't accept any money from me, but I'm going to open a savings account in my name and Regina's. By the time she's ready for college, she'll have all the money she needs. And maybe Frank will soften by then. This will be just between us."

"Vivian, I can't—"

"Yes, you can. I told you once that in our family we take care of our own. Regina shouldn't get any less than my other nieces and nephews are getting." She started for the door.

"Wait. Give me your address before you go. The least I can do is send you a Christmas card."

Smiling, she wrote it down for me. "Hide it well."

"I will."

We shook hands.

"I'm glad you came," I said. "And I'm sorry about the way the situation is between us."

"You never know, it may change. I'm extremely patient. Running a business has taught me that much. Good-bye."

"Good-bye, Vivian."

I found Gloria reading the newspaper in the kitchen.

"No bad news, I hope."

"I'm not sure."

"Let's hear it."

"Not tonight. All of a sudden, I'm exhausted. If you don't mind, I'd like to go to bed."

"Go ahead. I brought along Dorothy Parker for just such an emergency."

For a long time, I couldn't get to sleep. I kept imagining what lye would do to someone's insides. *She was retarded.* I should have been told for our daughter's sake. Never mind *his* private torment. I had a right to know. And I would find a way to make him tell me.

IN the morning, we decided to take the kids on a walking tour of the campus and then to the zoo.

"I've been to the zoo," muttered Regina.

"You like the zoo. If you want, you can ask Susan to come."

"I don't want to go."

"All right then, you'll have to stay at Mrs. Lorimer's and I'll have to pay her. That means no money for you when the ice cream truck comes around."

"I don't want any ice cream."

"Remember that later."

"I will." Determined, as always, to have the last word.

Gloria and I packed a lunch, and after dropping Regina at Mrs. Lorimer's, drove off with Brian. The day was perfect, hot but dry, with huge clouds driven by a wind that occasionally touched ground. We parked at the edge of the campus and walked directly to Harley Hall, which housed the English Department.

"Ah, the return of the natives," said Gloria. "Let's see if Big Chief Denning's in."

The secretary told us Dr. Denning had gone to Tulane two years ago. Gloria looked at me in surprise. "Didn't you know that?"

"I never kept up with him. The only time I get out

here is when Frank and I come to a lecture-concert series or a play."

"You *are* a hermit."

I suggested we have our lunch at the botanical gardens behind the Natural Science Building. Gloria warned Brian not to touch the flowers. He ran around sniffing them and giggling.

"Over nine years ago," I said, looking around us.

"Nine years ago what?"

"I sat on that bench over there and took myself apart."

"Over what?"

"I'd had a fight with Frank. I should say I'd *started* a fight with him, and I couldn't finish it. I was so damned ridiculous, so proud. I came and sat here and had this big exorcism of my pride. Oh, God, was I filled with self-pity."

"You did grow up that year. I guess I resented it because I wasn't ready to do the same. I didn't want to lose my best friend."

"Gloria, am I still your best friend?"

She chuckled. "Yes, you always will be, no matter how far apart we live. I don't click with many people."

"Same with me. What you said a few minutes ago is true. I really am a hermit. Seeing you has made me realize just how much. I have no close friends at all. Oh, Frank and I play bridge with a few couples and there are a couple of people I like at work, but somehow we never manage to get together much outside of school. I guess my best friend is my husband. I don't know if that's wise, but that's the way it is. Besides him, you're the only other person I can really talk to —or *want* to talk to."

"What about your father? You used to be able to talk to him."

"There's too much disappointment and disapproval there now. On his part. He's never quite gotten over my quitting school. More than that, he's vehemently

against Frank's political views, and—I hate to say it
—I don't think he's as fond of Regina as a grandfather
should be. She can be a terrible hellion, which you've
seen, but he's not very understanding of her, the illness and all."

"And she doesn't look like you, either."

"What has that got to do with it?"

"Sometimes a great deal, unconsciously. You disap-
point him by leaving school and marrying Frank and
then you have a child that looks entirely like Frank, so
your father feels cheated all the way around. I'll bet
if you had another baby, that looked more like you,
he'd treat it differently."

"I wouldn't want that."

"Of course not. Look, once you start your own family, you've got a double load. You have to manage
your parents as well as your children."

And maybe your husband too, I thought. I was still
thinking of what Vivian had told me, still burning
over Frank's secretiveness. For some reason, Vivian's
information made me think of the night Sylvia had
slept over. Was Frank sleeping with her and keeping
that a secret too?

We smoked a couple of cigarettes and watched
Brian. Now and then, with an exaggerated gesture of
delicacy to convince his mother, he would reach out
and stroke a flower and give her a smile that said: "See,
I'm not hurting them." Again, I felt a twinge of jealousy.

"I'm going to hate to see you leave," I said impulsively. "This time, let's not lose touch with each other."

"*You're* the hermit. If you can tear yourself away
from your sanctuary, you're welcome at our place anytime. All three of you."

After an hour at the zoo, Brian got bored. When
I picked him up and carried him to the car, he buried
his fingers in my hair and murmured, "Fire." I thought
of Regina's hands in Sylvia's hair and how I had over-

reacted to it. I cautioned myself about overreacting to everything Vivian had told me.

When we got home, I called Mrs. Lorimer. She said Regina was outside playing, so I told her to send her home when she came in. Brian took a nap for an hour, then went out to play in the sandbox Frank had put in the vacant lot. Around four-thirty, Gloria went up for a shower while I set up the charcoal grill in the backyard. I began making the salad in the kitchen. As I was washing the vegetables in the sink, I looked out the window and saw a patch of red move behind the tree near the sandbox. I stood still, squinting, trying to make it out. What I saw next was the point of a stick protruding from the other side of the tree. Just as I was struck by the possibility of what it was, Regina jumped out and cracked the stick over Brian's head. He went forward, face down in the sand. Regina dropped the stick and ran. I flew out the back door yelling for her to stop, but she continued on without a backward glance. When I got to the sandbox, I saw the blood running down each side of Brian's ear. But what frightened me more was his face: his mouth was drawn back in a sob that couldn't escape and his skin was purple from the lack of air. I grabbed him up and slapped his back until his breath returned in little hitches; finally, he was able to scream. I carried him into the kitchen, where I patted his head with a wet dish towel. The profusion of blood terrified me, and I yelled for Gloria.

"My God, what happened!"

"Regina hit him with a stick." She looked at me incredulously. "I saw her. We'd better get him to the hospital. I think he's going to need stitches."

Gloria held him on her lap while I drove. His sobbing slipped into faint whimpering and he closed his eyes.

"Don't let him go to sleep," I said.

"You don't think . . ."

"I don't think anything. Just don't let him go to sleep."

The cut required six stitches, but the doctor assured us he would be all right. However, just to be safe, he told Gloria to be alert for any signs of dizziness or wavering in his walk.

When we drove into the driveway, the whole place looked disturbingly peaceful, as if nothing had happened. There was a thin line of smoke coming up from the charcoal grill; the three huge oaks blotted out the descending sun and colored the air a soft blue-gray. There was no sign of Regina. Gloria sat with Brian in the living room, cutting up an apple for him, while I searched the house. I looked under beds, opened closets and checked the basement and garage. As I was deciding my next move, the phone rang. It was Mrs. Lorimer.

"Mrs. Mattison, Regina wants to spend the night here."

"I'm sure she does. I'll be over to get her right now."

"She says she's afraid to come home."

"Just keep her inside until I get there."

I went out the back door and picked up the stick she had used on Brian and brought it into the kitchen. Then I started for Mrs. Lorimer's. When I reached the edge of her yard, Regina came barreling out the front door and went running in the other direction. I started after her, kicking off my thongs as I ran. As I rounded the corner onto the next street, my foot came down on something sharp. It was just enough to throw off my gait, and the big toe of my other foot slammed into the edge of the sidewalk. Strangely enough, the pain was more of an inspiration than a deterrent; I sped up and caught her in the next block. She had been screaming all the while I was chasing her, so there was quite an audience on hand, on lawns and porches and at windows. I got hold of the collar of her red shirt and yanked her backward so I could get a grip on her arm. Immediately, she began to pull.

"Stop pulling or so help me I'll break it!"

Mrs. Lorimer, who had been following me, arrived in time to hear this. She scowled and took a step toward me.

"That's no way to talk to a child."

"This is none of your business," I snapped.

"It's my business when I see a child being threatened."

"Would you like to know what this *child* did?"

"I don't care what she did. It doesn't excuse—"

"There's a three-year-old in my house who has six stitches in his head because of her!"

"I didn't, I didn't!" Regina screamed.

"Don't bother lying—I saw you do it. Now start walking!" She continued to pull in the other direction. "If I have to start pulling you, you're going to be sorry."

"Mrs. Mattison, maybe it would be wise to wait until you've calmed down."

"I'm not waiting for anything." I began to pull Regina the way a cowboy might pull his horse out of mud. Mrs. Lorimer walked alongside us.

"I want Daddy!"

"Maybe she could stay at my place until her father comes home."

"She's coming home with me."

"I want Daddy! My throat hurts!"

After the distance of one block, she realized my strength was greater than hers; she gave up pulling and stumbled along hesitantly. Mrs. Lorimer walked with us as far as our yard. Her cue to stop was my emphatic good night.

As soon as we got into the kitchen, Regina pulled back at the sight of the stick. I let go of her arm and picked it up. "Do you know that that little boy had to have his head sewn up?" My hand tightened around the stick as I looked into her face: there were Frank's eyes, his high forehead, his long, thin jaw line, but there was none of his softness. That face was a wilderness to me; all my anger gathered in my throat and I had to fight not to cry. "Do you realize how badly you *hurt* that boy?"

No answer.

"Would you like to see what you did? Would you like me to show you his stitches?"

Gloria came in. "Irene, he doesn't know what hit him. I don't think we should even bring it up."

Regina turned and sneered at her. That was all it took. I snapped the stick in two.

"Upstairs." My tone changed both their faces. For the first time in the past two years, there was fear in Regina's eyes and I savored it. "Upstairs. Now."

"I want Dad—"

"If you say that one more time, it'll be worse. Now get moving."

She went ahead of me, looking over her shoulder as we climbed the stairs. I followed her into her room, closed the door and pulled her over my knee. When I raised my hand, I realized I still had the stick in it. I dropped it, yanked down her shorts and panties, and slapped until my hand burned. She fell back on the bed, screaming.

"You have exactly half a minute to get quiet. If you don't, you'll get more. With the stick." To prove it, I picked it up. She turned her head and cried into the pillow. "I'll tell you right now, if you *ever* do what you did today, I'll beat you until you can't stand up. And don't think for a minute your father will be able to stop me."

When I got downstairs and saw Gloria and Brian, I felt I couldn't be in the same room with them. I sat in the kitchen to gather myself, but when I saw the flies feasting on the raw steaks that were supposed to

114

have gone onto the grill, I burst out crying. Then I felt Gloria's hands on my shoulders.

"I'm so ashamed, I don't know what to say."

"Shh, don't say anything. You just sit there while I get these steaks on." She put them under the broiler and slipped a block of frozen spinach into a saucepan.

"I don't think I can eat."

"Of course you can." She took out the plates and began setting the table.

"Oh, Gloria, don't! Yell at me—do something!"

"Yell at you for what?"

"You must be angry; you have to be!"

"I was, but not at you. And after I heard what went on upstairs, I don't think I'm angry with *her* anymore."

"What she did is inexcusable. I'll never forgive her for it."

"Don't say that. She's had her punishment. In fact, I think our being here is her punishment. We can stay at a motel."

"I wouldn't blame you if you did. But I wish you wouldn't."

"We'll see."

In an obvious effort to lighten my mood while we ate, she got Brian to chatter about the flowers and the animals he had seen that afternoon. But the boy's readiness to be cheerful and the bandage on his head depressed me even more.

"Something has to be done about her," I said as we washed the dishes. "As soon as Frank gets home, I'm laying down some new rules."

"Don't get worked up over it again. The trouble will be over when we leave."

"No, it won't. She's got the mistaken idea she runs this house. I'm going to see to it that idea goes right out the window."

Gloria agreed to stay the night. When we took Brian upstairs, I got the cold, sick feeling that maybe Regina would attack again. I went to her room while

Gloria tucked Brian in, and found her asleep clutching the Howdy Doody puppet Frank had given her. There was only contentment in her smooth brow and purring lips, but when I kissed her cheek I could smell the salty aftermath of her tears.

Downstairs, Gloria tried humoring me. I was ready for it. She widened her eyes dramatically, shook back her hair and ran her fingers through it, and said, "Whew, what a day! Mah deah, ah think we deserve some refreshment." She took out a joint and plopped down onto the couch.

"I don't think I should. Maybe I'll have a drink instead."

"You'll have some of this. You are going to relax."

I was in the mood to be told what to do. I wanted her to take me by the hand and lead me into oblivion.

She took two deep drags. "Now let's think pastel thoughts. Lightness and air, that's our need."

"Talk to me. Tell me about California," I said, taking the joint from her.

"Well"—she laughed—"that should take about two minutes. It's the epitome of contradiction and if you enjoy analyzing that sort of thing, it's rather amusing. Let's see, we have sunshine and smog, the ambitious and the idle, a richness of imagination and a poverty of style, an air of permissiveness and stringent laws, a desert kissing an ocean. Let's see, what else. . . ."

The grass was not pulling my mind away from the afternoon; it was doing just the opposite. I went on asking typical questions about California, her job at the college, where she and Pat had taken vacations. As animated as she was, I could not be distracted by the new chapters in her life or by things I'd never seen. I could barely even recall what Pat looked like.

The telephone rang. It was Frank.

"I called you earlier but there was no answer," he said. "I wanted to get through before Regina went to bed."

I wanted to tell him what Vivian had said and what Regina had done to Brian. I wanted him to know how cheated I felt, but I *didn't* want him to come running home. I needed another day or two alone with Gloria.

"Irene? Hello?"

"I'm here."

"Is anything wrong?"

"No. I was sleeping. How's your demonstration going?"

"There were some beatings and arrests. Tim's in jail. We're going to the ACLU tomorrow to see what they can do."

"You mean you might be arrested?"

"That's not what I said. Irene, you sound funny. Are you all right?"

"How do you expect me to sound when you tell me someone's been arrested?"

"I shouldn't have told you. I'm sorry."

"It's a little late for that, isn't it?"

"Honey, why are you mad at me?"

"I'm not mad. Where are you now?"

"We're at Sylvia's cousin's house."

"Who's 'we'?"

"All of us."

How cozy, I thought. But I said nothing.

"Is Gloria there?"

"Yes; she's sleeping." I glanced guiltily at Gloria.

"Are you having a good time?" he said.

"Wonderful."

"You don't sound it."

I heard a click on the wire.

"Is somebody listening in there?" I said.

"No, there's only one phone."

"Maybe somebody's tapping the wire."

"Daddy! Daddy! Come home, please come home! They're being mean to me!"

"Get off that phone," I said.

"Regina?"

117

"Daddy, please come home *now!*"

"I said to get off that phone."

"Regina? What's wrong, honey?"

"She hit me, she chased me and hit me, please come home!" She began to sob.

"Get off that phone this minute!"

"Irene, what's going on there?"

"Daddy, please come home *now,* please, please!"

"Get off that phone, young lady, before I come up and pull you off it!"

"Daddy——"

"Don't talk to her like that," he said.

"What did you say?" My voice was burning.

"I said"—his voice softened—"I just asked you not to talk to her like that."

"And how *should* I talk to her?"

"Daddy, please, before she hits me again!"

"Irene, what's *going on* there?"

"Ask your daughter." I hung up. When I turned to Gloria, I suddenly burst out laughing. "God, aren't telephones wonderful, the way you can just hang them up?"

Gloria was not amused. She looked at me apprehensively. "Don't get upset again. I shouldn't have given you the grass."

"Oh, what the hell. Let them play me for the villain. She can tell him whatever she wants. I'm not going near her. I've had enough of her for one day."

In a few minutes, the telephone rang again.

"It's me," he said. "Now tell me what's happening."

"I'm tired, Frank. Nothing's happening."

"Damn it, what are you keeping from me!"

"You're a great one to be asking that question."

A tiny pause, then slowly: "What do you mean?"

"Nothing, nothing, nothing. Look, Frank, it hasn't been a pleasant day and I'm tired. Regina hit Brian over the head with a stick. He had to have six stitches."

"Stitches?" Another pause. "Well, what did he do to her?"

"He didn't do a goddamn thing to her!"

"Irene, take it easy."

"Don't tell me to take it easy! 'What did he do to her?' It seems to me your first question would be to ask how he is."

"Is he all right?"

"Yes, he's all right."

"I'm coming home. I'll take the first plane I can get."

"Fine. Exactly what *she* wants. Now she's learned the power of tears and hysteria."

"Stop it, stop making her sound so conniving. She's only a child."

"Yeah, and Hitler was a child once."

"I'm not going to argue with you. I'm coming home."

"You do that. And when you get here, I'm leaving. I'm going someplace with Gloria for a couple of days."

"I'll be there as soon as I can."

After I hung up, I made us whiskeys with soda. Gloria kept quiet, waiting for me to talk.

"I suppose I sounded like the proverbial harridan."

She shrugged. "You were angry." Then: "But you're angry at more than just Regina. Something was bothering you last night after Vivian left."

"Yes. But I don't want to talk about it until I've spoken to Frank."

"Of course."

"And I want you to do a big favor for me. Frank made me promise never to let Vivian come here. I'm going to tell him I ran into her downtown on the street today. I want to say you were with me."

"All right." She grinned. "Looks as if Regina wasn't the only one who was a bad girl."

We sat quietly for a while, sipping our drinks. The voice I had used on the telephone kept ringing in my head, circling round and round one figure—Sylvia. It made me squirm to admit my jealousy; verbalizing it would make it easier.

I told Gloria about the night Sylvia had stayed over and how she impressed Frank and Regina. As I continued my description of her, Gloria's face changed. She looked as if she was hearing about someone she already knew.

"I wish you could meet her sometime," I said. "I'd love to hear your appraisal."

"Frank's quite fond of her?"

"He's enamored of her social consciousness."

"In California I've seen that kind of social conciousness shoplifting in stores." She fell pensive, and I watched her.

"What are you thinking?"

"Nothing."

"Liar." I grinned. "You're thinking Sylvia's the same type he used to see before he met me."

"Is that what *you're* thinking?"

"Yes."

"And you don't like her being in Chicago with him?"

"I don't like her being with him, period. Sometimes I can't believe how naïve he is, and when I tell him he is, he just accuses me of being cynical. He has this attraction to underdogs *just because* they're underdogs. That's the way he sees Regina because of her illness."

"You certainly don't fit in that category."

"Maybe I'd have more leverage if I did."

The next morning, Frank called again.

"Is everything ironed out?" he asked almost shyly.

"She's still mad. She's not speaking to me. We had a quiet breakfast and she went out to play. What time are you getting here?"

"That's what I called about. I'd like to stay a couple more days. I want to help straighten out this business with Tim."

I asked myself whether Sylvia had talked him into this or whether he had considered what I had said the night before about giving in to Regina's demands. I figured the least I could do was to give him the benefit of the doubt and encourage him to stay. With that settled, I still wanted to get away from the house and Regina to relax with Gloria. I called my mother and asked if I could bring Regina to Cedar Run to stay with them for a night or two. She conferred with my father and called me back to say they would come to our house because my father wanted to see an old college friend who had just been hired by the university. Regina was impassive when I announced that her grandparents would look after her for a day or two.

Gloria and I took Brian and drove eighty miles to Lake Hammond, where we got a room in a motel with a swimming pool. We had a day and a half and two nights of solid relaxation, but as we prepared to leave, a foggy depression settled over me. I knew I was going to miss her terribly and I began to resent our living so far apart.

We went directly from the motel to the airport in Detroit. We said practically nothing to each other all the way. But when we stopped for coffee in the terminal, it was Gloria who launched into resolutions for the future.

"Even hermits have telephones and stationery," she said, grinning. "Since you and Frank both have vacations at Christmas, why don't you come out and stay with us."

"Maybe we will, or maybe next summer."

When the announcement came for boarding, she gave me a firm hug and said, "Well, off to our separate lairs." I kissed Brian good-bye and he gave my hair one last stroke. Impulsively, I took out my manicuring scissors and cut off a small chunk above my ear and wrapped it in a tissue.

"There," I said. "He can have fire anytime he wants it. And before it goes gray."

"We're going to be seeing a lot of you before it goes gray."

This final assurance of hers lifted my depression. Driving home, I told myself there was no reason why Frank and I couldn't get to California once every year.

When I arrived, Regina burst out of the house, asking when her father was coming home. "Probably tomorrow," I said, and she questioned the "probably." When she asked me to call him, I realized he had forgotten to give me the number and I had forgotten to ask for it. Had he intentionally neglected to give it to me? I was too distracted by this thought to notice the coolness between Regina and my father. Then at one point, when I had answered her third demand that I call Frank, my father turned to her and said firmly: "Leave your mother alone."

"I don't have to," she shot back. "She's *my* mother."

"What did I tell you about that back talk, young lady? Do you want more of what you got yesterday?"

"Kenneth." My mother, warning him and soothing him, in the tone I knew so well.

"What did she get?" I asked.

"She got a swat on her butt."

"What for?"

"Ask her. She knows what for."

"I didn't do anything," she protested immediately. "He's just mean."

"Regina."

"He is. He's your dad, he's not mine."

"But if I were your dad, you'd be a changed little girl."

"That's enough," I said.

We were saved by Susan, who appeared at the back door to ask if Regina could come out. Regina hesitated, so I promised them both ice cream when the truck came around. They went out to play on the tractor-tire swings.

"Buying her off," muttered my father.

"Give me a break, will you? Now tell me what she did to get a spanking."

"She refused to go to bed. She said I wasn't her boss. Then when I picked her up, she tried to kick me. And when I swatted her, she said her daddy would beat me up when he got home."

I shrugged. "She's upset. It's the first time Frank's been away from her."

"Maybe he should be away from her more often."

"Kenneth!"

"What kind of a crack is that?"

"It's not a crack. It's advice."

"Well, I don't like it."

"I don't expect you to, but you'd better listen to it. He's spoiling her rotten and you're helping him do it."

"I'll be the judge of that."

"You know, it's usually the parents who discipline the child and the grandparents who spoil it. Not the other way around."

"Then don't discipline her."

"Someone has to. Maybe you don't mind her talking that way to you, but she's not going to do it with me."

"Kenneth, leave her alone."

"Thank you, Mother." I turned back to him. "Now let's drop it. If you have nothing to say that's pleasant—"

"That's right, something you'd *like* to hear."

"—then you can leave. You seem to forget this is my house, not yours."

" 'He's your dad, not mine,' " he said, mimicking Regina.

"Kenneth, what is the matter with you?"

"You know what it is, Mother? It's that damned male pride that can't stand a little girl talking up to it. Thank God Frank doesn't have that handicap."

"You're right, he doesn't have any pride. Maybe that's why you married him."

It was well below the belt, and I was more stunned than angry. But I quickly realized how I could zero in. "You can think that if you want. But just remember he's got one thing you don't have. He's got his Ph.D. Now go peddle your sour grapes elsewhere."

He stood up. "Maybe Regina is more like you than I thought. But at least you waited until you grew up to kick me."

My mother's consolation at the door—while my father raced the car engine in the driveway as a signal for her to hurry up—was that he and I would make up after we had had a few days to cool off.

"Do you think I'm a bad mother?" I asked.

"Of course not. And neither does he. He's just mad at Regina, so he's taking it out on you and Frank."

"Do you think she's spoiled?"

She hesitated. "Not really spoiled, but a little high-strung. You're going to have to be both patient and firm with her and that's a hard balance to maintain." My father honked the horn. She squeezed my hand and kissed me. "Don't worry about your father. He'll brood for a few days and then he'll be ready to apologize. Give Frank our love when you talk to him."

FRANK came home the next afternoon, sunburned but haggard.

"I suppose you heard about the confrontation," he said.

"What confrontation?"

"At the convention. Haven't you seen the news?"

"No."

He went into elaborate detail about the hecklings and the beatings and the arrests. They had managed to raise the bail for Tim's release and were laying plans for his lawsuit against the Chicago police. My interest and attention were half-hearted, but I managed to hear him out to the end.

"Where's Regina?"

"She's outside. Frank, there's something I want to talk to you about. And I want to discuss it calmly."

"What is it?"

"A couple of days ago Gloria and I ran into Vivian downtown."

"Vivian!"

"Yes. I didn't recognize her at first, but she recognized me." Already his eyes were blazing. "We had just a short conversation and . . . Frank, why didn't you tell me about your sister?"

"Tell you what?" His voice nearly cracked. "I told you a long time ago she was a troublemaker."

"I'm not talking about Vivian. I'm talking about Regina."

His head jerked up. "Regina?"

"Your sister Regina."

"What—what did Vivian tell you?"

"More than you've told me. I'd like to hear something from you. I'd like to know why you've kept this from me."

"She died." He looked away at the window and said it again, whispering. "She died."

"I know that. She killed herself in that horrible way. But I want to know why you didn't tell me."

"It's an ugly story. I didn't see the need."

"You didn't see the need? She was retarded, for one thing. And you named our daughter after her without my knowing it. Now I want to know why!"

"I . . . owed it to her. She was too young to die, and that way."

"Why did she do it?"

"She *was* retarded—not severely, not so you could tell it at a first or second glance. I think it was worse for her that way. And she was pretty too, except for that empty look in her eyes."

That empty look in her eyes. As soon as he said it, it hit me: the photograph I had found in his desk drawer the day I was packing everything to be moved to the trailer. His sister Regina must have been the girl in the picture—*and* the reason it had so conveniently disappeared in the moving.

"But," he continued, "the kids at school were no worse to her than her own brothers and sisters. They tormented her, and the older she got, the more they piled it on. I looked after her but it didn't do much good, because as soon as my back was turned, they were after her again."

"Where were your parents all this time?"

His voice turned venomous. "Have you ever watched parents quietly disown a child? I saw it happen. Regina had no protection except my promise to run away with her. Finally, that was all she talked about and I kept promising and promising. Then I got that scholarship, so I told her she'd have to wait a year or two. We were sitting under the dead oak in the backyard when I tried to explain it to her, but she stood up and backed away from me. . . ."

Backed away. Like Wanda Hoople.

"There was nothing more I could say to her, so I let her go. That afternoon she took the lye from under the sink and carried it into the woods where no one would hear her scream."

"Oh, God!"

He was staring at the window and I followed his gaze. We saw Regina at the edge of our vacant lot, saw her look up at Frank's car in the driveway and break into a run for the house.

"Frank, you could have told me this before. Why do you feel you have to carry something like this alone?"

"I told you once what I came from. I was raised in

a cesspool and I want to keep you out of it. You and Regina."

"But, darling, you're not *them*."

His voice broke. "I don't know what I'd do if you ever left me."

"Frank, there's no reason to leave you."

"Promise me."

"Of course I promise."

"And promise you'll help me keep Vivian and the rest of them away from us."

"They can't hurt us."

"Promise me: don't ever let them in this house or near Regina."

I nodded.

She came through the kitchen and dining room, squealing, "Daddy, Daddy," and jumped into his lap. Her hands fisted against his chest, she scowled and said, "Don't go away anymore!"

Gently, he pulled her head onto his shoulder and stroked her hair. "I won't, pumpkin, not without you."

But she was not reassured. Even as she clung to him and accepted his stroking, her scowl remained.

I think that if we could recall a nightmare in its entirety, we would find that the real horror of it lies somewhere in the middle, when you can't remember the beginning, which got you to where you are, and you can't foresee any logical end to it. Looking back now, I can only guess where our nightmare had its beginnings. I say this because it proceeded slowly and I had no feeling of momentum until very nearly the end. That momentum became apparent when Regina entered high school at fifteen and it continued to build for two years, growing into a monstrous inevitability which I would have to face with a gun in my hand.

For me, one of the beginnings was Hugh Lance's heart attack in the school parking lot. The next day he was dead and within two years the school was in a shambles. His replacement, Jack Rand, who had connections at the board of education, neither liked nor understood kids and covered up the fact by running the school with a limp hand. Easily intimidated—I suspected he had been bullied as a child—he became a pushover for the troublemakers in the building. He never walked the halls as Lance had done, and instead of dealing with the increasingly rowdy behavior during assembly programs, he simply canceled them. When I sent a boy to his office because he had KISS MY BALLS embossed on his T-shirt (T-shirts, tank tops, shorts and halters were now standard dress in warm weather), Rand sent the boy back with a note which said that according to the constitutional dress code, the boy was allowed to wear what he pleased. My run-ins with Rand increased, as did several of the other teachers'. Fifteen students could fail your class and Rand couldn't have cared less. But if just one failed and that one contested the grade and threw a fit in his office and brought in parents and made *his* life miserable, then you were sure to be "investigated for unfairness and incompetency." Realizing he could not control the students, he turned his frustrated rage, blindly and arbitrarily, on the staff. Fortunately for me, two incidents occurred that made him keep his distance. One day during a free period, I rounded a corner in the hallway to find him just a few steps ahead, walking in the same direction. At the end of the hall, two boys obviously cutting class were loitering and preparing to light up cigarettes. Rand approached them and said timidly, "You boys had better get to class. A teacher might find you here." He gave an involuntary little jump when, right behind him, I said,

"A teacher *has* found them." The boys shuffled off (no need to hurry, since tardiness was a negligible offense) and Rand squirmed under his smile before he slunk away. The second incident was even more to my advantage. At faculty meetings, we all complained about the graffiti in the halls. His response was that that was the result of faulty surveillance by the teachers. When I pointed out that there were almost no graffiti in the rooms, the teachers' territory, and that we could not be in two places at once, he resorted to his usual out: he wasn't responsible for the change in society's values and if kids didn't respect property, that wasn't his fault. The next day after school, I went to the custodian and got a wire brush and cleanser and a bucket of water and took them out to the front of the building, where we had a five-foot-high, ten-foot-long stone slab with chrome letters that spelled out AARON PECK HIGH SCHOOL. For five months, we had had to look at the spray-painted insertion of two letters, so that the name read "Pecker." I went to work with the steel brush and cleanser. A few minutes passed before a car stopped and a man got out with a camera. He was a reporter for the local paper and asked if I minded having my picture taken. His thrust-forward face and eager eyes had "muckraker" written all over them and I was more than willing to cooperate. He wanted to know how long the "er" had been there and why the custodians weren't doing this job. I told him they had their hands full *inside* the building, and besides, it was up to the principal to give the order. He asked if the principal was in the building and I said I doubted it. He asked if there were any other teachers still in the building; I said three or four. Next, he asked if Rand always left before his teachers did. I decided not to overstep myself on that one: I simply answered that I didn't keep tabs on him. Then he left me and went into the building. In the next evening's paper, there was a front-page story about Peck, accompanied by my picture. The story was continued on a back page, with photographs of the obscenities in the hallways. Rand was furious and when he called me into his office, he accused me of setting him up with the reporter. I told him exactly how it had happened, but he threatened he would have my job. I replied that he couldn't *do* my job and that if he threatened me any further or tried harassment, I would give the reporter a call. For a month after the story appeared, the whole building changed. The graffiti were eradicated; kids who were cutting classes and roaming the halls were rounded up and sent to the deans; and "inappropriate" clothing was prohibited. At the end of the month, the campaign dissolved. Rand went back to hiding out in his office and the casual chaos settled in once again.

Obscenities were no longer restricted to angry outbursts. They were implanted in the very fabric of social communication. Conversations in the hallway during passing and in the classroom before and after the bell were laced with that verb-turned-adjective "fucking," used for emphasis in both positive and negative descriptions. "Shit" was reserved for anything difficult or distasteful, as in "This book is shit"; "Don't hand me that shit"; "That's a crock of shit." "Suck" remained a verb and was generally applied to all things oppressive: school, homework, teachers and niggers all "sucked." "Prick" and "cunt," of course, were the favored ascriptions for anyone objectionable. Although there were few occasions when any of these words were said to my face, there was a lack of compunction in most of the students insofar as letting me overhear them. If I confronted a student about his/her language, the stock response was disbelief or amusement or "I didn't say it to *you*." Once, a snappy girl told me I shouldn't be listening in. This is not to say I had no rewards in the classroom or that every day was a misery. However, the general tone of the school, fostered by Rand's permissiveness, began to take its toll on my energy and patience.

And so did Frank and Regina.

By the time Regina finished the seventh grade, she had gone through puberty and reached the height of five foot eleven. She acquired a lovely shape, which she proceeded to undermine by slouching with her shoulders curled and her pelvis thrust forward. And because her face was plain and undistinguished, she took to make-up with a vengeance. She would not step out of the house unless her face was rainbowed in iridescent color. For two years running, the arguments went on between her and Frank about her appearance. I bowed out entirely after the day she turned to me and said: "Don't tell me how I should look. *You've* always been pretty." When I assured her she would be quite attractive if she cleaned up her face and her posture, she looked as if she were tolerating a consummate liar. Then, under her breath, she growled, "I don't know why I had to look like *him*."

And so began the rearrangement of relationships among the three of us. All those years of Regina's keeping her distance from me, of Frank's indulging her and actually reveling in her every whim, of my own abdication due to frustration and fatigue—all those years seemed to evaporate in the face of the reversals that came. Gradually, boys entered Regina's circle of friends. They gathered in our recreation room for dancing and Ping-Pong, and Frank would go down to see if they were having a good time. Regina complained bitterly about "being spied on" and told me she wouldn't mind *my* coming down to meet her friends but to keep Frank away.

"What's the difference who comes down?"

"He's out of it," she said. "He wants to know everybody's name."

"Nothing wrong with that. It's being sociable and showing good manners."

"It's being nosy. He wants to know their parents' names and where they live. He's like a cop or something."

The next time he went down, I went with him and watched. One of Regina's girlfriends had brought along a new boy. He was watching the Ping-Pong game, waiting his turn. Frank approached him, shook hands amiably, then proceeded to do just what Regina had described—asking the boy about his parents, where they lived, even where they came from.

Upstairs, I told him I thought he was being too overbearing.

"There's nothing wrong in finding out about her friends," he said. "There's a lot of drugs around and you never know who might be peddling them."

"You're not going to find out that way. You're making them uncomfortable."

"Are you faulting me for being interested? All I've heard from you about your school is 'parental apathy,' how the parents don't show up for PTA meetings and open-school conferences."

"There's such a thing as a happy medium."

Frank's surveillance continued until Regina announced to me that she and her friends would not be meeting in our house anymore. Instead, they would gather someplace where they would be left alone. At this point, she shut Frank out of her circle of attention almost entirely. She barely spoke to him at all, restricting her conversation to grudging answers to his questions. If she needed to be driven somewhere, she asked me to do it. When she practiced her French for oral quizzes, she would come to me even though Frank had had two more years of the language than I had and his ear for it was better than mine. I was put on the tightrope between them. It was easy to see how Regina felt suffocated by him, and a selfish part of me saw some justice in her about-face because all those years that he had won her attention and her affection cheaply, with indulgence, he had not worked at winning her respect. Of course, it was too late for that. Still, it pained me to see how deeply she was hurting him. But I sensed in him something more than hurt. I sensed panic. Not wild, hysterical panic, but the kind of panic that is kept in check. Sometimes, in the middle of the night, I would hear him get up to go to the bathroom, listen to him pause at Regina's door, open it, close it, and come back to bed. Something, something was moving in on us.

The pressures of school, the uphill battle with Rand, the friction between Frank and Regina, and perhaps the fact that Gloria now had four children made me decide to become pregnant. We had visited Pat and Gloria almost every year since that Chicago summer and I had watched her family grow. The idea of our having a second child was not new to me, but whenever I discussed it with Frank, he had always presented a firm argument for how much I would miss teaching. But that argument no longer held any ground now that the school seemed to be crumbling. Naïvely, I thought a baby would be the best thing for us all.

I got plenty of encouragement from Gloria via long distance. Her second had been another boy, and Pat had wanted her to stop there. Her third pregnancy disappointed him, but when it produced twin girls, he cut back on his office hours to spend every available minute with them. Gloria's favorite story was the one about how Pat liked to sit and watch the babies sleep. One day, he came running out of their room and hustled her back to it. "Come here—listen." She listened, then asked what the big deal was. "Don't you hear it? They're breathing together, *in unison!*" And he looked down at them as if they were the eighth wonder of the world. I could just picture Frank, Regina and myself pushing each other out of the way to take care of the baby.

But that was not to be the case. When I got the doctor's confirmation, Frank's reaction was more than disappointment. It was horror. The color left his face, he stared right through me and said, "But *how?*"

"The way it usually happens."

"But how did you let it happen?"

"I just did. My, what a wonderful reception."

"I'm sorry. But we can't. . . ."

"Can't what?"

"Regina's fifteen!"

"What difference does that make?"

"It's just so . . . ridiculous."

"I don't see what's ridiculous about it. Do you remember that day you came back from Chicago and we talked about your family?"

He winced. "What have *they* got to do with this?"

"You made me promise to help you keep them away from us and I agreed. Since then, we haven't seen hide or hair of any of them. Including Vivian. Maybe *that's* the problem. We've become so solitary. Barry's way out in Texas, Neil's up in Vancouver, my best friend lives thousands of miles away, and we see my parents twice a month at the most. What's wrong with expanding our own family? I'm sure it'll be good for Regina."

"There's nothing wrong. You're right." But there was no conviction in his voice.

Regina's reaction was not as severe, but it was far from what I wanted. She gave me a long, clinical look and said: "A baby? You're too old." After a few weeks she did warm up to the idea, but with more amusement than enthusiasm. Frank said little if anything about it. I had the peculiar feeling he was watching me the same way he had been watching Regina—with panic. I kept telling myself he would change once the baby was born; the fact that the baby was *not* born showed me how wrong I was. When I lost it in the fourth month, he made a pretense of disappointment. But I could sense his relief. And after the doctor warned me against trying for another, his relief became obvious. I slipped into a quiet depression, which he tried to lift me from with candlelight dinners and little gifts. I didn't want his offerings of comfort. I began to think that if thoughts could kill, *his* thoughts had killed the baby. Within a month or so, he went back to keeping unreasonable tabs on Regina, and my feelings of menace returned.

During the next year and a half, Regina put the finishing touches on the wall that would shut out her father. In his presence, she no longer stooped to sullenness or insolence, for she had found that her most effective revenge was to ignore him. Yet he took her punishment unflinchingly, keeping her at an early curfew and insisting upon being given her exact destination (or destinations) whenever she went out with her friends.

The night she introduced us to Virgil Evans, I saw a flickering of something alien in Frank's face. Perhaps that was the beginning of the real momentum, because from then on nothing would be the same.

Regina had had exactly three dates by the time she entered her junior year of high school. Whether this was due to her intimidating height, an overeagerness to please, which hid a cache of jealousy and resentment, her unglamorous appearance next to her prettier friends, or any combination of these, I could not say for sure. (Had she gone to Peck, I might have had more ready answers. However, neither of us thought it a good idea for her to be in the school situation with me, although Frank wanted it that way. So she attended Old Central, eight blocks from our house.) What *was* obvious to me was her jealousy over her girlfriends' popularity with boys. Friday night was stag night: the girls all went out together. Saturday night was reserved for dates. It was this night that Regina sat at home, sulking and turning down every offer of consolation. Now and then, she would let slip a sour-grape criticism of her friends: they were boy-crazy or they had no taste and would go out with anyone who asked them. At these times, I saw that familiar look on her face, the one that had been there the day she sent Frank out into the vacant lot to drive the kids off the swings and the day she had begrudged Brian her coloring book. What was missing now was the gratitude, the worship, she once had for her father. Without her noticing it, I would watch her from the corner of my eye while she looked him over as though he were some kind of distasteful specimen.

"Why did you marry him?" she asked outright one day when we were alone in the car.

"What a thing to ask. I fell in love with him."

"What with?" Her voice was cool and hard.

"Of all people, it should be obvious to you. Your father's a rare man in his own way. He's intelligent and kind and conscientious and . . . humble."

"What else?"

"I think that's plenty."

"Didn't you ever go out with any handsome men?"

"Yes; I just never met a handsome man who has what your father has."

"Maybe you didn't look around long enough. Your friend Gloria found one."

"You can't always help who you fall in love with."

"If you'd married someone else, I wouldn't look like *him*."

"If I had married someone else, you wouldn't be here."

I was well acquainted with the preoccupation teen-agers have with looks, but I was also aware of how Regina would tune out if I started in on the topic of "other qualities."

"I wonder what the baby would have looked like," she said.

I didn't answer. The baby was not a favorite topic

136

of mine. It only rekindled feelings of resentment for Frank, feelings which would distract me from defending him to her.

"We did heredity in biology last year. It seems weird to me I didn't get anything from you. It's all *him*. If anyone looked at you and me together, they wouldn't think you were my mother at all."

What she said was true and I had to think quickly. "Sure they would. You've got red highlights in your hair and you've got a very good figure. You certainly didn't get *that* from your father. In fact, sometimes you remind me of Grandma."

"Which one?" she said pointedly.

"Grandma Rutledge, of course."

"How come he hasn't got any pictures of *his* family?"

"They were very poor. They probably couldn't afford a camera."

"I'll bet they were all ugly, every last one of them."

"That's not true. Your Aunt Vivian—" A twinge of guilt stopped me.

"What about her?"

"She's a very striking woman and *she's* very tall."

"How come I've never seen her? Or any of them?"

"It's very complicated. It's the way your father wants it."

"Everything's the way he wants it."

"Never mind that. Your father is not ugly and neither are you. I wish you would get that out of your head."

"It's easy for you to say."

I waited a moment to think out my words. With Regina, they always had to be carefully chosen. "Since we're on the subject of your father, are you aware of how you've been treating him?" She rolled her eyes and put on that "Here we go" expression. "You know, he'd give up the world for you."

"I don't want him to give up anything for me," she said flatly.

"You've been shutting him out completely."

"I don't like him breathing down my neck."

"Regina, I wasn't an only child, but I was an only daughter. My father was very possessive of me too."

"He's always watching me. He gives me the creeps."

"He loves you."

"I don't want to be loved like that."

If she only knew just how much she was *my* daughter. That desire for independence, the rigid adherence to her own opinions, even the callousness—I had had them until I met Frank.

Her withdrawal from Frank was so complete that it included his friends as well. Bernie and Sylvia and Sylvia's husband, John, who had lavished attention on her for years, were now dismissed as "a jerk" and "a dog" and "out of it." She seemed to be shaking all identification with Frank, and although she didn't move completely into my corner, my company was always preferable to that of her father.

It was in her junior year, in late September, that she lost her appetite and sat dreamily at the dinner table. She spent most of her time in her bedroom. The eye make-up was toned down, the lipstick grew lighter, the rouge disappeared altogether. The second Thursday in October, she announced she had a date, and on Friday at seven-thirty, Virgil Evans rang the doorbell.

He was as handsome as anyone the movies or TV had to offer. Just half an inch taller than Regina, he had the solid, sinewy build of a swimmer. His sandy hair was not fashioned in the popular layered look but cut close to the scalp, with a part on the right side. His features, strong and angular, were softened by large brown eyes and full, almost overripe lips. When he smiled, he showed slightly gapped teeth, similar to Frank's. Frank shook his hand and invited him to sit down. Regina said they couldn't or they would be late for the movie. Frank said they could come back to our house for a snack afterward. Regina rolled her eyes at me with that all-too-familiar message "Get him off my back." But Virgil liked the idea. Regina's face changed. It was apparent that any idea Virgil had would be just fine with her.

It was when Frank closed the door after them that I saw that alien look on his face. He stood there gripping the door handle, his eyes squinted and his jaw pushed forward. For a moment, he appeared to be calculating something; then his lips tightened and he opened the door with a furious yank and glowered at the street as they drove away.

We both sat in the living room grading papers. Now and then, I would look up to find him staring at the floor. At ten-thirty, he began checking his watch, which he continued to do at ten-minute intervals until they walked through the door at eleven forty-five. I went into the kitchen to put the pizza in the oven. I wasn't gone five minutes when Regina burst in.

"He's starting again!"

"What?"

"Asking all those questions about Virgil's family, where they live, everything!"

"He does have the right to know a little bit about a boy who takes you out."

"Then *I'll* tell him! I don't want him asking questions. He never stops. Will you please go in and shut him up? I'll watch the pizza."

When I got to the living room, Virgil was telling Frank how he had just recently come up from Florida to live with an aunt after his father died. Right now, he was looking for a job until he entered the community college the following fall.

"Where in Florida?" said Frank.

"Fort Lauderdale."

"What was your father's name?"

"Same as mine—Evans." Virgil smiled.

"I mean his first name."

"Frank, really." I turned to Virgil. "He's writing a book about first names."

Virgil laughed. But Frank was not to be put off. "What was his name?"

"Philip."

"What kind of work did he do?"

"He was a handyman."

"Did he have a business?"

"Not really. People called him for odd jobs. But he did pretty well for himself."

"You were born in Fort Lauderdale?"

"No, in Canada in a house trailer. They were on a fishing trip."

"Are you a Canadian citizen?"

"No. They registered the birth later, in Florida."

The questions continued. Although Frank's tone was conversational, I felt an urgency behind the questions and I think Virgil did too. Finally, I stepped in.

"What do you plan to study in college?" I asked.

"Not history or English." He chuckled. "They've always been my worst subjects. Maybe phys ed or social work." He talked readily about his love of sports. I tried to keep my face looking interested while I observed Frank. I could see he was itching to jump back in.

"Regina said you met at a football game," Frank said.

"That's right."

"How did that happen?"

"I was sitting next to her."

"Since you don't go to that school, how did you happen to be at one of their games?"

"You know Central has been the class A state

champ quite a few times. They have a big following."

"That kind of news gets all the way to Florida?"

"No, I found that out when I got up here."

"All this question and answer is making me hungry," I said. "I think we should eat."

As we moved toward the dining room, I brushed Frank's arm and whispered, "Leave him alone now."

While we ate, Virgil and Regina told us about the movie. Virgil did most of the talking and Regina hung on every word. It was both touching and amusing to see the transformation in her, all that hard brass turning to putty. Already I was drawing parallels between her and myself at the time I had met Frank.

She walked Virgil out to his car and Frank watched from the window. When she came back in, he was waiting for her.

"Did you have a good time?"

"Yes. Until we got back here."

"Honey, I'm just interested in who you see."

"You're just interested in ruining things for me! If he doesn't ask me out again, I'll—you'll be sorry!"

"If he likes you," I said, "he'll ask you out again."

She turned to me. "I'm not bringing him in this house again if *he's* here!"

Frank flinched. I wanted to take a crack at both of them, at Frank for his ridiculous behavior and at her for handing out orders. "No fighting," I said. "It's too late."

"Regina, I didn't mean to make you uncomfortable."

"Oh, yes, you did! You're always butting in, you're always asking questions. I'm sick of it. Just leave me alone." She ran upstairs and slammed the door.

Frank sat down with a long sigh. I knew we had to discuss this and I was anxious to get it over with.

"She's right, you know."

He looked up and looked away. He wasn't even going to challenge me.

"If you don't leave her alone, she's going to turn her back on you entirely."

No answer.

"The Frankenstein monster turned on his creator."

"I don't think that's amusing."

"It's not supposed to be. She's growing up and you had better start accepting that. You always wanted her to have everything, but now that she's found something she wants, it seems you're going out of your way to sabotage it. I don't understand it."

"I'm not sabotaging anything. I'm simply concerned."

"*I'm* concerned, but I'm not playing interrogator."

He said nothing. He wasn't going to talk. But I knew how to get a reaction from him.

"If we had had the baby, you might not be so pre-occupied with running Regina's life."

"I'm not running her life." Then: "I'm sorry about the baby, you know that."

"No, I don't know that. Maybe losing it was a blessing. Maybe you wouldn't have had enough love to give it."

"That's a rotten thing to say."

"I can't help feeling it's the truth. But since it's not here, it doesn't matter, does it? What does matter is Regina. And you. You're going to be very unhappy if you don't let her grow up on her own. A five-year-old or a ten-year-old may enjoy being coddled, but Regina is sixteen. She doesn't want you that way anymore."

He sat staring at the floor. There was no point in going on.

"I'm going to bed," I said. "Are you coming?"

"Later."

As I walked past him, he reached out and grabbed my wrist. "Irene, please be patient with me."

"It's not my patience you have to worry about. It's Regina's."

WITHIN three weeks' time, Virgil Evans was bringing Regina home from school every day. He would stay for an hour, drive off, then return around nine o'clock, after Regina had finished her homework. We let them have the recreation room to themselves until ten-thirty. They went out every Friday and Saturday, and Virgil always had her home by 1 A.M., her curfew time.

There was absolutely nothing in the boy for Frank to criticize. He was bright, personable, considerate, and had a sharp, mature sense of humor. But I could see that Frank was looking for something to criticize. Quietly, he watched the boy like an apprehensive cat, and I found myself watching *him* watch.

I can't say exactly when Frank's nightmares began. I can only say when I first noticed them, between Thanksgiving and Christmas. Several times I awakened to find him thrashing and gritting his teeth. One night he fell right out of bed. When I questioned him about the nightmares, he said he didn't remember them. But the one I remember—will always remember—woke me early one Sunday morning. There was a mumbling which slowly shaped itself into words, and I heard "Regina, come back." I heard it twice. I rolled over and saw him twitch and open his eyes. In a daze, he looked right at me and said, "She's going." He then closed his eyes and went back to sleep. I got up, sat in the rocker and smoked cigarettes. He slept fitfully for another two hours.

His loss of sleep began to show. He left for work groggy and came home exhausted. He looked attentive only when Virgil was in the house. He had run out of questions for the boy, but there was always the watching, the constant watchfulness.

This change in Frank coincided with the change in Regina. Her first case of romance softened her considerably and I was delighted. Although her entire time schedule was shaped around Virgil, I didn't mind in the least. In all her sixteen years, she was the most pleasant, the least demanding she had ever been. She looked contented, and more than anything, I hoped this experience with Virgil would spawn some self-confidence in her that would remain even if he left her one day. For a while, she seemed to lay aside her resentment of Frank, but she certainly had not buried it. It exploded in my face the afternoon I came home from school to find her and Virgil waiting for me. They were sitting on the couch when I came through the door and both of them stood up immediately. That one urgent gesture spelled trouble; all I could think of was: Oh, God, they're going to tell me she's pregnant. But one glance at the rage in Regina's face told me the topic was going to be Frank.

"He's crazy! He's out of his mind!" she said.

"Take it easy," said Virgil.

"What are you talking about?"

"Him! He's spying on Virgil!"

"Regina, be quiet. Mrs. Mattison, can you sit down for a few minutes?" I sat. "A few days ago, my aunt told me she thought a man was following her. I didn't pay much attention to it because she does like to exaggerate. Yesterday, she said he drove past the house a couple of times and parked out in front for a while. The way she described him, it sounds like Mr. Mattison. She described his car too."

I sat there not saying a word, because I had nothing to say.

"I've known from the beginning he doesn't like me. I don't know why he doesn't. If I did, maybe I could do something to change it."

Only if you traded places, then he'd like you. I didn't need to say it, only think it. The dark suspicion that had taken root in the back of my mind was beginning to spread its branches.

"Virgil's right," said Regina. "He hasn't liked him from the beginning. But he's not going to get away with spying on him. I'll move out!"

"Don't be silly," I said. "I'll take care of this."

"You've said that before and he's still the same. He's *worse!*"

"I promise you there will be a stop to this."

"Mrs. Mattison, I don't want to make trouble, but my aunt—well . . ."

"I understand. Take my word for it, it won't happen again."

I asked him to go home and to stay away for a day or two. I let Regina go up to her room while I thought out what to say to her. I didn't want to panic her, didn't want her to see *my* panic. In the kitchen, I took a slug of brandy, then went up to her.

She was lying on her bed in her bra and panties, doing her homework. It would have been easier for me if she had had clothes on.

"I want to talk to you about something and I don't want you to be embarrassed by it. I want you to know you can trust me. Whatever we say to each other will remain strictly between us. I won't discuss it with your father and I don't want you to discuss it with Virgil."

She looked surprised, not apprehensive. That encouraged me.

"What I ask may be difficult for you to answer, but remember that it's just as difficult for me to ask." I drew breath. "You've been avoiding your father for a long time now. Even before you met Virgil. I want you to tell me why."

"You know why."

"I want you to be specific."

"He watches me. All the time. I'm sick of it. Now he's spying on Virgil."

"Let's stick to you. Has he ever said or done anything *specific* to make you . . . embarrassed or afraid?"

"He'd like to embarrass me but he can't. A few weeks ago he asked me if I was sleeping with Virgil."

"What did you tell him?"

"I told him it was none of his business."

"And *are* you sleeping with him?"

"Yes. I love him."

"Regina, have you thought about the consequences? Like getting pregnant?"

"He uses something."

"Those things aren't very reliable." God, I thought, how these kids just jump right in.

"You could get me some pills, then."

"I don't know; we'll have to talk about that later. Has your father said anything else or *done* anything to make you uncomfortable? Anything at all?"

"Just that he's always around, watching."

"From now on, if he does anything to upset you, will you come and tell me in private?"

"Sure. If you can *do* anything about it."

I wasn't certain she had understood my questions fully. But I couldn't bring myself to be more specific.

That night, I was more specific with Frank. I waited until he was in bed reading. With no preface at all, I asked him point-blank: "Why have you been spying on Virgil?" He looked up, disbelieving but guilty. "Well?"

"What do you mean?"

"You know what I mean. You drove past his house and you parked out front. I call that spying. Do you realize you've terrified his aunt?"

"I don't believe he has an aunt. At least, not in that house." He laid the book down. "Don't you see there's something about the boy that doesn't jell?"

"What, for instance?"

"Just look at him—he could have his pick of girls. Why does he want Regina?"

Soon after I had met him, *I* had been told by Gloria and my parents that I could have my pick. But it was a point I couldn't make to him. "You can't explain those things, you know that."

"It's obvious he's using her."

"It's not obvious to me. And what if he is? That's a chance everyone has to take."

"I don't want him using her."

"Frank, you have no say in the matter. And the crazier you act, the more appealing Regina will find him." His face was set against anything I had to say, but it changed with my next statement. "I want you to leave them alone. And I want you to see an analyst."

"What!"

"You heard me. I've had it, Frank. I've had it with your nightmares and your delusions. You want to know something? My school's gotten so awful that everyone counts the minutes, waiting for the end of the day. I don't. Because I know what I'm coming home to isn't going to be much better than work. You're making both Regina and me miserable and now you're starting in on Virgil and his aunt. You need help and I can't give it to you."

"You honestly believe that?"

"I believe it enough to tell you this: there's something terribly wrong in this protectiveness of yours. If you won't go to an analyst, I'll leave you. And I'll take Regina with me."

"Irene!"

"I mean it. You find somebody by the end of the week and you make an appointment."

When I got into bed, he turned off the light and slid toward me.

"Please don't."

He pulled away and lay on his back. "You'd really leave me?" he whispered.

"If you force me to."

I was drifting off when he spoke again. "Trust me, Irene. You know I'd never do anything to hurt you."

"But you *are* hurting me. I'll trust you when you start getting help." *And after I get some information.* I decided then that he wouldn't touch me again until I had had a talk with Vivian. And maybe not even after that.

LONG-DISTANCE information gave me the number of her lumber company. I dialed twice and hung up both times before the second ring. Standing there with the phone in my hand, I couldn't shake the memory of Frank's kindness to the blind boy, Larry, or the looks of adoration on the faces of those students he tutored in our living room at midterm and finals. He was still the same man and that man couldn't be capable of . . . Then I remembered the rumors about the girls, the *young* girls, coming to his apartment that summer I lived with Gloria and he lived upstairs. And I saw Sylvia's hand going under a sheet, with him accepting it. Was that another man, hidden from me all these years but forced to surface now to draw breath? One of the teachers at school had been married ten years and then discovered the two-year affair his wife had been having with another woman. And I had thought at the time: How could he have been so blind?

The third time I dialed, I let it ring through. A man answered. I asked for Mrs. Snell.

"Who's calling?"

"It's a personal call."

"She ain't here right now. She's—just a minute."

I heard some kind of rustling and the man say sniggeringly, "Says it's personal."

"Hello."

"Vivian?"

"Yes."

"This is Irene, Frank's wife."

Slight pause. "Is something wrong?"

"I was wondering if I could come and talk to you."

"What about?"

"I'd rather not say over the phone."

"Is it about Frank?"

"Yes, it is. Could I drive up tomorrow?"

Another pause. "I'll come there."

"We can't meet here."

"I assumed that," she said. "You name a place to meet where I can have a drink."

We settled on a restaurant at the edge of town near the expressway she would be coming in on.

Dinner that night was totally silent. Regina gulped down her food in five minutes and left the table. Frank picked at his and stared at the wall. When I came back from the kitchen with the coffee, there was a slip of paper near my napkin. On it was a name and telephone number.

"One of the graduate assistants goes to him. He's supposed to be good."

"Did you get an appointment yet?"

"Next Tuesday at eleven."

There was nothing more to say. Any word would have been the wrong one. I wanted him to see the analyst, knew he *had* to see one, and yet I cringed at his quick compliance. He wanted me to be pleased, but he looked more beaten and drained than I had ever seen him.

As soon as he went up to his study, Regina came down and motioned me into the kitchen.

"Well?" she said.

"It's all right. We had a talk."

"A talk? You've had talks with him before and nothing's happened."

"It's taken care of."

149

"What's taken care of? What did he say?"

"He knows he's been wrong."

"That's *it?*"

"What do you want—blood? I am doing the best I can. And you yourself could make things a little more pleasant by being kinder to him."

"You don't care what he does to me, do you?"

"Regina, get out of here before I slap you." A ridiculous threat. She towered five and a half inches over me. "I will handle this my way."

"You'd better."

The next day, I called school and said I was sick, but I left the house just as if I were going to work. I had three hours before I was to meet Vivian. I went to two shopping malls and browsed through the stores, rehearsing what I was going to say to her. The more I rehearsed, the more my courage began to waver, and I felt nauseous. I knew I would have to have a drink before Vivian, but I needed more than that.

I went into a phone booth and called California.

"Irene!" said Gloria. "Is anything wrong?"

"No. Why should something be wrong?"

"You've never called at seven-thirty in the morning."

"I'm sorry. I forgot all about the time difference. How is everyone?"

Brian had taken up scuba diving and was in the throes of his first romance. Ray needed glasses and was having fits over having to wear them. The twins, Amy and Amanda, were already taking a gymnastics class. And Gloria and Pat were planning a whole month in Europe. All good news. Predictable good news. When they first married, I had thought it wouldn't last a year. Now they were going to Europe for a month. Second honeymoon. Away from the kids. It wasn't what I wanted to hear. I wanted something to be wrong that I could help put right. I wanted to say, "Look, Gloria, it's not all that bad, look at it this way" or "I think you should do this, now get hold of yourself."

"Where in Europe?" I asked.

As she went through the itinerary I began to cry. We had never been to Europe. We had never been anyplace without Regina.

". . . and the college extended my leave of absence, but I don't think I'll be going back. Believe it or not, I've gotten to like it here at home. Say, aren't you supposed to be at school? . . . Irene? Hello?"

"I've got a cold."

"You sound like you've been crying."

"I think I'm getting an allergy. Anyway, I was bored and I wanted to catch up on you and Pat."

"One day away from the job and you're bored? You *are* a model of the work ethic. Anything new there?"

"Nothing much. Regina has a boyfriend and she's head over heels. That's about it. I have to run out on some errands now. I'll give you a call in a couple of weeks."

"No, it's my turn."

I got to the restaurant half an hour early and ordered a double Scotch. Gloria's words stuck with me: *Believe it or not, I've gotten to like it here at home.* At the same time they depressed me, they made me determined to be straightforward with Vivian.

Age had been good to her: she arrived looking exactly as she had ten years before. What was more astonishing was the resemblance between her and Regina. Assessing her dignified posture and her self-assured, long-legged stride, I thought how good it might be for Regina to use this woman as an example.

"Hello, Vivian. I'm glad you could come on such short notice."

"You made it sound urgent. No one's sick, I hope."

"No, nothing like that. But I do need to talk to you. And I'd like to keep this just between us."

"That goes without saying." She eyed my drink. "I thought you were a teetotaler. Now where did I get that idea?"

I wondered if this was a digging reference to the grass I had been smoking that night she came to the house to see Regina. She settled back into the booth and ordered a martini.

"I don't know exactly how to begin," I said. "I don't know what to ask. I guess I'd like you to just start talking about Frank."

"What in particular?"

"I'd like to hear what the rest of you think of him."

"We don't all think exactly alike. Naturally, we've all been hurt by him, the way he cut us off. Let me ask *you* something. Has he cut you off too?"

"I don't know. I'm not sure. But he is alienating Regina. Lately, he's been so . . ."

"Possessive."

It wasn't a question; it was a statement. I felt a chill.

"Yes, possessive. In the most unreasonable way. Nothing I say seems to penetrate. He was always a reasonable man." She pursed her lips and lowered her eyes. "Wasn't he?"

"If he is a reasonable man, then that makes the rest of us look pretty awful—it means his reasons for cutting us off are valid. I really don't prefer to look at it that way."

"Vivian, what *are* his reasons for hating—for avoiding all of you?"

"Hate is the right word. Frank's always been good at hating."

I hate people who just breed.

"But what are the exact reasons? Does it have anything to do with his sister Regina?"

"Has he told you anything about her?"

"That horrible story about the lye—the one you

told me—and how she was retarded and wanted him to run away with her."

"Run away with her?" Her eyes widened. "Run away with her? She wanted him to *leave her alone.*"

I knew then I should leave, that I had a sufficient glimpse of the entire picture. But I didn't move. "What do you mean—leave her alone?"

"Regina was slow, but she was sharp enough to sense something peculiar in Frank's attention. He watched her like a hawk night and day. He used to want to stay home from school to be with her. She never made any friends because she could never get away from him. Finally, I guess she couldn't stand it anymore."

"That's not enough to make a girl drink lye."

"I suppose not." She hailed the waitress and ordered another drink for each of us. Through the window I could see it was beginning to snow heavily, the wind whipping the flakes into a gauzelike curtain that obscured the highway. I wanted to jump into that wind and whiteness, have it shake me up and set me down on some new, firm ground.

"Then what *would* make her do it?" I said.

Vivian looked into her drink. "Something she never spoke of. She didn't even leave a note."

"What couldn't she speak of?"

She shrugged. "None of us ever *saw* anything. But after her death, Frank never looked any of us in the eye. And he couldn't wait to get out of town and off to college. I would like to think he hates us because he hates himself. That's what I would like to think."

"Where were your parents while all this was going on?"

"Irene, being poor is a full-time job. My father had to worry about getting food on the table and clothes on our backs. That was his main concern and everything else was just frills. He and my mother didn't have time to investigate every mood one of us had.

Some things they did see they probably had to turn their backs on and hope for the best."

"I'm sorry. I didn't mean to imply . . . I know a little of what you're talking about."

"Do you?"

"Regina—*my* Regina—has always been outside my grasp. And now she's turning on Frank . . ."

"Turning?"

"She doesn't want anything to do with him. And I'm getting to the point where I can't blame her. I don't know what to do anymore."

"Are you thinking of leaving him?"

"I'm trying *not* to think of it."

"Have you thought of getting him professional help?"

"He's already agreed to see an analyst."

"Then why don't you wait awhile and see how that works out? Besides, if you left and took Regina with you, it might set him off."

"Set him off?"

"I've seen his temper. If you need a little moral support now and then, you know where to reach me."

"Thank you, Vivian. I appreciate it."

She asked me questions about school and I told her I had just about reached the end of my rope there too.

"What's wrong with this country," she said, "is that there's no allegiance anymore, particularly to the family."

"I guess you're right."

"I know I'm right."

We said good-bye in the parking lot, with the blizzard blowing all around us. She repeated her offer of being available if I needed her again.

"I wish you had told me years ago what you told me today."

"Do you think you would have listened?"

"I might have."

"I doubt it. Besides, I don't know if I would have told you. Quite selfishly, I wanted Frank to be happy. Maybe that was wrong. There's no way of predicting how things are going to turn out. Take this car, for instance." She swiped the snow on the trunk of her black Lincoln. "Thirty years ago, not a single person in Ridgeway would have dreamed that a Mattison could own a car like this. Now I've got three lumber-yards and the same people who used to spit at me are kissing my ass. We've had offers to join the country club, bridge clubs, every kind of organization in town. But we don't belong to anything. We belong to our family. And we take care of our own. If you're patient with Frank, maybe it'll all work out for the best."

"Maybe."

I had two hours before the time I normally arrived home. Traffic was at a crawl. I did not want to kill the time by driving around. Fortunately, the radio announced that all schools were closing early.

Heading for home, I was a little heartened by Vivian's optimism. Virgil's car was parked out front and that made me feel better too. But as I came in the back door, I was greeted by Regina's shouts from the recreation room.

"Get out! Get out of here!"

I heard Frank's voice, low and firm, then Virgil's: "Mr. Mattison, I don't know why you have it in for me. If you want me to leave——"

"No!" said Regina. "If you leave I'm going with you and I'm not coming back." Frank mumbled some-thing and she shot back with: "Just try it and see!"

I stood still, my purse and my keys still in my hand. Frank came up the steps. He looked exhausted as usual, and he gave a start when he saw me. Whatever there was in my face, it made him lower his eyes.

"I have had it with you," I whispered, choking with rage. "Maybe you think I was joking when I said I would leave you. I'm not joking. I'm telling you right now, I don't want you to say another word to that boy. Whatever room he's in, you make sure you're not there. And I don't want you alone with Regina."

"Irene!"

"You heard me. When you see that doctor on Tuesday, you'd better be ready to level with him. I'm giving you exactly three months. If you don't start making some changes during that time, I'm going to see a lawyer."

His jaw tightened and I could see his eyes misting. But I was not going to buckle under any tears. I went upstairs, closed the bedroom door, and sat down to watch the blizzard. It seemed appropriate that there was chaos outside too.

FRANK kept the appointment and every one after it. Around me, he walked on eggs and avoided all direct eye contact. A hard silence settled between us. I found myself in some amorphous emotional territory where revulsion mingled with pity. During the day, pity dominated as I weighed the facts of his unfortunate childhood: poverty, passive neglect on the part of his parents, small-town and small-minded social exclusion, and finally the emotional trauma he must have suffered over his attraction to his sister and her reactionary suicide. But at night in bed with him, I huddled close to the edge and my thoughts ran from facts to suspicion. Why had he chosen the name Regina for our daughter without telling me the source of it, if not because of some dark allegiance to his sister? Had he consciously intended our daughter as a replacement for his sister *from the very beginning?* Were all those accounts he gave me of his brothers and sisters really true or had they been a ruse to gain my support in keeping away the only people who knew his secret aberration and might suspect a repetition of it? Why was he so relieved when I lost the baby—because its presence would only accentuate his strange devotion to Regina? These questions would run through my mind as I stared at the philodendron outlined against the street-lighted window shade. I clearly remembered the night we had fought over the other one and how he had regretted its being the source of our fight. Now he was seeing an analyst to try to get rid of some other source that would keep us apart. One minute, I knew I had to stand by him so long as he was willing to fight this horrible thing in him; but the next minute, I wondered if any success on his part would truly erase my revulsion, which might survive on memory alone.

For two months, silence reigned. Frank's and mine were rooted in embarrassment, but Regina's silence had a smugness to it, as though she had accomplished some private kind of victory. During meals, while Frank and I sat clenched and barely ate, she took second helpings and prolonged the ordeal by eating slowly, all the while looking perfectly content with her silence. Occasionally, when I found it intolerable to just sit there, I would ask some question about school or her friends. Sensing the desperation and awkwardness of my gesture, she would reply as briefly as possible and usually with a smirk. I could not help resenting this posture of hers, especially when I would catch a glimpse of Frank. At the table he never looked at her, and that was when I pitied him the most. There was shame and apology in his face, so obvious I was certain Regina must see it too. I had to keep reminding myself that she knew nothing of the *other* Regina and therefore could not fathom the anguish her father was going through.

At the end of February I took another day off from work, for a dental appointment. Early in the afternoon, after I returned home, the phone rang. It was the dean of girls at Old Central. She explained that due to the growing rate of truancy and forged excuses, it was now school policy to check with the parents after the fifth absence in the semester. Regina, she said, already had six, and the semester had just begun. I assured her there was some mistake, that Regina had not missed even one day of school. She then gave me the dates of absence, verified by all Regina's teachers. I said I would check with Regina and get back to her. When I hung up, I was angry, but I was also relieved that the call had not come through to Frank. This matter would have to be settled privately between Regina and me.

"I want to know where you've been on the days you haven't gone to school."

"You sound funny." She giggled. One side of my mouth was still numb from the dentist's Novocaine.

"Never mind how I sound. Answer my question."

"Just hanging around."

"Hanging around *where?*"

"I went downtown a few times. Once I went to a movie."

"You were with Virgil, weren't you?"

"Once."

"Don't lie to me. He's the only reason you'd skip school for." She sighed and rolled her eyes. "And you forged my name on those notes you took in, didn't you?"

"Yes, I forged your name."

"And that doesn't bother you?"

"So I took a few days off; what difference does it make? I'll get the same grades I always get."

"That's not the point. The point is you lied."

"They make you lie, them and their stupid notes."

"I'm not going round and round with you about this. When I call the dean, I'm going to tell her the truth."

"Oh, stop playing the teacher. I'll get two weeks' detention!"

The fact that she expected me to lie for her came

as no surprise. "Well, you can tell your father and hope he'll get you off the hook—in school, at least." The scowl on her face assured me she had got the point. "You take your detention and we'll keep this between us. And no more cutting, or the next call the dean makes might be to your father."

That night, she was far from imperious at the dinner table. She sulked and ate little.

A week later, I had to give one of the teachers a ride home to the south end of town. He lived two blocks from the restaurant where I had had my meeting with Vivian. After I dropped him off, I pulled up to a stoplight right next to the restaurant. The right-of-way traffic was coming off the expressway ramp. I looked at the restaurant, recalling that day with Vivian, and I felt vaguely guilty because I hadn't talked to her since. By now, she probably thought I had simply used her to get the information I wanted. And I had.

I turned my attention back to the traffic just in time to see a familiar-looking car shooting down the ramp, racing to make the light. When it passed through the intersection I saw Virgil driving. Regina was sitting next to him.

At home, I waited an hour and a half for him to drop her off. Frank was upstairs in his study, so as soon as she came through the door, I led her into the kitchen.

"Did you serve your detention today?"

She knew something was up and wisely chose not to lie. "All right, what do you want me to tell you?"

"Where did you and Virgil go today?"

A tiny flicker of fear crossed her face before she was able to compose herself. "Go?"

"Yes, go, as in *travel*. Where did you go?"

"We went for a ride."

"The question was *where*."

She looked me over carefully and I could almost

159

see the wheels turning in an attempt to guess exactly how much I knew.

"We went for a ride in the country."

"Apparently you don't remember what we talked about last week. Apparently you wouldn't mind getting another two weeks of detention."

"They didn't give me detention."

"Regina . . ."

"That's the truth."

"Why didn't they give it to you?"

"I don't know."

"I can check this so easily."

"Go ahead and check."

"You didn't go to school today, did you?"

"I was supposed to go on a field trip with the natural science class. I just didn't feel like it."

"You kill me. I let you off the hook with your father, the dean doesn't give you detention, and yet you go ahead and brazenly pull the same stunt. You must *want* to be punished. You know, if I brought your father into this—"

"Go ahead. Who cares!"

I could see she *didn't* care. That frightened me.

The next day I called the dean and asked if I could see her at four o'clock. When I arrived, she stood up to shake hands and offered me a seat. Her deep, throaty voice on the telephone had led me to believe she was my age or older. I was surprised to find her a young woman not yet thirty.

"I don't want to take up your time," I said, "so I'll get right to the point. I want to know why Regina wasn't given the customary detention for skipping school."

"Well, we felt—*I* felt—that in Regina's case, the punishment would be redundant. She was quite ashamed of herself and in view of her scholastic average and the satisfactory appraisals from her teachers, I thought it best to give her another chance."

"Believe me, she used that chance. She skipped school yesterday."

She lowered her eyes to the pencil she was playing with. "I see. Mrs. Mattison, until this semester Regina had no record of truancy. Do you have any idea why she should suddenly begin skipping school?"

"I certainly do. She has a boyfriend."

"Yes, she's told me about him. But I don't think Virgil is the reason she's skipping school on these particular days."

Virgil. Hearing her say the name so casually, as if she knew him, bothered me.

"Regina has *discussed* the boy with you?"

"Somewhat," she said. "She's very fond of him. And the fact is she told me he doesn't like her staying out of school."

"Doesn't like . . . ! She spent yesterday with him when she was supposed to be in school!"

"I think she would have skipped school without him. I think he's the most positive factor in her life right now."

"In what way positive?"

"He seems to be giving her a certain balance, a comfort she needs right now."

"Comfort from what?"

"She seems to be under a strain."

"What kind of strain?"

"Haven't you noticed it?" she said.

"What kind of strain?"

"She feels a lack of freedom because her father doesn't like Virgil."

"Her father is opinionated and overprotective," I said quickly, "but he certainly hasn't impinged upon her freedom. I don't know what you mean by this 'lack of freedom.'"

"I mean it in the psychological sense. She feels her father is watching her in a certain way."

"What way?"

She would not have had to answer. The sudden evasiveness in her manner indicated she had been told more than she was going to tell me.

"She couldn't exactly describe it to me," she said.

"Can *you* describe it?"

"I wouldn't attempt to without knowing a few more facts."

If that was my cue to provide those facts, I ignored it. "I don't want Regina to know I've been here," I said. "But I do want her to be given detention for skipping school yesterday."

"If you want. But I don't think that's going to solve the problem."

"It might be a start."

Driving home, I tried to sort out my feelings over what Regina had done. It angered me that she had taken this situation to someone else, an outsider. But I was frightened by the possibility she didn't trust me enough to tell me everything. Her unyielding harshness with Frank had seemed perverse—unless something had *already* happened.

For two days, I watched them closely. Frank was the same with her as he was with me—withdrawn, his shoulders hunched and rounded in an attitude of self-protection. Regina was self-possessed and untouchable. Around Frank she showed no fear, barely any resentment. She simply acted as if he were invisible. When Virgil came into the house, Frank dutifully hid himself in his study.

Regina got her detention and gave me smoldering, knowing looks the whole week. Suddenly, it was as if I were the one, not Frank, who was oppressing her. By the end of the week, I was so exhausted from sleeplessness, I went to the doctor and got a prescription for sleeping pills. And I decided to break the silence with Regina.

"Do you want your father to move out for a while?"

"No, not really," she answered casually, too casually, as though she had *expected* me to suggest it.

"Then he's not the reason you were skipping school?"

She sighed deeply, her usual signal that this was something she didn't care to discuss.

"Regina, what did you tell Miss McPhee about us, about your father?"

I expected an outburst, but she seemed merely indifferent. "Not much," she answered.

"She seems to have gotten the idea your father is the reason you've been skipping school."

"What does *she* know?" She shrugged.

"Did you use your father as an excuse to get out of that first detention?"

"No."

"Then why did you mention him to her at all?"

"She asked me what things were like at home."

"What did you tell her? Did you tell her anything you haven't told me?"

"I don't know what you're talking about."

For the next few weeks, I had the feeling of treading stagnant water. Frank slunk around the house and said nothing. When I asked how he was doing with the analyst, he would put on a wounded look, as if I had made the most blatant accusation—the very thing I wanted to steer clear of. Regina didn't pay much more attention to me than she did to Frank. She was animated only in the presence of Virgil. I knew she was much too wrapped up in him, but that necessarily had to be the least of my concerns. Perhaps it was this sense of treading that made me wish something—anything—would happen. Perhaps this is what sent me into Frank's study late one afternoon before he got home.

In the back of one desk drawer, tucked beneath some papers, was a gun, loaded. Under it, single pages from a Fort Lauderdale phone directory were folded in a square; all contained complete listings for the name Evans. And there was a letter from the Fort Lauderdale Health Department, which said that on the basis of the information given in the request, they were unable to locate the birth certificate.

I took the gun to our room. I pulled out the bottom drawer of the dresser and put the gun on the floor, then pushed the drawer back in. I had already given Frank my ultimatum. A month and a half remained. I would wait.

THE gun took up a permanent position in my mind. In the middle of teaching a lesson or pushing a shopping cart down the aisle of the supermarket, I carried a picture of its stubby barrel and deadly cylinder, and with that picture I remembered Vivian's words: "I've seen his temper."

In magazines and in the family living section of the newpapers I saw scores of articles about the increasing divorce rate and the common tendency at middle age to reassess one's marriage. I found most of the personal interviews laughable (although I was incapable of laughing) because the discussions of "changed values" and "looking for new purpose" remained abstract, nothing more than little sociological essays. But a gun was concrete. So was the letter from the Fort Lauderdale Health Department. And there was Vivian's story, and there were the circles under Frank's eyes and mine from sleeplessness. Everything pointed to the plain fact that nineteen years of marriage had not created a profound intimacy but instead left me stranded with a stranger. And to what degree was that my own doing? How many clues had I ignored over the years?

Driving to and from school, I had fantasies of running away, just stepping on the gas and aiming for Los

Angeles and that Southern California sun which seemed capable of burning out your past and leaving you contentedly empty. The one thing I wanted most was to feel empty so I could sleep again.

By March, Regina had been going with Virgil six months. If one day passed without her seeing him, she was ready to jump out of her skin. I set no limits to the time she spent with him. When she was gone from the house and Frank was in his study, I could at least be alone.

The second Saturday in March, Virgil and Regina were going to Detroit to see a play. Virgil came by that morning and had breakfast with us. Dressed in a steel-gray three-piece suit and sporting his wide, gap-toothed smile, he looked more handsome than ever, the archetype of America's Prince Charming. All through breakfast, Regina hung on his every word and took her eyes off him only to get the fork to her mouth. Although I found her too subservient to him, I had to admit she looked the happiest I had ever seen her. Even her coloring had changed. Her cheeks were pinker, her eyes glistened, her face looked fuller. It was saddening to realize that the most Frank and I could draw from her was a smirk or a sneer.

That morning, Frank was a little more at ease with Virgil and almost friendly. When they were ready to leave, Frank even walked them out to Virgil's car. From the dining room window, I watched him look over the car, ask questions and climb inside to inspect the dashboard. Maybe, I thought, just maybe he was beginning to get a grip on himself. This thought, however, was whittled down to wishful thinking by the end of the day. He refused lunch, went through two stop signs on our way to the supermarket, ate only a few mouthfuls at dinner, then planted himself in the living room to wait for their return.

"Maybe they'll want something to eat when they

get back," he said. "What time was that play supposed to be over?"

"Four-thirty, five."

"It's seven o'clock now. They'll probably be hungry."

"I doubt it. They'll probably have dinner along the way."

"They didn't say anything about stopping for dinner. Did they say anything to you?"

"No."

"Maybe they'll be a little hungry anyway. When they get back, they can come in and have a little something. Even if they did stop and eat, they should be back pretty soon. If they stopped, it would probably be along the expressway, and someplace quick. I don't imagine he'd take her to—"

"Stop it! Just—stop it!" If you don't stop it, I thought, I'll walk out of here tonight.

He settled back and hid behind the newspaper he had been pretending to read.

They pulled into the driveway at eight-thirty. Frank bounded through the dining room and kitchen and out the back door. In a minute, Regina and Virgil came in alone.

"Where's your father?"

"In the garage."

"Doing what?"

"Who knows?" She looked annoyed. "Virgil's tired; he wants to go home. What did you want to talk to him about?"

"What do you mean?"

"Daddy said you wanted to talk to him."

A dull freeze came over me. What was he doing out in that garage? "I—I just wanted to know how you liked the play."

"I didn't think it was so bad," said Virgil, "but Regina didn't like it. The end was kind of a disappointment, but I guess they work on those things before they get to New York."

He went on with his review, but I had my eyes on Regina. The tilt of her head told me she was wondering the same thing I was. As Virgil continued talking, she turned and went to the dining room window. Obviously seeing nothing, she started for the kitchen, but before she reached it, Frank reappeared. His fists were clenched at his sides.

"What are you up to?" she said.

"That's what I was going to ask you."

"What are you talking about?"

"You know what I'm talking about and so does he. Sit down, both of you."

"I'm not sitting—"

"You'll do as you're told." There was a new, solid authority in his voice and Virgil was the first to bow to it. When he sat down on the couch, Regina joined him.

"Now where did you go today?"

Virgil gave a puzzled smile. "To Detroit."

Frank moved in closer on them. "I'm going to ask you just once more and I want the truth. Where did you go?"

Regina was fuming, but Virgil looked questioningly, helplessly at me.

"Frank," I said, "what are you doing?"

"Tracking down a lie, that's what I'm doing. They didn't go to Detroit."

"Mr. Mattison, we've got the play programs in the car. I can show—"

"Anybody can get you play programs. What about the ticket stubs? They'll have the date on them."

Virgil turned to Regina. "Have you got them?"

"No, I haven't. And he's gone crazy."

"Stop this right now," I said.

"I checked the mileage on the car before they left this morning and I checked it again just now. They've gone a hundred and fifty-five miles. Round trip to Detroit is at least two hundred and ten!"

For a minute no one said anything. Finally, Virgil spoke up. "Mr. Mattison, you must have made a mistake. We were in Detroit."

"A hundred and fifty miles is seventy-five each way. Where did you go?" He leaned over and put his face in front of Virgil's. *"What are you?"*

"Frank!"

"Get him away from us!" Regina cried.

He grabbed the boy by the front of the shirt. "I want to know right now!"

Regina tried to stand, but Frank pushed her back onto the couch. It was the first time he had ever laid a hand on her that way. Instantly, I thought of the gun.

"Seventy-five miles each way," he said to Virgil. "In what direction?"

"Frank, let him go."

"In what direction?"

I got up and went to the phone.

"Stay away from there, Irene. All I want is an answer from him."

I began dialing Bernie Golden's number, shaking so badly I missed a numeral and had to start over. Frank rushed to me and pressed the button to cut me off. I looked him squarely in the eye and whispered, "You're sick. You're so sick I'm beginning to hate you."

"Don't say that. Don't—" His eyes finished the plea.

"Let him go home," I said. "Go upstairs and wait for me. Go now before I walk out of here tonight."

He left.

"He's nuts—he's out of his mind!" said Regina.

"That may be, but he's suffering too. You can see he's suffering. Now tell me, did you really go to Detroit? That's all he wants to know."

"Yes, we went to Detroit!"

"Just like those days you *said* you went to school?"

"So you're on his side now?"

"I'm on my own side, and I want the truth. The two of you are driving me crazy. It's not just him. Now I have to worry about whether or not you're showing up at school or if you're really going where you say you are."

"Mrs. Mattison, we really went to Detroit. He must have read the mileage wrong."

"All right, Virgil, all right. You can go home now."

"Oh, that's just fine!" said Regina. "And I'm supposed to stay here with that lunatic!"

Virgil turned to her. "He'll calm down after I'm gone."

She walked him out to his car. I waited twenty minutes. Instead of giving her the customary signal with the patio floodlight, I slipped out the back door with the intention of apologizing to Virgil. I had taken only a few steps when I heard them giggling in the car, then Regina broke into a shrill laugh. I went back into the house and signaled with the light.

When she came through the kitchen she had a faint smile on her face as though none of the last hour had happened. She breezed past me without a word.

The nightstand lamp was on when I walked into our bedroom, and Frank was lying with his arm over his eyes. I undressed in the bathroom, put on a nightgown and sat down in the rocker.

"You're pushing me to leave you. That's what you really want, isn't it?"

"That's the last thing I want."

"I can't believe that. It comes down to one of two things. Either you're not making any effort to overcome this perv—this obsession, or else it's entirely out of your control. But whichever circumstance it is, I can't live with either one."

"It's not what you think, Irene. It's not at all what you think."

"Then what is it?"

That pleading look again, but no explanation.

"I found the gun," I said.

"I know you did."

"Then you know what I found with it."

"Yes."

"Tell me why, then. Where did you get the gun?"

"It was just an impulse. I'm glad you took it. I never would have used it, anyway."

"Frank, the gun is loaded."

"It came that way."

"What did you have in mind—putting bullets in our heads while we were asleep some night?"

"Jesus, Irene, don't!"

"You haven't got much time."

"I know that better than you do. Trust me a little longer."

"I told you my time limit and I'm sticking to it. After that . . ."

After that, I didn't know.

Two days later, on Monday, I was teaching my second class when one of the office secretaries came to the door with a telephone message. It was from Vivian. I was to return the call as soon as possible. My next period was free, and I went directly to the phone booth.

She answered on the first ring. "Vivian? It's Irene."

"Can you talk?"

"Yes. What is it?"

"Frank was just here."

"What!"

"I called you just as soon as he left. Irene, I think he's dangerous."

"What did he do? What did he say?"

"He was raving. What little I could make out was about Regina. He said I had turned her against him and turned you against him. You didn't tell him about the talk we had, did you?"

"Not a word, I swear."

"I didn't think so. But he really lit into me. I was afraid he was going to hit me."

"What else did he say?"

"It was all a jumble. He kept mixing up the two Reginas and saying how nothing was his fault. That's what he kept saying: 'It's not my fault.'"

"Oh, God!"

"I just wanted to warn you. But you can't tell him I called you. For *my* sake."

"No, of course not. Vivian, what am I going to do?"

"You're going to be careful. Don't do anything to rile him up or make him suspicious. You might have to have him committed for a while . . . you know? . . . Irene? Hello?"

"Yes, I'm here."

"Just be careful, will you?"

"Yes. And thank you."

"Don't thank me. I'm sorry it's turned out this way. If you need any help, you know where to reach me."

I sat there in the booth, just trying to breathe. When I was able to think, I got the operator and told her to make my next call collect.

"Gloria, it's Irene."

"Well, we're back to the early morning calls." She chuckled.

"Gloria, I need you here. Can you come today?"

"What's wrong?"

"Everything!" I began to cry. "Everything *you*

171

thought would be wrong nineteen years ago. God, you must have been looking into a crystal ball."

"Take it easy. Tell me what it is."

"Frank. He's sick, so sick, and there's nothing I can do! I'm going to have to have him committed or else I'll kill him!"

"Stop that. What are you talking about?"

"First his sister, now his daughter. He's in love with Regina and he got himself a gun."

"What!"

"Please, can you come? I need you here."

"Do you know what you're saying?"

"I know I sound hysterical—I *am* hysterical—but it's the truth."

"All right, honey, take it easy. Do you think you can hang on until tomorrow? I could come tomorrow."

"Yes, as long as I know you're coming."

"All right, then. I'll call you as soon as I get a flight."

"Leave the message for me here at school." I gave her the number.

"I'll call the airlines right now. You're sure you'll be all right tonight?"

"Yes. Just come."

I got through the day on that single expectation. After school, I checked my mailbox in the main office and found Gloria's message. Her plane would arrive the following afternoon at five.

AT dinner, Frank didn't touch a thing. He sipped on some wine and stared at the table. But he did not appear passively lost in thought; on the contrary, he had the look of someone who has just made up his mind.

"Virgil's picking me up in half an hour," Regina announced casually. "We're going to the movies."

"You're not going anywhere," said Frank.

She ignored this and started eating her pie. I waited. When the pie was gone, she picked up her plate and carried it to the kitchen, then came back through on her way upstairs.

"You heard what I said." His voice was hard enough to make her stop and turn to me.

"Are you going to let him start in on me again?"

"You step one foot out that door," he told her, "and I'll call the police. I don't want to do that to you, but I will if you force me."

"Then do it." But there was little conviction in her voice.

"I will."

Again she looked at me, but I turned away. If I just get through tonight, I thought, Gloria will be here tomorrow. Regina ran upstairs.

"I'm sorry," he said.

"Sorry for what?"

"I know what I'm doing, Irene." When his hand touched mine, it was like a jolt and I pulled back from it.

If you know what you're doing, then you're hopeless! If you know what you're doing, then you know you're driving me crazy!

"Irene, listen to me."

"I'm tired of listening to you. I'm tired of looking at you. Leave me alone tonight."

I went up to talk to Regina. Her door was closed, but I could hear her talking on the phone. She said, "Please, please," just before I knocked. She told me to wait a minute, then lowered her voice. When she hung up, I went in.

"Was that Virgil?"

"No. Betty Riley." One of her friends.

"I hope you haven't said anything to her about
. . . us."

"I haven't."

"Regina, I want you to do what your father says.
Just for tonight. He's more upset than usual."

She looked afraid. "What about tomorrow night and
the night after? He'll find an excuse whenever he
wants."

"I know, but I'm thinking of a way . . . ." What—
to have him committed? Arrested? "I want you to
stay away from Virgil for a few days while I decide
what to do about your father."

"All right, a few days."

Frank hid in his study. Downstairs, I tried watching
television, but my mind was on Gloria. Regina sat
with me, next to the phone, and chewed on her finger-
nails.

"Expecting Virgil to call?"

"Yes. If I can't see him I can at least talk to him."

When it rang she picked it up. "It's for you," she
said, and handed it to me.

"Irene, it's Vivian. Don't talk, just listen. I've been
thinking over what Frank said today and I'm worried
about Regina. The way he kept mixing up the two
of them . . . My hands have been cold all day. I don't
trust him."

"I know, I know."

"Look, I have a plan. Let me bring Regina up here
for a few days, maybe until the end of the week, while
you figure out what you're going to do. Frank would
never think of looking for her here."

"But how?"

"I can pick her up in front of her school tomorrow
afternoon. You can call the school and tell them she
won't be in the rest of the week."

"What about my parents? I could send her there."

"You mean they know about all this?"

"No, I couldn't tell them."

"Well, you'd have to tell them, because I'm sure that's the first place he'd go looking for her."

"You're right. But your place is such a risk. If he ever found out . . ."

"Isn't there a bigger risk having her *there*? Irene, you didn't see him as I did today. Believe me, if you had . . . Please, let me do this one thing for you, and for her."

"Yes."

"What's the name of the school and what time does she get out?"

"Old Central on Pershing Avenue. Three o'clock."

"I'll be out front. You remember my car—the black Lincoln. I'll have on a green coat."

"Okay. Maybe someday I'll be able to repay you."

"Don't worry about that. I'll be there at three o'clock sharp. When I get back here with her, I'll ring you once and hang up to let you know everything's all right."

"About what time will that be?"

"Let's see, it's seventy-five miles, so it'll be an hour and a half, approximately. About four-thirty."

I was to pick Gloria up at the airport at five. "Make it six-thirty."

"Fine. One ring." She hung up.

"Come into the kitchen." Regina followed me in and sat down at the table. "Listen carefully. You've heard me mention your Aunt Vivian before. That was her on the phone. You're going to stay with her for a few days up in Ridgeway. While you're gone, I'll have a chance to think what I'm going to do about your father. She's going to pick you up in front of school tomorrow, but you're to tell no one where you're going, none of your friends or that Miss Mc-Phee, no one."

"Not even Virgil?"

"You'd better not. If your father questions him, at least he won't have to lie."

"Do I really have to go?"

"Yes. For my sake as well as yours. You can take your school books with you. But remember, not a word to anyone about this."

Later, when I went upstairs to bed, I passed by Regina's door and heard her talking on the phone again. I couldn't make out the words, but I distinctly heard her giggle and then laugh shrilly. It made me feel uneasy, and I almost opened the door. But I moved on to the bathroom, thinking maybe she really didn't fathom the seriousness of the situation. And maybe it was better she didn't. After all, she was still a child.

THE next morning, I drove her to her school before I went to mine.

"Remember, don't say anything to anyone. She'll be here at three. Black Lincoln, green coat. I'll call the school tomorrow and tell them you won't be in for the rest of the week."

"Come in with me now and tell them."

"I can't. I'll be late."

"It'll just take a minute. If you do it in person, they won't be suspicious."

"Suspicious of what?"

"I've got a record now for skipping. If you call them up they might not believe it's you. They might send a truant officer around."

Despite the inconvenience, I was impressed by her concern for details. If a truant officer did come to the house while Frank was there, it could be disastrous.

We went together to the main office, where I spoke to the secretary in charge of attendance. Just as I was explaining that Regina was going out of town, I was aware of a pink blouse next to me. In it was Miss McPhee. When I turned to her, she was looking at Regina sympathetically. Something in me resented that look, for it implied she knew exactly what was going on. We exchanged a quick greeting, then Regina walked with me to the front exit.

"Listen," I said, "if that Miss McPhee calls you in today to ask where you're going, don't tell her anything."

"She won't call me in."

"If she does."

"I won't tell her."

I bluffed my way through the day by giving the kids surprise compositions to write. I concentrated on how I was going to tell Gloria about Frank, and how I was going to tell Frank about Regina's absence.

A little after five, Gloria got off the plane, looking as beautiful as ever: tanned, sleek and self-possessed. I felt first a pang of jealousy, then a seething rage at how my life had been turned around. Years ago, anyone with eyes and minimal intelligence would have predicted that her marriage with Pat was doomed to end shortly or drag on miserably. But here she was, four children later and her marriage still intact, being summoned to witness the bitter closing rites of *mine*.

I stood at the chain-link fence outside the terminal and watched her come down the stair ramp and walk across the runway. *You cheated on your husband and are living happily ever after. Your husband wanted you to have children. You want to stay at home. Your husband has no secrets. You're living in never-never land and I'm living in hell!* To regain myself I had to turn away and walk into the terminal. In my attempt to squelch that unwarranted bitterness, I let my memory run back nineteen years to the one warning which had many voices—Gloria's, my father's, Dr. Denning's and, the night of the wedding party dinner,

Vivian's. But I had ignored all the warnings, dismissed all the clues; all that courage and optimism on my part had been nothing more than romantic arrogance. Besides Frank, there was no one to blame but myself.

When she came through the door into the terminal, her face fell at the sight of mine. I knew very well what I had come to look like the past few months—the half moons under my eyes, the ashen complexion, the absence of animation in my face—but seeing her reaction to it made me feel like a crone who has had a floodlight turned on her. By the time she reached me and put her arms around me, my throat had swollen so, I couldn't speak. I clung to her, silently, while we waited for her luggage, and I held on all the way to the car. I gave her the keys and asked her to drive. We held the silence throughout the ride. When we got to the house, I made drinks, stiff ones, and sat her down in the living room. "Frank won't be home until six-thirty. We'll have time to talk first." I sat next to the phone, and part of me waited for Vivian's signal. "I can't mince words, Gloria, or give you a long preface. I want you to think back to when I first met Frank. I want you to remember anything *specific* you didn't like about him. Something he might have said or something you might have seen that I didn't." She cocked her head questioningly. "I'm sorry to put you on the spot, but I want you to be honest with me."

"You know I will be."

"I didn't listen to you then; I didn't listen to anyone. But I'm ready to listen now."

"We went over this a long time ago. You know my reaction to Frank was more a reaction to losing you. You were my mentor, my mother, a hundred things, and he was a threat."

"But if it had been a *different* man, would you have felt what you felt toward him?"

"I'm not sure. Maybe. If you had fallen as hard as you did for Frank."

"But aside from me, what was there about *him* you didn't like?"

She lit a cigarette and looked through the smoke she exhaled. "I guess his magnanimity. The way he was always polite to me, almost unctuous, when I insulted him and treated him like shit. I thought he was either a saint or a sap or a phony, and I certainly didn't want to believe he was a saint. But then, maybe he was just smart. Maybe he figured treating me nicely was going to win him extra points with you. If that was the case, he was right."

"Yes, he was right. And I wonder now how many other things he counted on. What I wonder most is *why* he wanted me."

"Certainly you know by now."

"No, I don't. For years I thought I did. I thought I did." I knew I had to say it then or else I would never be able to say it. I had to look her in the eye and say it. "He wants Regina the way he had his sister! He wants to sleep with her. It's all he thinks about!"

At first, nothing in her face registered what I had said. Her eyes drifted to her drink and back to me. "How do you know?"

"It's so obvious, it's pathetic, the way he hovers over her, the way he hates her boyfriend. He's been spying on the boy, practically tracking down his family tree, hoping he can find something—God knows what— to use against him. He's a spectacle and he's gotten to the point where he's not even trying to cover it up anymore." I poured it all out. The beginnings of his surveillance, the immediate antagonism he displayed toward Virgil, and finally Vivian's story, which he had hidden from me all these years. "I keep telling myself this doesn't happen to people like us, you can't live with someone this long without knowing him. But I don't know him! Suppose we had had a son instead of Regina? Would this thing have stayed buried or would he have wanted me to keep having children until he got a daughter?"

"Irene, you don't think this was *planned,* do you?"

"He named her Regina, didn't he? And oh, so casually, as if the name just popped into his head. He never said a word about *that* sister. And why has he kept his family away from us? I'm telling you, I don't know what to do. One day I think this is something that has nothing to do with his love for me, that it's a sickness and he's fighting it. Then the next day he pulls the same old tricks and I think no, he *wants* to follow this perversion to the end and he's planned it that way and there's nothing I can do except let him go crazy and get him into an institution. But at the same time I can't take a chance on what he might do to Regina. Or to Virgil. I'm caught. And I'm tired. I'm so goddam tired, I'm almost numb."

"How much has he admitted to?"

"He's seeing an analyst."

"Has it helped?"

"Not that I can see. You can't reverse a lifetime in just three months. But something has been touched off in him. He drove up to Vivian's yesterday and babbled about Regina and his sister. But he kept mixing them up. It's the first time he's been back home in over twenty years. I cannot believe it's a good sign."

"Has he been violent with you?"

"No, never. Just the opposite. He keeps asking me to be patient."

"And obviously you have been. Why haven't you left him before this? Why haven't you tried a separation?"

"I would have to take Regina with me and that could be the very thing that would make him snap. And . . . I can't section myself off. That's the problem. I still love him. Sometimes it absolutely repulses me to think it, to admit to it. But if this thing of his is something people can have and get over, then I can't just run out on him. I love him and want to help him, but the thought of him laying a finger on Regina . . . I think I could kill him if he did it."

"Maybe you could send Regina away. To a private school in another town."

"She'd never be willing to leave Virgil. That's another problem I haven't begun to deal with. I'm sure she's been sleeping with him from the beginning. If she ends up pregnant, I don't know what that would do to Frank. But I want you to see him, I want you to watch him when Regina doesn't show up for dinner."

She winced slightly. "Like watching a fish on a hook."

"And what have *I* been?"

"Take it easy, honey. I wasn't criticizing."

When Frank came home, he took one look at Gloria and stopped cold. Gloria played her part perfectly. She was cheerful and breezy and right on cue with a story of how her mother was considering a property investment and wanted her here to look at it. Frank smiled and went through the amenities by asking about Pat and the kids. But as soon as she turned her back, he gave me a wounded look mixed with fear and accusation.

Gloria took care of the dinner conversation by rattling on about the trip to Europe she and Pat were going to take and a dozen other things I barely heard. I sensed the close attention she was paying to Frank, and I wondered if he sensed it too. Finally, when Gloria paused, he looked at his watch and asked where Regina was.

"She'll be late," I said as casually as I could.

"Where is she?"

"Some club meeting."

"What club?"

"French, I think."

"Her French club meets every other Thursday. This is Tuesday."

"I think this was a special meeting about fund-raising. Anyway, she's having supper with some of her friends."

"You mean at one of their houses?"

"Yes, that's what I mean." My tone of voice told him he had gone far enough. He asked nothing more, but he stopped eating and took to his wine.

After dinner, he sat in the living room with us. He faced the window and kept staring through it. After less than an hour, he excused himself by saying he had work to do in his study.

As soon as he was out of the room, Gloria turned to me and said, "There *is* something wrong with him. I can feel it. He's absolutely panic-stricken."

For weeks, I had longed for an outside confirmation. Now that I had it, I began to shake and my whole body seemed to race downhill into my stomach. I couldn't talk, I didn't want Gloria to talk, so I turned on the television. And waited.

At nine, he came downstairs and announced he was going out for ice cream.

"And take a little ride past Virgil's?" I said. "You needn't bother. She's not there."

He paused. I knew he wanted to maintain the charade about the ice cream because of Gloria, but he also wanted to know what I knew.

"Did she call you? I didn't hear the phone ring."

"No, she didn't call and no, the phone didn't ring. I know where she is."

He managed a small chuckle. "Where, then?"

"She's on a little vacation. She'll be gone for the week."

I watched Gloria. She kept her face turned to the television, but I saw her swallow hard.

"Irene, I don't think this is anything to joke about."

"I don't, either. Especially since the joke is on me."

"Gloria, would you excuse us for a minute?"

"Sure." She started up from her chair.

"Stay where you are," I said. Then to Frank: "Does it bother you that I have someone here on my side?"

"Is she with Virgil?"

"You see?" I said to Gloria. "Everything comes back to Regina. His darling daughter. His *desirable* daughter."

"Stop it. Now where is she? What do you mean—'for the week'?"

"She's where you'll never find her. I want her away from here while I decide what to do about you. I'm going to see a lawyer. If it takes the truth to keep you away from her legally, then I'll tell the truth."

"Tell him whatever you want. Only tell me where she is right now. Is she with Virgil? Is she? Because if she is, she's in danger!"

"In danger," I mimicked. "No, she's not with Virgil. She *was* in danger, but she's not going to be anymore."

"Irene, don't toy with me. For her own good, tell me where she is. You can't play this game; you don't know what's involved. Tell me where."

I said nothing. Gloria watched. The next thing I knew, I was pulled to my feet, my shoulders gripped in Frank's hands, his face red and furious in front of mine.

"Tell me, goddammit, tell me! You don't know what might be going on!" He began shaking me. "Tell me, tell me!"

"Take your hands off her." Gloria was standing and her voice was hard. "I said take your hands off her." He turned and looked at her. She didn't make a move and neither did he. He just stared. "Take your hands off her *now*." His hands fell away from me. He looked as if he were going to be sick. The three of us stood there and then Gloria backed up and turned off the television. Frank collapsed into the chair I had been sitting in and put his hands over his face.

"How perfect!" he gasped. "How perfect you should be here now!" He dropped his hands and looked at her. "You were right, Gloria. You tried to save her from me at the very beginning. You were right and I should have let you do it. But now it's too late." His face drew back in a smile. His shoulders and chest began to shake, but it took a few seconds for me to realize he was not laughing. He was crying. "And so it's time to tell, and you might as well hear it too. I admired you, Gloria, and it's hard to fight someone you admire. Sit down, both of you. I don't want you standing over me this way. Please sit. Over there, together." We sat down on the couch. "You're right, Irene, everything comes back to Regina. I knew when she was born it would have to. I tried to think it wouldn't; I just willfully underestimated them. But they're strong. They're so goddamn strong, it's frightening."

"Who's strong?" asked Gloria.

"Vivian. My so-called family. The kind of family neither of you would know anything about. And there's no reason why you should, except that through me Regina's part of that family. She may not recognize it, but they do. They'll try to claim her the way they tried to claim me and my sister."

His big hands hung limp over the arms of the chair, but he was breathing like a runner.

"Regina died because of them—and me. I wouldn't take her away. I promised her I would and then I didn't. I told her to wait but she couldn't wait and I just closed my eyes to it because I wanted to get out my own way, I wanted to wait until it was convenient for *me*. By then it was too late for *her*. And then she was dead." He took a deep breath and shuddered. "Irene, I must tell you something I should have told . . ." He turned his face away. "Vivian is my mother."

Gloria and I looked at each other. Her eyes said the same thing I was wondering: Was he going to become so irrational that we would have to call the police?

"Frank, Vivian is your sister."

He nodded, not looking at me. "Yes, that too." He drew breath again. "Regina and I were hers and my father's—"

"Frank, maybe you should—" But Gloria squeezed my arm and shook her head, indicating I should let him continue.

"From the beginning," he said, "I knew there was something different about Regina and me, the way my mother—or who I thought was my mother—looked at us, the way the older ones looked at us. I understood it with Regina—she had that clouded look, she was 'slow'—but I couldn't understand why they looked at me the same way. We seemed to amuse some of them and embarrass the others. Except Doris, the oldest, and my . . . mother. Doris hated us and the other one hated us and pitied us at the same time. Sometimes when we were sleeping, they would come in together and Doris would hold the pillow over our faces so no one would hear us scream and my—the other one would beat us with a piece of garden hose. Doris said if we ever told anyone she'd kill us. One night, Vivian came in and caught them. She knocked her mother to the floor and dragged Doris into the house—"

"Into the house?"

"Regina and I didn't sleep in the house. There was a shack in the backyard, an old toolshed. They put a wood stove in it and that's where we slept. Vivian used to clean it and get wood for us until I was old enough to do it. Then, this one night, Vivian caught Doris, and from what we heard from the others, she beat her to a pulp. The next morning Doris was gone for good and from then on my—Vivian's mother never

185

stepped foot into the shack. She ignored us most of the time, but once in a while I'd catch her looking at me and I'd think she was going to cry. I remember once this hot, hot day she called me into the house and gave me a glass of lemonade and said, 'Listen, boy'—she never called me or Regina by our names—she said, 'Listen, boy, today ain't half as hot as the fires of hell. You got to watch out. God's already paid your sister by making her feeble-minded and I'm sure he's got something waiting for you too. You just remember you belong to him because even the devil belongs to him, even Vivian.' "

He stopped and seemed to mull this over in his head. But I could mull nothing over. To me, it was a story about someone I didn't know.

"When I was ten or eleven I began to realize why the others were crowded into three bedrooms while Vivian had her own room. Sometimes my father slept in there with her, sometimes my brothers Tom and Jack. They were the nicest to us besides Marian. Marian worked in the dime store and she used to bring us candy and little toys until Vivian made her stop. They hated each other. Later, Marian met a man, only she never brought him to the house. They moved away to get married and we never heard from her again. The night before she left, she came out to say good-bye to us and she told me to watch over Regina and keep her away from Vivian. I asked her why; she said in a few years I'd *know* why. And of course she was right. One night, Vivian and Jack came out and took Regina into the house. When they brought her back she was crying, this dull moaning. I asked her what happened. She slid her hand down her stomach and said they had hurt her. The next day she helped me nail metal prongs on the doorjamb and I got a board to stick in them. About a week later they came for her again and they broke the door down. Jack and Tom held me down and Vivian took

Regina inside. Then Vivian came back and they left. That's when—when she told me Regina and I belonged to her. She stroked my hair and told me I didn't have to mind anyone but her and my father and they would take care of us. She kept saying how someday we'd all get even with Ridgeway; she'd see to that personally. We'd have money and they'd come crawling to us and then *we* could laugh at them. She said we didn't need any outsiders, not if we all stuck together. Then she started"—he shuddered—"she started kissing my neck. She said we all had to love each other, her and my father and Tom and Jack, Regina and me. The rest of the family didn't count, not if they ran out the way Doris and Marian did. I got away from her and ran for the house. In my father's room, they—Regina was in the bed making that dull moaning and my father was saying, 'It's all right, Daddy's here, Daddy's going slow,' and he was moving on top of her and when he saw me *he smiled. . . .*"

Through his words I could hear that dull moaning. It was coming from inside my head. I glanced at Gloria. Her mouth was slack, and her California tan looked tawny.

". . . Regina called to me, she called my name, but I couldn't move, and then—then he got off and Jack got on and I began to scream, and I ran to my moth—Vivian's mother's room. She was sitting there in her straight-back chair with the Bible in her lap. I begged her to stop them, but all she did was smile and say, 'They're none of mine, God has sent me a sign, they were conceived in lust but I've put lust aside, they're lust's children, they're none of mine.' She closed her eyes and started praying for me. I yelled for her to come and help me, but she didn't move, she only smiled and said, 'You can't shout down lust, boy, you have to put it aside.' "

He stopped and closed his eyes. His hands were still hanging over the arms of the chair and his veins stood out like a network of tubing. When he spoke again, his voice was distant and strangely metallic, like a noise traveling down a long, narrow pipe.

"After a while, Regina didn't cry when they took her in at night. Vivian was working at Leo's lumber company and bringing home more money than her job was worth and she was buying Regina presents and dresses. For a long time, I didn't do anything. If someone looked at me sideways at school or on the street, I was afraid they'd found out about us. I had to keep reminding Regina not to tell anyone. Then one little thing happened and it changed me and it changed Regina." He glanced at us briefly, then stared out the window. "This girl asked me to a dance. She was afraid to ask me because her father was a drunk and her brothers were hoods and her sisters were whores and the whole town knew it."

"Wanda Hoople," I murmured.

"Yes. The whole town knew about her family but no one knew about us. When she asked me, she stood there, ashamed of what *she* was, and waited for me to answer. But I couldn't answer and she backed away from me like I was some kind of a prince she had no right to approach and I wanted to say, 'It's not like that, you don't know who I am,' but I didn't say anything, I didn't say a word. After that, in school, she'd slink past me with her head down and I wanted to say . . . I couldn't say it. I couldn't say it to anyone. So I turned it on Regina. One night I told her not to go with them when they came for her, I told her it was a sin, it was filthy, and she'd rot in hell for it. She started crying and moved toward me, but I pushed her away and when they came to get her, she started howling. She ended up telling Vivian what I'd said, so the next day Vivian took me for a ride in the car Leo had given her. We parked on this country road way out of town. She told me there was no place in the world for Regina and me except with her. She told me to keep my dirty mouth shut around Regina and to stop putting ideas in her head. But it was too late to undo what I had done. Regina kept after me to take her away and I kept promising her, but . . . I kept seeing her as one of *them* and sometimes when she touched me I wanted to jump out of my skin and leave her with them. But she kept begging me to take her away and I kept saying later, later. Then I got the scholarship to college. All I could think about was privacy and no noises in the night and no one to look after but myself. I told her she would have to wait, wait until I got to college, and then maybe in a year I could come get her. She said she couldn't stay there without me. She said she'd follow me, she'd go wherever I went. She knew what was really in my mind. You'll never come back, she said, you'll never come back and I'll rot in hell. And then I—" His voice broke and the words came out in spasms. "I told her she could never follow me because where I was going they wouldn't let her in. The next day she took the can of lye into the woods where no one would hear her scream. And she must have died screaming. When I found her, her mouth and her eyes were wide open." He was crying again, without sobbing, and his hands were fisted. "Vivian knew why she'd done it. And she told me I was going to pay for it. I could run off to college or the North Pole, it didn't matter where, but she'd know where I was, and someday I was going to pay for it. But those few years in college, it all slipped behind me like a story I'd been written out of. They left me alone. Until our wedding. Then I knew that nothing had slipped behind me; I knew that the worst was *ahead* of me."

Slowly, he turned and faced me, and he waited. But my tongue was only a blur in my mouth, and there were no words to focus it.

"That day Vivian came to the hospital, I knew. I knew she was just beginning. Then I started hoping.

Hoping she would get some fatal disease or smash up her car. But she's invincible. She's proven that much."

"Why . . . why didn't you tell me at the beginning?"

"I never planned on a beginning. When I left Ridgeway, I had accepted the fact I could never marry anyone. I thought just to be away from them, to breathe my own air, would be enough and I could live alone. But it didn't turn out that way. In a way, it was a blessing not being attractive, because I never had to fight girls off. But there was a kind of girl who *was* attracted to me. Girls like Regina and Wanda Hoople, girls who hid in corners and thought the world was made for everyone else but them. And I found that somehow I made them happy. For a while that was enough. Until you came along."

He squinted and turned away as if the very memory were some harsh glare he couldn't endure.

"You came along like some cruel joke. At first, I thought . . . I even thought Vivian had hired you to lead me on and mock me. That's why I avoided you until I ran a check on you through the registrar's office and convinced myself there couldn't be any connection. But for months after that it was worse. I used to stand in front of the mirror and ask myself: 'What does she see in me? What can she love?' I decided a hundred times to tell you, but I always backed off. Then that day your parents came to my apartment, I saw who you came from and what you came from, and you held me up to them like a prize, and they took your word for it. I decided then I'd do anything to keep you and I *have* tried . . . to keep you." He turned and looked at Gloria. "But *you* knew something. Every time I was around you, I felt naked, and I asked myself: 'Why doesn't Irene see what Gloria sees?' You were a bigger threat than Vivian was. If Vivian ever tried to approach Irene, I had a story all set to counter hers. But you were a stranger and yet you sensed something; there was no way of fighting you. I had to leave that to chance."

"Frank, it wasn't that . . ." She didn't finish. I watched a tear drop from her jaw.

For a while none of us said anything. My only reaction was numbness. There was a hazy pattern forming in my head, but as it began to grow clearer, I drew back from it. Perhaps I was frightened of arriving at it by myself and needed it told to me.

"And what about Regina?" I said.

"They want her," he answered, almost whispering. "They're using Virgil. I'm almost sure he's one of them."

"But you're not completely sure."

Dear God, let the pattern get hazy again, let it disappear! Let every word he's said be a lie! Let him be insane, just let him be wrong!

"He's never lived in Fort Lauderdale. There's no record of his birth there, if that's his right name. There's no aunt living in that house, just him. Irene, it's not crazy—there's something in his face when he defies me with that smile: he looks at me the same way Vivian used to. His eyes, his teeth . . . From the beginning I suspected . . . Remember that day they were supposed to have gone to Detroit? I checked the mileage, remember? They'd only gone a hundred and fifty-five miles. Ridgeway is seventy-five miles one way, round trip is a hundred and fifty! Suppose he's been taking her up there already!"

The expressway ramp, the day she was skipping school with Virgil. They had come from the north, the same direction Vivian had come from the day we met at the restaurant. I had that picture in my mind, but I couldn't speak it. I could only speak against it.

"That couldn't be," I said. "He couldn't have taken her to Ridgeway. She would have known who Vivian was."

"Why would she? She's never seen her."

What about today, I thought, when Vivian picked her up at school? What about last night—wouldn't she have recognized Vivian's voice on the phone if Virgil *had* been taking her to Ridgeway? It didn't jell. It was preposterous, as fantastic as the story he had told me about Vivian.

"Frank, I've seen your birth certificate. I saw it when we got married. Vivian's name was not on it."

"No, it wasn't. There was no doctor. They didn't register the birth until later. Naturally they didn't put her name on it."

"Then you have no proof."

"No, Irene, I have no proof. I have no proof that I love you, either, or that I've never looked at Regina the way you think I have." He moved forward in his chair. "I know I'm a selfish man, Irene, and a coward. I lost my sister because I was selfish and cowardly, and I lied to you because I was selfish. I couldn't risk losing you *that way*. But now I don't want to lose you *or* Regina! You've got to tell me where she is!"

I couldn't answer. If all this was some elaborate lie just to get Regina back home . . .

"You'd better tell him," said Gloria.

She looked at me and there was pity in her eyes. Pity where there had once been blind adoration. I wanted that adoration back, I wanted to be the rock again, I wanted to return to Irene Rutledge and start all over again.

"Tell him."

"She's at Vivian's."

"Irene, you can't joke about this. This is ser—"

"She's at Vivian's. Vivian picked her up at school today."

His face registered nothing. Until he looked at Gloria.

"My God! How!"

"I sent her. Vivian called me yesterday and told me you were up there raving."

"But why did she call *you?*"

"Because she was afraid for Regina. She offered to take her. And she was concerned about *me.*" Defensive now. "That's something I haven't had the past six months—someone being concerned about me."

He leaped from the chair. "I have to go get her!"

"You're not going without me. I'll call her and tell her we're coming together."

"No; they'll hide her someplace. They'll keep her from me!"

"Don't call," said Gloria. "We'll just drive up there."

"No," said Frank. "I'll go alone. I don't want you to see them. I don't want them to dirty you with their looks."

"You're not going alone."

"We'll all go," said Gloria.

He started for the door.

"Frank, if you leave this house without me, I'll call Vivian the minute you're gone." He stopped. "I'm going to get some answers tonight all the way around. I'll be back down in a minute."

I started for the stairs.

"Irene, we can't wait!"

"I'll be down in a minute."

Upstairs, I pulled out the bottom drawer and found the gun. I emptied my purse on the bed and stuck the gun in it. Just as I was about to switch off the light, I looked at the philodendron I had bought for Frank back in college. I wanted to shoot it to pieces and reclaim myself.

As I started downstairs, I tried dismissing everything he had told me as a fantastic, convoluted lie. He himself had implied that he had betrayed his sister Regina

193

and, in a way, Wanda Hoople too. Perhaps the story he had told me was manufactured to betray Vivian. I almost grinned at the thought that maybe betrayals, like death, came in threes.

ON the expressway, I had to tell him three times to slow down. The third time I spoke sharply, and Gloria pressed my arm admonishingly. Sitting in the middle, I sensed a bent-forward rigidity in the two of them, as if their bodies were accelerating the engine. But I didn't want speed. I wanted the car to stop and time to stop so I could think. My mind was filled with fragments, all of them terrifying yet unconnected. My body was limp and there were intervals when I had to *think* to breathe. For reassurance I slipped my fingers under the flap of my purse. The dull, cold metal of the gun calmed me until we reached the sign that said RIDGEWAY CITY LIMIT.

We crept along the main street, the only moving car. With the exception of two bars, everything was closed. The shadowy mannequins in a dress shop window, a night light burning in a hardware store, the darkened movie-house marquee—they all gave the one message small towns give when they lock up for the night: You Belong at Home. We stopped at a light, a ridiculous ritual on this empty street, and I looked at Frank. His eyes were fixed on the pavement ahead and they would remain there all the way to Vivian's. The word "hometown" struck a sardonic note in my head.

Within two blocks, the main street became residential, then gave way to overgrown empty lots, a trailer court, and finally a woods. Frank turned right onto a gravel road. There were no streetlights and there was no moon. The countryside was a blur; the road was all that was left of the world.

Then the headlights went out.

"What are you doing?" The darkness made me whisper.

"I don't want them to see us," he answered.

"Is that it?" asked Gloria.

I turned to where she was looking and saw the lighted windows of the house, which was set back a good hundred yards from the road. The light was splintered by a profusion of trees, most of them pines and evergreens. Very slowly, the car moved forward and gradually I could make out the driveway. Frank pulled into it, then angled the car so we were blocking it. He took out a handkerchief.

"Hold this over the light when I get out. Gloria, you cover up the one by your door."

"I'm not holding anything," I said. "I'm going with you."

"Irene—"

"I said I'm going with you."

"I am too," said Gloria. "I'm not staying out here alone."

He hesitated, then told us to get out on his side. We started up the blacktop driveway.

"We could be shot," I said, "sneaking up like this."

"Quiet."

The closer we got, the more impressive the house became. It was a large two-story affair with cathedral peaks and redwood siding. On one side of it was a swimming pool and bathhouse, on the other a four-car garage. The garage doors were closed, with two cars parked in front of them, neither one Vivian's. The back end of another car protruded from the other side of the garage. At first it was a mere outline in the darkness, but as we neared the front door of the house, there was just enough light from the drape-covered window to indicate its color. The recognition went through me in a tremor. The car was Virgil's.

"I'll stand to the side of the door. You and Gloria ring."

"Why? What are you going to do?"

"I don't want them to see me first."

We were too close now for me to protest. I thought: Thank God he hasn't got the gun.

I looked through the little diamond-shaped window in the door as I rang the bell, but all I could see was a hallway that ran into darkness. There was a large archway and a glow of light on the left, undoubtedly the living room. I rang again. I turned to Frank and Gloria and said maybe everyone was in bed. When I turned back to the window, it was filled with a man's face, and I let out a gasp. The man was Leo.

He opened the door and looked at me quizzically, then managed a small smile.

"This is a surprise," he said, eying Gloria.

He stepped back, Gloria and I stepped forward, and then I saw his face darken as Frank came into view.

"Hello, Frank. We didn't expect you . . . in our home. Vivian will be surprised."

Frank pushed past him. Leo made a slight gesture to block him, then checked himself. Gloria and I followed Frank to the archway, which overlooked the sunken living room. Everyone's eyes were on the archway as we moved into it. The initial silence must have lasted only a few seconds, but it seemed painfully long as Vivian looked first at Frank, then at Gloria, and finally at me. Her face seemed to flicker like a jewel held up to the light: surprise gave way to amusement, amusement to satisfaction. Her head began to nod slowly, knowingly, and her mouth formed a faint, faraway smile. I looked away, at the room and the others in it. Vivian was seated in a white overstuffed chair next to the round metal fireplace. On the sofa opposite her were two women, a chubby brunette and a rather regal-looking redhead. In the two chairs flanking the sofa were an innocuous-looking man in his early fifties and Virgil. Virgil did not look at me; he was watching Frank. The only light in the room came from the logs burning in the fireplace and from a small lamp on the table near the window. The dark redwood paneling muted the light before reflecting it, softening the shadows in its glow. It was partly the lighting, partly the open spiral staircase which climbed to a second-floor hallway, and partly the three steps that separated the room from where we were standing, that gave me the feeling this was a room you *sank* into. There were no ornaments, no pictures on the walls, and all the furniture was large and modern and comfortable. It was a room designed for the body, not the eye: there was nothing to look at except the fire and each other. I looked at the fire first, then at Vivian.

"Hello, Irene," she said, still smiling. "I hadn't expected this from you. I hadn't expected this at all." She closed her eyes and opened them on Frank. "Did you threaten *her* too?" she said to him.

"How about a drink?" Leo said from behind. The rest of them had drinks. The man and the two women on the sofa looked as if they had had several. Even Vivian was glassy-eyed.

"Where is she?" said Frank.

"Just a minute," I said. "I have a few things to say and I don't want Regina to hear them."

"Then come in and sit down." Vivian motioned us to another sofa, against the wall nearest us but outside the center circle. Gloria and I sat on it, but Frank sat on the steps. "This is my brother Tom, his wife, Alice, and my brother Jack's wife, Helen."

We all nodded. "This is a friend of mine, Gloria Malone." I turned to Virgil. "What are you doing here?"

"I was waiting for Regina outside the school," he said sheepishly. "She said I could come."

"And where is she now?"

"Upstairs, sleeping," said Vivian.

"Have you ever been here before?" I asked Virgil.

"Here? Why would I have been here?"

"What about the day you were supposed to have gone to Detroit?"

"That's where we went."

"Frank says the mileage on your car showed you couldn't have gone that far."

"I told you before, he must have gotten the numbers wrong."

Leo freshened all their drinks at the bar near the staircase. He seemed genuinely amused by me.

"What about those days Regina skipped school with you? Where did you go?"

"We rode around. Out in the country."

Frank jumped up. "What days? When was she skipping school?"

"Sit down, Frank," I said.

"When did this happen? I want to know—"

"Sit down."

"You didn't tell me?" There was hurt and disbelief in his face, but something else too. Repugnance. It chilled me, but I was not about to be distracted. Nineteen years ago, I had let my emotions snuff out my reasoning and common sense. I had married him and accepted his conditions on faith. Now, as I faced him and Vivian together, there could be no emotions, only hard and brittle logic. Gloria was with me; once again, I could be the rock. If Frank was lying, she and I would take Regina without him.

"Vivian, Frank says there's an error on his birth certificate."

"What kind of error?"

"An error in the parenthood."

"Well"—she chuckled—"he wasn't adopted. I hope he hasn't gone so far as to deny us."

"Then you're saying there's no mistake on the certificate?"

"I don't know. I'd have to see it."

I blurted it out. "Frank says you're his mother!"

Her eyes slid from me to Frank. "You told her that?" He didn't answer. "Well, well, well. What else have you told her?"

"That Virgil is—belongs to you," I said.

"I see. Anything more?"

"That Regina was your daughter, that your father and he"—I nodded toward Tom—"took advantage of her repeatedly until she couldn't stand it anymore."

"And what do *you* think of such a story?"

"I want to know the truth!"

"Irene," said Frank, "let's get Regina and go. She's not going to tell you anything."

"What do you say, Vivian?"

"What do *I* say? I say how is it possible you've lived with a man for almost twenty years without knowing him? You've lived with him, slept with him, paid the bills with him, had a child by him, and now, all of a sudden, you want the 'truth.' You've seen him around Regina, you've seen her reaction to him. Don't you trust what you see, Irene? Don't you trust yourself?"

The question hung in front of me like a distorted mirror. *You are the rock! Answer her! Gloria, say something!*

"You don't trust yourself," she went on. "The day you asked me to meet you, I knew that." Frank turned to me, blinking incredulously. "That's right, Frank. She's already come to me for answers. And her questions told me more than I told her."

Wait a minute, I'm running this! You're supposed to be helping me!

Frank and Vivian and the rest of them stared at

me and nobody said a word. I watched Virgil get up and go to the bar for more ice and return to his chair. The movement was too casual for a first-time guest. And sitting there in the circle with the rest of them, he looked just a bit too snug.

"Did you tell me the truth, Vivian?" My voice sounded tiny. Her eyes seemed to diminish it.

"What would you like to hear? What would ease your mind the most? Which story, Frank's or mine, would be easier to adjust to?" She waited, but I couldn't answer. "Can't make up your mind?" She turned to Gloria. "What about you? I assumed you were brought along to help her. Two little peas from the same pod. You almost look alike."

Gloria spoke up, acidly. "You're a great one to be talking about peas and pods, with the *festoon* you've got here." She nodded in the direction of the group. "I happen to believe Frank."

Vivian smiled, "Well, then, Irene, there's your answer."

Frank stood up again. "That's enough. Where's Regina?"

Vivian brushed him off with a glance and looked at me. "Shall I let him go upstairs?"

"I—" I looked at Frank. His face was flushed, his eyes wild. He took a few steps across the living room in the direction of the spiral staircase. Immediately, Leo and Tom and Virgil stood up.

"You stay put," Vivian snapped at Frank. "This is my house and Regina is here with Irene's sanction. It's up to her whether or not you'll go up there."

There it was, there was the proof. She said it was up to me. They weren't holding Regina, there was no design on her, she would be delivered to me when I said so. It was up to me.

"Well?" said Vivian. "Shall I send him up?"

I couldn't look at Frank. I couldn't look at any of them. "No, I . . . no."

"Irene, for God's sake," Gloria whispered.

For God's sake, what? Nineteen years ago you saw something wrong. And you haven't seen him when he's around her! You haven't seen him when he's crazed! I can't stand any more of it and if he has lied to me—

Frank made a forward lunge. Tom rushed him with his arms up while Leo moved in from the side. The three of them toppled the chair as they fell to the floor. Virgil picked up a heavy glass ashtray and held it in front of him like a tambourine.

"Put that down!" said Vivian.

They grappled on the floor behind the sofa the women were sitting on. The women didn't move. I jumped up and ran to the sofa. Leo had Frank pinned down, with his knee in Frank's back, while Tom twisted Frank's arm.

"Don't hurt him!" I screamed. "Don't hurt him!"

"They're not going to hurt him," said Vivian. *"You've* already done that quite sufficiently." She got up and walked over to Frank. She planted her feet near his head and looked down at him. When she spoke, her voice was soft and caressing. "You don't have to struggle anymore, Frank. I'm sorry it had to be this way, but you had to be shown. I told you once she would never understand. Her kind can't. You can see Regina in a few minutes, but I have something to say first. Tom and Leo will let you go if you behave yourself. Will you promise?"

"Let me go." His voice was deep and miserable.

"Promise me first. I told you you can see Regina soon. I always keep my word. You know that."

"Wait," I said. "What are you doing?"

"You keep quiet," she answered, still looking at Frank. "Do you promise?"

"Yes," he gasped.

The men came up off him. For a minute he didn't move. Then he pulled up onto his elbows, his knees, finally his feet, and dragged himself past Vivian and me to the archway steps.

"Sit down," Vivian said to me. "Over there next to your friend."

Gloria had been standing during the fracas. Now she was glowering at Vivian and not about to sit. "Irene, let's get out of here and call the police."

"You're not as smart as you look," said Vivian. "There's no need for the police. What would you tell them? You just sit down until I'm finished talking."

I sat, pulling Gloria down with me. I picked up my purse and put it back in my lap. Vivian stared at the two of us, grinning.

"You snot-nosed middle-class bitches kill me," she said. "You think the police can take care of your lives just because you pay your taxes. Virgil, get me a drink."

He took her glass to the bar. He hadn't asked what she was drinking. He knew. I saw the expressway ramp before me, his car coming down it, Regina inside. My lungs shriveled.

"I don't want to hear anything," I whispered. "I want Regina. I want her now."

"You'll get Regina, but first you'll hear me." She sipped on the drink Virgil gave her, hesitated, then nodded approvingly. "Five minutes ago, you wanted the truth, so now you're going to get it. First, I had to see how far you'd go, and you went far enough. Didn't she, Frank?"

He was sitting on the steps with his head in his arms. He did not look up or answer.

"I had your number a long time ago," she said, "that night before your wedding. I could tell you had your whole life set up like some goddam dance card. The first step was the big wedding, the big cake, the big degree from college sticking out all over your big smile. And you were big on manners too. You were so anxious to please, even when you saw how Frank felt about me. And later, when I came to see Regina when your friend here was with you—" Frank's head snapped up and he looked at me with huge eyes that made me turn away. Vivian smiled at him. "That's right, Frank, you didn't know about that. Even back then, she was riding the fence." She turned to me. "The truth is I am Frank's mother. That night before your wedding I told him to tell you. And I told him again that day at the hospital when you took Regina home. But he's always been stubborn and now he's paying for it."

"You don't need to say anything more." My stomach was filling up with disgust for both her and myself.

"Yes, I do, for your own benefit, so you'll know what *not* to do when you get Regina back. You see, you're going to have her for a very short time and I don't want you tampering with her. She's made her choice, the choice Frank should have made a long time ago. Instead, he chose to knock his head against a wall." She turned to Frank. "And it hasn't been worth it, has it, Frank? She doesn't understand you, she never could understand you. You're a different breed; it's as simple as that. No matter how hard you try, no matter how many degrees you get, you're still my son. You're still one of us."

"I'm going to be sick," I mumbled. Gloria slipped her arm around my shoulders.

"*You're* going to be sick? Well, go right ahead, because now you'll know how I felt watching you and your little family at that wedding party dinner. You'll know how you turned my stomach that night you let me in to see Regina and then again when we met at the restaurant. I know your kind, Irene. I grew up watching them. So smug in their position, so complacent with their dusted and simonized skeletons tucked away in their closets, so quick to point their fingers at someone else's misfortunes. Stupidly, I was jealous of them until my father taught me not to be.

He taught me they weren't the only army in the world; we could make our own. And we have, haven't we?"

"Yes, we have," said the redhead, and the brunette nodded.

"It's sick, it's so sick," I muttered.

"Sick, is it? What would you know about it? When I was fifteen, three boys raped me behind a church. They were *your* kind and I was just a Mattison, so you can guess who would be believed and who wouldn't. I told my mother and father. My mother looked down her nose at me and prayed at the same time. But my father did something about it. He took me into his bed and showed me it didn't have to be that way. And my brothers showed me too."

"Please, no more." I slumped against Gloria.

"Too indelicate for you? Let me tell you something. This family has something you and Frank never had and never will have. There are no secrets between us. We take care of our own, we protect each other."

"The way you protected your daughter?"

"Yes," she snapped. "I protected her well until Frank polluted her mind with his filthy talk and drove her crazy. She was loved. My father loved her, Jack and Tom loved her, I loved her. How do you think the rest of the world would have treated her? I'll tell you how —they would have turned her over to social services and stuck her in a home run by the state. All my mother could do was pray for her." She grinned. "Those who can't do, teach—or pray. I don't teach or pray. I run a business and we all share in it. No one in this family has to go *outside* to make a living. And we all make a very good living. I've taken care of that." She took a long swallow of her drink.

"Who does he belong to?" I asked, pointing at Virgil.

"I gave birth to him," said the brunette, "but he belongs to all of us."

"If your husband is Jack, that makes Virgil Regina's cousin," I said.

"Who her husband is has nothing to do with it," said Vivian.

"What do you mean?"

"Virgil *might* be Jack's. Or Tom's. Or even Leo's."

"Oh, Christ!" Gloria whispered.

"There's no ownership in this family," said Vivian.

"What do you call it, then?" I said. "The way you've got them all under your thumb?"

"No one's under anyone's thumb. If anyone wants to leave, they're perfectly free to do it."

"And then a few years later you go after their children."

"Only in Frank's case. He *owes* me something. He took my daughter away and he took himself away. If he'd stayed, I could have forgiven him for what he did to Regina. Or maybe if I'd had another child. But I couldn't. Cancer took care of that. So my only contribution to this family is my granddaughter, and I want her."

"You'll never get her," I said.

"You're wrong, Irene. We already have her. And you have no idea how easy it was. I was very skeptical when Virgil first brought her here last October. I thought I would have a losing battle on my hands, but as it turned out, Regina was very anxious to join us after she got to know us."

"You're lying."

"Regina is in love with Virgil. And Regina is pregnant."

Frank let out a sharp groan. I slipped my fingers under the flap of my purse.

"I think you'd better get Regina now," I said.

"I hope you're prepared for this."

"Just get her."

Vivian nodded at Virgil. He stood and went up the spiral staircase. Everyone was silent, and I thought:

It'll all be over in a few minutes. We'll go away from here and never talk about it again. Regina will go to school tomorrow, I'll go to work, Gloria can fly back to L.A.

But these thoughts died with the next sound. Regina's laugh, shrill and empty, came from upstairs. I had heard it before, the night she and Virgil returned from their supposed trip to Detroit. I had heard it when she talked on the telephone to Virgil. It was filled with mockery and arrogance, perfectly matched now with Vivian's face.

"You know, don't you, that you can be prosecuted for what you've done."

Vivian chuckled. "There you go with the police again. This is a private family matter, even though you've dragged your Siamese twin here into it."

"I'll make it public if I have to."

"Irene, please," Frank moaned. "Don't talk to her."

"I'll drag you into court and show what you've done."

"And what have I done?"

"You abducted her, you and that . . . offspring."

"You're being silly. You *sent* Regina here. To get her away from her father. Even Miss McPhee knows that."

"Miss McPhee? What has she got to do with this?"

"Miss McPhee has been quite concerned about Regina's welfare. She's taken a personal interest. And I'm sure she'll take an even greater interest when she finds out Regina is pregnant."

"What are you talking about?"

"I'm talking about a little do-good twit who I'm sure resembles you. You're a teacher. How would you react if one of your students told you her father had . . . funny ideas? Miss McPhee had quite a reaction."

"No," Frank was whispering, shaking his head. "No, you didn't. You couldn't do that."

"*I* haven't done anything. I've never seen the woman. But Regina's been very close to her."

"What are you getting at?" I said.

"You want it straight and simple? Here it is. Regina has chosen to come to us. When the time comes, she wants to have her baby here. You're not to stand in her way. If you do, you'll get your police and your courtroom and your public testimony, only I'm afraid you and Frank will be on the receiving end. Just a few words to Miss McPhee about the *possible* paternity of the baby, a few tears from Regina. That should set a few wheels in motion."

"For God's sake," I screamed, "he's your son! Are you going to sit there and tell me you would push your own filth off onto him?"

"Call it whatever you like. Now aren't you suddenly the loving and protective wife, once you're sure of your facts!" She leaned forward in the chair, her eyes slitted. "He was my son and then he left and then you took him. I'm just taking back part of my own. We'll keep Regina. You and Frank have each other, for whatever *that's* worth now."

Another shrill laugh from above, approaching the stairs. I looked up and saw Virgil descend. Then came Regina, wearing a pink satin robe. Behind her was a tall man with salt-and-pepper hair. He held her hand all the way down the steps. I turned and looked at Frank. He was leaning forward, his mouth open and his eyes frozen.

"Jack," he whispered. His other brother.

Jack smiled and rested his arms on Regina's shoulders so that his long fingers dangled near her breasts. His face was flushed, Regina's hair snarled and sweat-soaked. For some time, no one spoke. Then Jack gathered Regina's hair in his hands, twisted it into a tail, and laid it over her shoulder. He moved to the bar for a drink. Regina sat down on the arm of Virgil's chair.

"Have you told them everything?" she said to Vivian.

"Yes."

"Regina, don't," said Frank, his voice quivering. He put out his hands. "Come to me and we'll take you home." She looked at him blandly. "We'll go home and forget all about this."

"We're not forgetting about anything," she said. "I'm going to have a baby."

"We'll take care of that. We'll get a good doctor. We'll all go away if you want to."

I listened to him beg, and I remembered my thoughts about betrayals earlier that night. The betrayals here *had* come in threes. He had been betrayed by his mother, his daughter—and his wife.

"We can go anywhere you want. We can go to California. You can rest on the beach. We'll all feel better in the sun."

Regina's eyes shifted to Gloria and she gave her a once-over smirk.

"And later you can go away to school. It'll be a new start. We'll all start over again."

"I've already made a start."

"No, honey, they've tricked you. It's not what you think it is."

"No one's tricked me," she said flatly, shaking the hair from her shoulders. "You're just jealous."

"No, Regina, that's not—" His voice broke.

My fingers moved farther under the flap of my purse. "Don't you talk to your father that way." I was crying and hating myself for it. I wanted my rage to be firm and awesome. *Where was the rock?*

"You don't have to stay," she said.

"Go get dressed. You're coming home."

She looked questioningly at Vivian. Vivian nodded and said, "For the time being."

Regina stood up and started for the staircase. She grinned at Jack.

"You weren't raised this way!" I said, more to Jack than to her. "There's no *reason* . . ."

She stopped and turned. She gave me a long, leveling look, not like a defiant daughter, but like one woman assessing another.

"You should be happy," she said. "Now you can have him all to yourself. That's what you've always wanted, anyway. Now I'm out of the way."

"That is not true and you know it!"

"Yes, it is. It's just the way you are."

"The way I am? And what is that, Regina?"

"You've always gotten whatever you wanted. You're pretty and you're selfish——"

"Regina, they can't make you beautiful! That's what it comes down to, isn't it? Like the time you were sick when you were little, and you wanted to punish people for something that couldn't be helped. That's what you're doing now—punishing us."

"If that's what you want to think."

"Do you know what you're doing to your father! You did all this behind our backs, you lied to me! You made me think——"

"You thought what you wanted to think. That's not my fault. Besides, if you found out, you would have stopped me. Now you can't. You've always gotten what you wanted; now I'm going to get what I want."

"Is *this* what you want? To be shuttled around from one to the other, to be used like—like an appliance!"

"I like it here," she declared. "We're all the same here. No one's any better than anyone else. You could never stand that. You have to be superior. You and *her*." She sneered at Gloria.

Gloria snatched the bait. "What you've just shown, Regina, is that she *is* superior to you." She struck the spot. Regina made a slight movement forward before checking herself. "And I'll tell you something else. It's easy to please a crowd. But try it with one person; it takes guts and it takes work."

"Save your sermons," she said, and went up the stairs.

Through my tears, Vivian was a smiling blur slowly bending forward in her chair. "I'm glad you came tonight after all. Better than putting it off until the end of the week. Who knows"—she chuckled—"you might have had Frank locked up by then. That would have been a little messy. I'd better go help her get her things together."

"You can't have her," I whispered. My fingers pushed forward under the flap until they found the metal.

"She hasn't decided whether she wants to finish out the semester at school. If she does, she'll stay with you until June. When the warm weather comes, she can wear those Indian tops that hide everything."

"I won't let you." *I won't let you do this to Frank.* I gripped the handle and dragged it toward me.

"If she decides to quit, she can come here immediately. I've already gotten her a doctor, so that's taken care of. That do-gooder Miss McPhee might try to poke her nose into this, but I think Regina can handle her. I'm sure the two of *you* will behave yourselves. You should know by now I don't make idle threats."

She started up from the chair, smiling. Smiling. She was still smiling when she saw the gun. The smile stayed, giving a little twitch with each shot. Half sitting, half standing, she seemed to be waiting for me to finish. I dropped the gun even before she dropped into the chair.

No one moved, perhaps because she was still smiling. Even with the low gurgling in her throat and the languid closing of her eyes, she smiled, drawing my breath away. The room turned inside out and there were only shadows. One of the shadows moved immediately to Vivian, bent over her, mumbled something to the other shadows, and then came to me. It was Frank. His arm went around me, and Gloria took my hand. Two figures appeared on the staircase. There was a scream, and the room went right again.

"You crazy bitch! You killed her! You killed her!" Regina broke away from Virgil and started toward me. "You ruined everything—you always ruin everything! You killed her, you bitch!"

Frank jumped up and held her away from me. She saw the gun at my feet and began kicking at Frank in her effort to get to it. My one hand stayed with Gloria while the other went forward to retrieve the gun. Gloria called my name, made a move for my other hand, but I slid away and held my arm up in warning.

I leveled the gun on Regina.

"Don't come near me," I said. "Don't touch me or so help me I'll put a bullet in that machine that's supposed to be your heart." She drew back. When the momentary shock slid from her eyes, a grin slid into her face. "So help me."

"You'd really like to, wouldn't you?"

"Right this minute, yes, I would like to very much. Just don't *touch* me. I don't ever want you to touch me again."

"Who in hell do you think you are!"

"I know who I am, Regina." *Don't cry, stop crying.* "And *what* I am is not superior at all if you're my daughter. Now get away from me and stay away."

She yanked herself free from Frank and joined the huddle surrounding Vivian. Leo came out of that huddle. His lips were white, his face nearly purple. He started toward me.

"You stay away from me too," I said. "I want everybody to stay away from me."

Jack grabbed Leo's arm and pulled him back into the huddle. Frank sat down next to me and stroked my arm.

"Give me the gun, Irene. I won't let any of them near you."

I gave it to him and collapsed against his chest. Gloria stroked my hair.

"I love you, Frank, I do love you."

"Shhhh. I know. I'm here."

I didn't wake up until the police arrived. I don't know exactly how much time elapsed, but it had been time enough for Regina and Virgil to escape. After I had fainted, Frank had carried me up to one of the bedrooms. Leaving it, with one of the policemen gripping my arm, I was certain that it was Regina I had shot. Not until I got downstairs and saw Vivian smiling in the chair did I remember what had happened. Everyone was gathered in the living room. The two women were crying softly, sitting in their original places on the sofa. I leaned against the bar, with Frank and Gloria on either side of me.

Everyone, including the police, seemed to be waiting for something. Something turned out to be *some-one*. The chief or the captain or whatever they call themselves arrived and took in the situation with one officious glance. He looked at Vivian dispassionately, then at me the same way. One policeman began to explain to him and finished with a long sigh of familiarity before he added, "Some family reunion, eh?"

ONLY two of the bullets had struck Vivian. The other two were found in the arm and the leg of the white chair. This, my lawyer told me, might prove beneficial to my plea of temporary insanity, but I can't remember the reason he gave. I can't even recall the trial in any sequential fashion. The wheels of justice move through verbal muck, advancing one day and sticking the next, while the people in charge argue over whether to push or pull. And my lawyer, Mr. Bates, informed me in no uncertain terms that my demeanor in the courtroom was adding extra weight to his load:

"Mrs. Mattison, I do appreciate the fact you are level-headed and cooperate with the court, but for credibility's sake your image in there has to coincide with the circumstances of our case. The jurors look more concerned than you do, and that is never a good sign. Your daughter's disappearance and her refusal to surface is extremely damaging. And I don't have to tell you what McPhee's testimony is doing for the prosecution. You've got to show some kind of reaction to things that are said, some *expression*. Otherwise, it's going to be uphill all the way to the end."

It was uphill until very nearly the end. Leo, Jack, Tom, the two wives, two of Frank's other brothers—all of them denied Vivian was Frank's mother. Frank, the prosecution contended, had manufactured the lie to delude me, he had defiled his retarded sister and driven her to suicide, and he had taken advantage of his daughter as well—hence her fear to show herself. Gloria's account of Vivian's admission and Regina's conversion pleased Mr. Bates: her frustration and rage coming out in tears (something *I* was incapable of all through the trial), she gave a vivid picture of Vivian's smug assurance and contempt. Although it made colorful copy in the papers, it ultimately would carry very little weight with the jury, for the simple reason that Gloria was outnumbered. One thing I had in my favor —and a very small thing, Mr. Bates assured me—was that Leo had waited almost an hour before calling the police, time enough for Regina and Virgil to disappear. But it was Frank's car they had taken and Frank could not figure out how they had got his keys. The car was found abandoned fifty miles south of Ridgeway.

Considering the flimsiness of our case, Frank and Mr. Bates proposed a new tactic: "Your husband and I have decided it would be best if he went along with the prosecution's accusations. They've already set it up for us; all he has to do is confess he purposely misled you. You'll have a chance that way, a very good chance." Frank squeezed my hand.

"No."

Mr. Bates leaned forward. "Let me put it to you this way: it's your *only* chance."

"He's not bowing to them and neither am I. I did it once; I won't do it again."

"Irene," said Frank, "if this benefits the case, what does it matter how we bend?"

"Because it's time to break it with them. They've held on to you all these years with the truth. I won't let them hold on now with a lie."

They left, but Mr. Bates soon returned alone. He sat facing me, but he watched the pen he was twirling between his fingers. He spoke deliberately.

"History is full of martyrs who died for the truth. I have my own theory that most of them didn't happen upon a cause. They went out looking for one, one they knew could fulfill their fame-in-death wish."

"I didn't go out looking for a cause."

"No, but when you found one, you took a gun to it. All right, you made a righteous accomplishment. Now you are being offered the opportunity for a second accomplishment—getting the verdict we want. And yet you turn down that opportunity."

"I won't buy a verdict with Frank's name."

"So you'll risk a prison term and a long separation from him? Mrs. Mattison, your husband needs you more than he needs his name. You committed murder for your daughter, but you will not bend for your husband."

"I did not commit murder for my daughter. I knew she was already lost to us before I fired that gun. I killed that woman for myself. I've had plenty of time to think, Mr. Bates, and I've thought about my motive. You talk about righteousness. My killing Vivian was not done out of righteousness. It was done out of humiliation and shame. Let me tell you something. I married a decent man. His decency, his integrity, his love for me, are as tangible as that pen you're playing with. For nineteen years, I had daily proof of them. But when he ran up against this—this plot, I chose to doubt him, to wipe out years of evidence with one single suspicion. I chose to believe Regina even after I caught her lying to me about school and I chose to believe Vivian, a perfect stranger, because she flattered me with some cheap sympathy. And so did I love him any better than his daughter and his mother did? Vivian knew I didn't; she told me so that night. And I shot her for it." I was proceeding calmly, rationally, and yet my throat tightened and the tears started down my face. "I'm no martyr. Far from it. I turned Regina over to his family and in a way I turned myself over to them too."

"You're distorting the situation. You seem to forget he could have told you the truth years ago."

"I haven't forgotten that. But with another woman he might have told the truth. Another woman might have made him feel safe." I took the pen he was playing with and held it tight to steady myself. "He spent all those years loving and protecting his daughter the best way he knew how. Maybe he did it wrong, but he did it single-handedly. But the failure isn't all his. It's mine too. And Regina's. *Mostly* Regina's—I can't help but believe that. I'm not going to offer him up with a lie to make Regina and myself look good. We'll just have to continue as we have been and hope."

"Then hope for a miracle."

Mr. Bates did his best to create a miracle. Our next witness was the reporter who had photographed me scrubbing the graffiti off the front of the school. It seemed most of the jurors were impressed with this, but some of them changed their expressions when the prosecution pointed out that this gesture of mine had been "extreme and reactionary."

We were nearing the end. When Frank would come to see me, he would don a smile and reaffirm his faith in the jury. But there was always doubt in his eyes when his words ran out. Invariably, I turned the conversation to the weather and world news. We never mentioned Regina.

I rehearsed facing the verdict, although I said nothing to Mr. Bates. My resignation seemed almost sacrilegious next to his perseverance. He was still stinging from my refusal to go along with his and Frank's plan, but at the same time this fed his determination to win. There was a growing glint in his eye whenever he turned that pen round and round between his hands.

It was a Monday morning when I entered the courtroom and saw the pen not in his hands, its customary place, but stuck squarely in his pocket. He gripped my arm and whispered in my ear.

"We may have ourselves a *deus ex machina*."

"What do you mean?"

"I have one more witness. Keep your fingers crossed."

"Who is it?"

"No one you know. Someone's volunteered to come forward. This might make all the difference."

After the opening rituals, the judge called upon Mr. Bates. "You wish to call another witness?"

"Yes, Your Honor. I call Wanda Lowell to the stand."

PECK High had its share of poor kids, mostly black and Mexican, but the relaxation of the dress code and the adoption of denim as the national uniform of youth had successfully eliminated the conspicuousness of poverty. Wanda Lowell was conspicuously poor. Her face was gaunt and sallow, her hair thin and lusterless. Her shoulders rounded to make a hollow of her chest, while her hipbones jutted forward like two tiny buttresses. The yellow and white in her dress cruelly accentuated her colorless appearance; the striped material did not match up at the seams. It was painfully apparent this woman had no time for, or perhaps no conception of, even modest vanity. I looked at her ankles, and remembering Frank's story, I half expected to see socks sliding down them into her shoes. Of course, she didn't wear socks. She wore white heels, dulled and cracked by several layers of liquid polish.

She was sworn in and gave the court her maiden name, place of residence, and former relationship to Frank. Mr. Bates began his questioning, and several of the jury leaned forward in their seats.

"Mrs. Lowell, will you please tell the court how you came to be here today?"

"I been reading about this in the paper and I seen the lies Mr. Mattison's brothers were telling about—"

"Objection!"

"Your Honor, Mrs. Lowell's testimony will clarify her accusation."

"Objection overruled. Proceed."

"Well, that's what they were," said Wanda Lowell. "It looked like no one knew Mr. Mattison's side of the story except me, so that's why I decided to speak up."

"Will you tell the court why you waited so long?"

"My husband didn't want me to get mixed up in it. I had pneumonia in January and lost three weeks at work. And I don't get paid for today, either."

Mr. Bates guided her through an explanation of how she had known Frank from the third grade on. She made it clear—and Mr. Bates underscored the fact—that the two of them had never been romantically involved.

"And you never went out with him on a date? You never had a romance with him?"

"He didn't have any money for dates. He never went out with anyone. He was too busy looking after his sister. She was retarded."

Several of the jury sat up and leaned forward.

"Now tell us about the evening you visited the Mattison house."

"It wasn't visiting; no one saw me. It was in the winter, around Christmas time. A couple of days before, I asked him to go to a school dance, the kind where the girls are supposed to ask the boys. I asked him in front of his friends and it embarrassed him. He didn't have any money to go to a dance. I wanted to tell him I was sorry, but in school there were always too many people around. I knew him and his sister slept in this shack behind their house and I was going home after a baby-sitting job and their place was on the way so I figured I could talk to him alone. I took the shortcut through a field so I wouldn't have to go past the house. Well, I got nervous thinking he might get mad at me for coming around at night. I stood behind the shack awhile, trying to make up my mind. Then someone opened the back door of the house and I heard voices coming. I was scared if I ran they'd see me, so I stayed where I was. I heard them pound on the door and Regina started crying inside."

"And who was it pounding on the door?"

"I couldn't see but I could hear them. Two young men and a woman. They broke the door open and—"

"They *broke* it open? Something was blocking it?"

"I heard something crack and then something heavy fell on the floor. They got the door open and there was this kind of fight inside. Somebody got knocked against the wall."

"Were you able to look through a window?"

"There wasn't no windows."

"This shack that Mr. Mattison and his sister slept in had *no* windows at all?"

"That's right."

"I see. Go on, please."

"I looked for a window. I come around to the one side, and then around the back to the other side, and there wasn't a window. I was standing just around the corner from the front when Regina and the woman come out of the shack. Regina kept saying she didn't want to go in the house, but the woman said it's all right, he loves you."

"Who was the woman?"

"Vivian Mattison."

"When she said 'he loves you,' did she say who the man was?"

"No. She just took Regina in the house and closed the door."

"What about the two men? What were they doing while Vivian and Regina were in the house?"

"They stayed in the shack. They must have been holding Mr. Mattison down, because he kept begging them to let him go. Then Vivian come out of the house and the two men went in. She went in the shack and there was some talking, but it was real low and I couldn't make out what they were saying. I moved around the corner close to the door and then all of a sudden it opened. I sort of squeezed myself up against the wall because if I moved the snow would crunch. Then I heard Mr. Mattison tell her he hated her and the rest of them and he was going to get the cops after them. She was standing in the door and she laughed and she said, 'You wouldn't call the cops on your mother, would you?' and he said she was a liar. She said the cops would haul him away to the nut house if he ever opened his mouth."

"And then what happened?"

"She went back in the house. She didn't even close the door to the shack. He had to do it."

"Did you go into the shack?"

"No. I ran home. I cut back through the woods and I fell on a stick. It stuck right in my leg. I still got the scar." She pointed to a spot below her right knee.

"Did you ever mention this incident to Mr. Mattison?"

"No."

"Why not?"

"It would've shamed him. That kind of thing you don't want no one to know."

"How soon after this December night did Regina Mattison kill herself?"

"Couple of months. April, I think."

"April ninth, to be exact. Did you ever return to the shack?"

"No. I never went near that house again."

"Did you have any contact with Mr. Mattison after he left Ridgeway?"

"No."

"Thank you, Mrs. Lowell." He turned to the prosecution. "Your witness."

Naturally, the prosecution did its best to discredit Wanda Lowell's testimony. How, after all these years, could she recall exact words, exact dialogue? What was her *real* interest in the defendant's husband? Was she secretly in love with him? Wanda grew indignant at the last question and told her questioner she was a married woman and a mother and she hadn't come here to be insulted. I watched the jury. They were impressed.

The wrap-up came on a day of record-breaking temperatures. Collars wilted, faces drooped, magazines and newspapers were used as fans. Among the jury I sensed a definite anxiousness for the whole thing to be over with. For some of them, what had begun as a privileged adventure had now degenerated into a ritual of tedium. In his summary, my lawyer flattered them, caressed and cooled .them with his mellifluous voice.

"Ladies and gentlemen, you have had the most difficult task any jury can have. You have sat through a trial which has proceeded mostly on hearsay. Yet a few facts have been produced which cannot be overlooked. One, Irene Mattison has devoted fifteen years to teaching children. She has been sensitive to their needs as well as society's needs. It was a child's welfare, her own daughter's, that drove her to murder. It was outrage over an unspeakable depravity that compelled her to pick up a gun and use it. It was Vivian Snell's clever deceit and vengeful disregard for a child's life that overruled the defendant's rational powers. And if we look closely, what other course of action was open to her?"

Not once did he turn his back on them. Instead, he leaned forward, seeking out one pair of eyes after another until he had enlisted them all. He orated but it did not sound like an oration. His tone suggested he was telling them something they already knew.

"And now we come to the question of why the defendant's daughter has failed to appear in her mother's behalf. We can't presume to know all of her motives. Regina Mattison is seventeen years old. Some of you may consider her a child, just as her mother did when it came time to protect her. But child or adult, she is a daughter who has dealt the cruelest blow to her parents—abandonment in time of need. And yet she betrayed her parents long before this. That betrayal began after the first trip she took with Virgil Evans to Vivian Snell's house. We would all like a ready answer as to why this girl joined this circle, this cult of people, so completely and willingly. Of course, the obvious temptation is to lay the guilt at her parents' doorstep. But before we succumb to that temptation, let us consider the vast number of parents, many of them good parents, who have lost their chil-

dren to various cults whose values are alien to those
they raised their children with. And let us consider
ourselves, let us consider how often all of us, as children, disappointed our parents in our pursuits. Quite
simply, there was something inside Regina Mattison
that made this group attractive to her, just as there was
something in her mother that made them repulsive.
When Irene Mattison pulled that trigger, she was doing the same thing she did the day she took a steel
brush to the wall of her school. She was wiping out a
plague that . . ."

And on he went until I began to cringe. I knew
what he was doing was necessary, but part of me
wanted to stand up and shout the real reason Vivian
was dead.

I felt more comfortable during the prosecution's
summary, simply because it put me on the silent defensive. Jack Rand, the principal of Peck, had cooperated
with the prosecution. Although he described me as
a "competent" teacher, he maintained I was "er-
ratic" outside the classroom and stated outright that I
had a contempt for authority. On the other hand, Mrs.
Lorimer, our old baby-sitter, worked grudgingly with
the prosecution once she found she was in over her
head. They extracted from her an account of my
terrible temper and my eagerness to return to work
while Regina was still sick. They referred to this
testimony as often as possible, and I would catch Mrs.
Lorimer giving me long, apologetic stares. But of
course the prosecution depended most heavily upon
Miss McPhee.

"You have heard from Mr. Rand how on numerous
occasions Mrs. Mattison had defied him and sought
subtle ways for revenge. You have heard from Mrs.
Lorimer how the defendant's temper on one occasion
made a dramatic snap when a minor situation slipped
out of her control. And most importantly, Miss McPhee
has testified how the defendant discouraged the

counselor-student relationship with her daughter." He paused and stepped backward to the corner of the jury box and pointed at me. "What you see before you is a woman who will do anything to control those around her. When she feels that control threatened, she becomes vindictive. We cannot say for sure what went on in the Mattison household, but it was something that drove Regina Mattison first to Miss McPhee and then to her father's family. There was something in that household that made Irene Mattison almost a recluse. She has had a strangely limited life. Acquaintances, but no close friends except for Mrs. Malone, who lives two thousand miles away. I submit that the defendant *chose* this excessive solitude to keep her own violent proclivities in check. She saw Miss McPhee as an intruder and encouraged her daughter to stay away from her. Vivian Snell was the second intruder, and an undeniable danger because she was a concerned relative and knew her brother only too well. That is why the defendant took a gun with her the night of the murder. Her rational abilities were very much intact. She knew that only violence could rid her of this opponent. She knew she was likely to come out the loser if there was a legal battle over her daughter. The murder of Vivian Snell was calculated. And now the defendant is calculating your sympathy. She is standing on the name of motherhood. But I ask you, where is her *daughter?*"

The jury went out. I lay in bed in my cell and smoked cigarettes during the six hours it took them to deliberate. I was prepared for defeat, for during those six hours, it wasn't Mr. Bates's summary I kept hearing. It was the prosecution's. During the few minutes I did manage to fall asleep, I dreamed of Vivian. We were holding hands, and although she had her own hair, she had my face, and the jury knew it.

Mr. Bates was holding his pen in his hand when we reconvened in the courtroom. The room was filled, the way it had been during the opening days of the trial. The jury filed into the box. Every one of them looked tired and empty; for the first time, it occurred to me to feel sorry for them.

I stood up to face them.

"We find the defendant not guilty by cause of temporary insanity."

I stood numb amid the cheering and booing until the gavel struck and Mr. Bates gently pulled me down into my seat. A sigh whistled through his teeth. "Your miracle came through. You'd better put Wanda Lowell on your Christmas card list."

WE send our Christmas cards now—the few we do send—from Long Beach. They are plain white laminated cards with "Season's Greetings" printed in red block letters. I find their simplicity soothing, and I have toned down my formerly flamboyant signature to match. Simplicity is the banner we live under; not even the holiday hysteria will set it aflutter. We have retired as far as possible from the past and past habits. Now time is there to be spent, not saved, and I've turned the burden of spending it into a luxury. It takes forty minutes to walk directly from our house to the Safeway supermarket where I work as a cashier, but I allow myself an extra twenty minutes to walk out of my way, to stop and admire a garden or to face the ocean and smoke a cigarette. I find nothing mystical about the ocean. Its surf is just another practical reminder that life is a series of simple repetitions: keep the wind down and storms at abeyance and your surf will continue with its regular rhythm. Of course, there's always the invisible, sometimes treacherous undercurrent. I feel that undercurrent now and then, unexpectedly, whenever I am taken unawares by a tall girl whose face momentarily resembles Regina's. Then the resemblance recedes, the undercurrent subsides, and the safe and soothing rhythm returns. . . .

Endings spawn beginnings, and so quite naturally the conclusion of the trial nudged us into our present routine, our change of place. The board of education dismissed me "with regret" and with the florid jargon bureaucrats use when only half committed to expediency. Public opinion, it seems, did not coincide with the jury's verdict. But the university made no move against Frank. It wasn't necessary. The number of girls who signed up for his classes plummeted to five, three of whom thought they would like to brush bodies with depravity and made advances to him. A number of the boys smirked their way through the term and asked pointed questions about the practice of incest among tribal cultures. Frank gave notice for a January departure, and we put the house up for sale. The agent warned us not to get our hopes up: our notoriety would attract a lot of curiosity-seekers not at all interested in buying a house, and once a buyer could be found, he would be certain to feel an advantage in the bargaining. For our own peace of mind, we were asked not to be in the house at all when it was being shown.

As it turned out, we sold it at a fairly small loss and went to stay with my parents for a month. My mother was valiantly cheerful and supportive and made a dress for me and a sweater for Frank. Her smiling intentions, however, were outweighed by my father, who looked as if *he* were on trial. His eyes seemed larger, liquefied, unable to focus—not on what he saw but on something within him. He was quiet most of the time, but it was a restrained silence. It broke the night he got drunk and cried in front of me at the kitchen table. He said I should never have married Frank, he had a feeling from the beginning something was wrong, it was Frank's fault the way Regina turned out, and my life was ruined, our marriage now only a charade. I didn't bother defending Frank against the insult, because I knew it was the only handle available to my father for expressing his long-term disappointment in *me*. And although I decided there and then it was time for us to leave, I resolved to wait a few days so my father wouldn't think he had driven me away. Two days later, Barry came up from Texas with his wife and kids for a week's visit. Assuming the role of brotherly protector, Barry spent his first night home making a blatant gesture of avoiding Frank. Later in the evening, Karen, Barry's five-year-old, crawled onto Frank's lap and asked him to help her with her puzzle. Under Barry's watchful eyes, Frank's hands shook in an obvious effort not to touch her in any way. She sat there smiling and babbling to him while he resisted her by quickly assembling the puzzle. When he finished, he told her to take it and show the others, then got up and played bartender to avoid sitting down again.

We left the next morning. We drove south, then west. Six days later we arrived in Los Angeles. Gloria and Pat helped us find a furnished apartment in Santa Monica, but after two months we felt hemmed in. We decided to rent a small house and found one here in Long Beach soon after Frank got his bartending job. It was easy enough for him to get because he wanted to work the day shift.

Our life here isn't exactly meager. We play bridge on Sunday night with neighbors and on Friday night with Gloria and Pat. We work in the garden, go to the beach, to the movies, and occasionally drive up to L.A. for dinner and a concert. Sometimes, on weekends, Gloria's son Brian and his girlfriend come down for a visit. Often, Frank and Brian will lose themselves under the hood of Brian's 1956 Pontiac, his proudest possession, while Sally and I play gin rummy under the porch awning. During those afternoons,

Frank is his most animated, working furiously on that Pontiac or mowing the lawn or joining us in cards. But Brian's visits are a mixed blessing. When he and Sally leave, I can see the depression settling on Frank as plainly as the Big Dipper settles on the treetop across the street from our front porch. We usually sit on the porch after Brian leaves and have two beers before bed. Rarely do we speak; we just sit and smoke and sip our beer. But it was on one of these nights I learned the truth about Wanda Lowell's testimony in court. A woman happened to pass by wearing white heels and I thought of Wanda with her dulled, cracked shoes.

"I wonder if Wanda Lowell's ever been to California."

"I doubt she's ever been more than forty miles outside of Ridgeway," said Frank.

"I wish there were something we could have done for her."

"We gave her a day's worth of revenge."

"Revenge?"

"Two days, really. The day she testified and the day you were acquitted."

"What kind of revenge?"

"She lied, Irene, and they believed her."

"Lied? How did she lie?"

"She came to see me and asked if there was any way she could help. She never came to the shack that night. I just told her the facts and the two of us worked out the story together. Then I took her to Mr. Bates. When I saw that *he* believed her, I decided it was worth the chance. She was happy to do it."

"To perjure herself? Didn't she want anything— money or . . ."

"She wanted conspiracy. She wanted to make one big slash at the whole town and get away with it. Besides, she believed us. To offer her anything would have been insulting. It would only have shown we didn't understand her reasons."

I said nothing more about it. I'm in no position to presume or refute someone else's motives. Not even Regina's.

June first will be Regina's birthday, but since it's my birthday as well, we will get through the day without mentioning her. We get through weeks at a time without mentioning her, and then one Friday night Frank will stay on at the bar drinking boilermakers and come home to talk about her. I sit and listen and nod and wait for his soft reminiscence to become self-recrimination as he slides into his "if only"s, past and future: "If only we had moved far away years ago, while Regina was still a child"; "If only Regina would contact us just to tell us about the baby." The first few times he did this, I felt myself being pulled along to share in the recriminations. But now I can refuse because I have my protection: all I have to do is picture that thin, lightning-like scar in Brian's hair, just above his right ear, the scar he still carries from Regina. And with the rhythm of a reprise, I tell myself responsibility has to stop somewhere, that what a child is taught and what it learns are not necessarily the same thing. The thought has never accomplished a full exoneration, but it keeps Regina at the distance I need in order to go on functioning.

The mornings after the boilermaker nights, Frank hurls himself into the present. He ferrets out the weeds in the garden or washes the windows or rearranges the furniture in the living room and then takes me to dinner. Regina is not mentioned again until the next boilermaker night.

Of course, she's always here, huddling between our thoughts, defining our opposite hopes for the future. Last Saturday, Brian came down and took us to Laguna to look at pottery and antiques. He brought us back and left at dusk, and Frank and I took up our customary positions on the front porch. A few minutes after the streetlamps came on, Frank leaned forward, gripping the arms of the chair, and squinted through his glasses. Coming slowly down the street from the direction of the highway was a green Chevrolet exactly like Virgil's. My heart backed into my lungs and stayed there until the car passed, revealing an old woman as its driver. I will never forget that momentary look on Frank's face, as if a prayer were about to be answered. When the car disappeared around the corner, it was *my* prayer that was answered.

It's natural, I know, to wish for hard and exact conclusions in life, and in that respect I am unnatural. Regardless of the consequences, Frank hopes for Regina's return. He would like to hold his grandchild and see part of himself and me in its face. I don't want that conclusion, that finality. I am resuming my position as the rock. I want nothing more than to be caressed by daily routine, working the keys of the cash register and then fixing dinner for two. The wrongs Regina and I did to each other may soften the longer we are separated, may evaporate entirely if we never meet again, and I am depending on her to recognize that. For she has my blood as well as Frank's and I pray that she too has become a rock, firmly planted and unwilling to travel the territory that keeps us apart.

No one who buys it,
survives it.

THE HOUSE NEXT DOOR

A terrifying novel
by
Anne Rivers Siddons

28172 $2.25

Coming in November

BALLANTINE BOOKS

G-1

Bestsellers from BALLANTINE

The best
in modern fiction from
BALLANTINE